FOR DEXTER

You were a good dog.

LOST GRACE

THE REMINISCENT EXILE:
BOOK FOUR

JOE DUCIE

Cedar Sky Publishing was founded in Perth, Western Australia.

This book also available as an eBook.

Written by Joe Ducie: www.joeducie.net

Cover artwork by Vincent Chong: www.vincentchong-art.co.uk

CONTENTS

THE FINAL RESOLVE

ACKNOWLEDGMENTS

Thank you to all the readers that stuck with me through the writin' times. It took some getting to, this book, and I hope you enjoy it.

THE FIRST RESOLVE

Wandering This Desert of Bastards and Whores as a Tequila Mercenary

"I have taken more out of alcohol
than alcohol has taken out of me."

~Winston Churchill

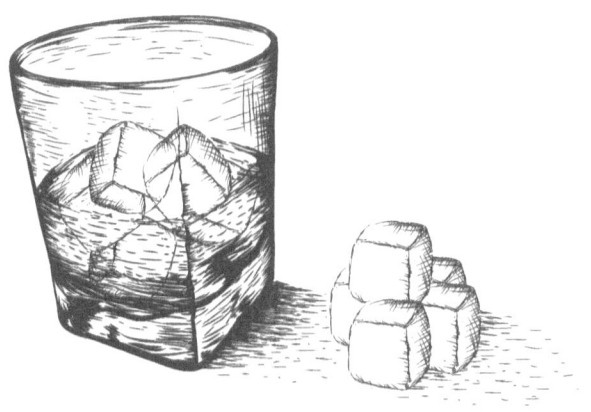

CHAPTER ONE

By Any Other Name

"Dark and getting darker"

Annie Brie handed me a takeaway cup of jasmine tea, steam rising in lazy, warm curls from the lip, just as something heavy shattered the front window of my shop. The object—a green bottle stuffed with a flaming white rag—bounced off the shelves bulging with thousands of books, and exploded in a wicked blast of purple flame on the hardwood floor between two narrow alleys of fiction.

Just before the Molotov cocktail detonated, I had eyes fast enough to read the label on the bottle: *Lagavulin 16*. Perhaps my favourite whisky in this, or indeed, any world. How dare they. Whoever *they* were.

Tendrils of flame, wildfire, found plenty of fuel in the haphazard stacks of books, stained with red wine, caked in dust, lining the floors and narrow passageways of my bookstore. I rose with a grunt as Annie took a step back, drew her service revolver (a gun she had recovered from her late partner, who had died hunting an abomination nearly a year ago now), and turned to protect my back, scanning the street through the small window alcove where we had been about to enjoy our tea. I was doing my best not to drink, best whisky in the world being thrown through my window or not.

Still, this was more than whisky. The purple flames spread fast, a wave of tingling heat reached me and soon turned blistering. I raised my hand, muttering under my breath, and caught the heat with a burst of Will enchantment before it could do more than singe the hair on the back of my knuckles. The energy in the fire was immense, however, and I felt the heat already working against my enchantment, looking to overflow the dam of power, and roast me—and Annie—alive.

I aligned my Will, cast silently as I clapped my hands together, and a burst of Arctic frost, colder than cold, fell from between my hands in a fat flow of liquid ice, which I wielded like a fire hose, and doused the flames from the Molotov.

Most of my books were protected, enchanted against damage, but the purple flame had eaten through those enchantments as if they were, well, paper and tinder. Which meant whoever had thrown the damn thing was aware of the Story Thread, the World Compass, and how best to kill around the protections that awareness offered.

"Clear on the street," Annie said. She stood in her dropped cup of tea—four bleedin' dollars from the café on the corner—knee-high boots splashed with jasmine. She glanced at me over her shoulder, jade-green eyes below jet-black hair, assessing the fire. "There's no one out there… that I can see."

Annie, who when we had first met at a grisly murder scene nearly a year ago, had had no clue of the secret truth of the world—of Will magic (magic was a hateful word), of monsters, demons, and the infinite number of other worlds that brushed up against this one, the original world, True Earth—was learning. Annie was learning. Whoever had decided to try and burn down my shop had waited until she returned with the tea—he, she, *it* had waited until Annie was back, with *two* cups. They had waited until they were certain I was in here.

Is this Atlantis business? Has she finally severed the celestial prison?

I stepped behind the counter and retrieved a sleek silver shotgun, carved with runes of power along the barrel, and loaded with nine rounds of specially designed ammunition capable of even annoying a Voidling. I punched a button on the cash register, the scent of burning pages, smoke in the air, a wreath around my head. I filled the pockets of my jeans and waistcoat with a handy bunch more ammo and stepped swiftly toward the front door.

The crude explosive had shattered the main window of my store, right through the *Books Bought & Sold* typography. A warm sea breeze—the Fremantle doctor—blew through the broken window. I scanned the courtyard outside, but it was mostly dark save for small pools of light from the streetlamps. The restaurants across the courtyard, food trucks, beyond the marble fountain at the heart of the plaza, were mildly busy for seven o'clock on a Tuesday, but none of the patrons seemed aware I'd just been attacked.

I walked out into Riverwood Plaza, the bell above my door chimed twice, shotgun at the ready, but none of my usual instincts, senses honed in years of training, war, and worse, seemed to be tingling. Whoever had thrown the cocktail had fled—either on foot or sideways into another world—almost as soon as it had been thrown. I cast a detection net just to be sure, a web of Will designed to pierce veils, but the net travelled all the way across the plaza before it hit anything living—the folks at the restaurants, enjoying their dinner. Nothing but human. Still...

"Anything?" Detective Brie asked. "It won't do much good to call this in, will it?"

I shook my head. A smile touched my face. "It's my business. Knight Infernal jurisdiction, Detective."

"Are you... leaving?" she asked. Her leather jacket clung tight to her lithe form and I could feel her heart beating alongside my own. That was the petal of the Infernal Clock resting in her heart, a crystal piece of pure celestial illusion—true magic. I had used the petal to bring Annie back to life after defeating (well, forcing a retreat) the Everlasting Scion on Diablo Beach. She did not know about the petal, and I hadn't brought it up. I didn't understand it myself, and the same thing had happened to me over eighteen months ago, when I had been killed in the ancient ruins of Atlantis, many, many worlds from little old Perth on the coast of Western Australia. Though it had been in one of the empty lease shops across the plaza here that Aloysius Jade had brought me back to life with the petal of the Clock. Confusing, troubling business.

"Declan?" Annie said. "You're staring at me."

I blinked, cleared my thoughts, and had the good grace to blush. I had been staring at her chest. "No, I'm not leaving. As far as attempts on my life go, this one was pretty weak. Come on, we'll head back inside. I've still got a story to tell you."

"About Atlantis—where you've been these last few months with your old girlfriend, Sophie's sister. Is that why she's not talking to you?"

I nodded. The net of Will cast over the plaza held steady as we stepped back into the shop. If anyone came within twenty feet of my door, I'd know it instantly.

We returned to the window alcove—the shattered main window would keep till the morning—and I mopped up Annie's spilt tea and then gave her half of mine. With a sigh, I sat back in the comfortable, whisky-stained leather couch, piles of books and papers towering over me on all sides, and placed the shotgun sharp-end toward the window across my lap.

"Thanks for getting the tea," I said. "And sorry I haven't been in touch before today." Last time I'd seen Annie, I had tasked her with taking and hiding my infant, new-born son—and not telling me where. The kid had two infamous parents. Myself, wanted and hated, with more enemies than I could count, and Emily Grace. Sweet Emily, who had turned out to be the Immortal Queen of the Renegades, my enemies during the Tome Wars, and more than that... Emily Grace had been Fair Astoria, one of the nine Everlasting—a race of malevolent *gods*, beings of immense power, who had steered the course of human history for millennia. Astoria had been one of the Everlasting not trapped away, which was too few these days.

Not to mention you released their Peace Arsenal, Declan, whispered a voice that sounded like my brother, King Jon Faraday. *No, not enough you release the Everlasting, you arm them, too.*

"How long have you been back in town?" Annie asked. "I've come by the shop most days, tried your number. Sophie and Ethan didn't know what to make of you. All they could tell me was that you were swept away… in the ruins of Atlantis. Along with Sophie's sister, Tal, who I was told was dead."

I nodded along. "Tal Levy was dead, but dead doesn't mean much these days." Again, the petal in my chest beat in sync with the petal in Annie's. How much did she know? Suspect? I needed to find a way to tell her the truth. The only reason I was back here, in true time, on True Earth, was because of that petal in her chest. It had been an anchor, a waypoint in the dark across time and the space between universes.

Annie's eyes kept scanning the dark street beside my shop through the window alcove. Looking for more would-be bombers. She had also kept her revolver drawn, resting on one knee, as she sipped her tea.

"It is really good to see you again," I said. "It was only a few months for you, but for me longer than that. I spent a year, Annie, ten thousand years ago in the past, with Tal… in the lost city of Atlantis. Before it was lost, here on True Earth. I was living in that doomed city, a wonder of architecture, of magnificence and Will—built by the Vale, an alien race, vaguely humanoid, damned to the Void so very long ago… I've been living in Atlantis, Annie. That's where I've been."

Annie masked her surprise, her doubt, with a sip

of warm tea. "OK, sure," she said. "How? Why? You... you what, you travelled back in time?"

"Across wastelands and heartlands," I said, shaking my head. "There and back again. Do you believe me?"

Annie considered, then nodded. "You have never lied to me," she said. "Well, never openly. You omit a lot of truths I would hear, though, Hale."

I thought about protesting that, but even the protest would be a lie of sorts.

"How are things in Ascension City?" she asked, her tone light, as if discussing the weather and not the seat of all power in the Story Thread. Ascension City, the homeworld of the Knights Infernal, my people.

"Preparing for war against the Everlasting, a war that will..." I ran a hand back through my hair and chuckled grimly. "Devastate the Story Thread, at the very least. The Tome Wars lasted a hundred years and unmade entire worlds, killed billions, created scar tissue on the face of reality that the creatures in the Void can exploit. A new war, a true war against the Everlasting, will make the hundred years of the Tome Wars look like kids throwing snowballs."

Annie licked her lips. "It's that bad?"

I sighed. "It will be. Unless we all come together, act against them. Unless I act."

"Then why aren't you?"

A lifeless smile touched my lips. "Because I fucked up, trying to be clever. And I want your advice, before anything else. And for you to give it, I need to tell you the truth—of my last year in Atlantis, of what I found, what I could *take*." I crushed the empty cardboard teacup in my hand and tossed it aside. My other hand had been stroking the shotgun, and I put a stop to that.

Annie held my gaze for a long moment. "There's a choice to be made, isn't there." It wasn't a question.

"Indeed."

"People will die no matter what."

"Sure as pepper sauce on my steak."

Annie Brie nodded once, sharply. Her revolver, dull gunmetal, sat menacing in the half-light. "Tell your story then, Hale. Then we'll see about this choice of yours."

REMINISCENCE THE FIRST

(One year before Declan and Annie have jasmine tea, in
Declan's measure of time.)

The Noble City of Atlantis,
Heart of the World

I was drunk on Atlantean rocket fuel and singing a
pauper's rendition of Billy Joel's *Piano Man*, a song
that wouldn't exist for about another ten thousand
years, when Tal Levy found me holding up the
universe in the marble bar just a few streets over from
the towering Vale Atlantia—the obsidian spire in the
heart of Atlantis.

"*You want me to play you a memory,*" I sang, kind-of-
sort-of-not-really in tune. "*But you're not really sure how
it goes, because I'm not really supposed to be here, drinking the
closest thing I've found to gin.*" The crowd laughed at me,
with me, as I swayed on stage in front of a floating
silver sphere that amplified my voice throughout the
bar. "*La…la…la…di-de-da…*"

Closest thing to gin, indeed, although it was more
of a sweet wine—mead, perhaps. The amber drop
packed a punch like clear liquor, and a man should
never drink anything stronger than gin before
breakfast. The time lag from the journey to Atlantis—
what I was calling the pounding headache and an
inability to find restful sleep—made it feel like five
o'clock in the morning all day long. Two weeks in the
Yet-To-Be-Lost-and-then-Found-Again-by-Me-in-

Ten-Millenniums city and I hadn't been able to shake the fatigue of the journey.

Tal slipped in at the back, through the glass entrance doors that led to streets paved with gold-inlaid cobblestones. She wore a strapless dress of red and black spun silk. *Of all the not quite gin joints in all the worlds…* Her soft eyes held me for a moment, judging and perhaps pitying, as the three-man band, playing instruments similar to guitars, drums, and trumpets—but no piano—struggled to match the swaying cadence in my voice.

"Open mic night at the Embleton, ladies and gentlemen," I said, as the music played on, snared me in its embrace. I held something that looked like a microphone, a small black cylinder with a soft glowing light, but the hovering sphere in front of me did the work of carrying my words to the farthest corners of the bar. Didn't feel right without a proper mic, though, felt too exposed. Always needed a weapon in my hand—whether it be a crystal sword or a crystal scotch glass. "My name is Declan Hale and I'm here most nights. Fun fact: I died once. It went *okay*, I guess." I raised my glass of amber wine – the sweet gin-like drop tasted like raisins soaked in oak casks and petroleum. Gin*ish*. I was on my second flask. "None of you understand a word I'm saying, but that's okay. Good music can span language… distance… and time, am I right?"

I laughed and so did the bar, my voice echoing against the high glass ceilings. A nice twilit sky, azure bruising toward purple, could be glimpsed through the glass. Most of the clientele in the Embleton knew me by now—the madman from the future who said Atlantis would one day, perhaps one day soon, be swallowed by the Void. I'd been here two weeks, yes, since unleashing the Everlasting's Peace Arsenal in the ruins of the city ten thousand years in the future, but it had taken me only half a day to find my new favourite haunt after being released from captivity in the Vale Atlantia. And only minutes after that to recast the translation enchantment so I could converse with the bartender.

Though a universal language transcended time and space in bars and taverns. Sit at the bar, drop a coin, and wait for a glass to magically appear.

Tal took a seat at one of the round tables. An inch of sawdust coated the wooden floors to catch spilt drink. The lights were dim, a burnished half-light under the twilit sky, casting the blue marble of the bar a darker shade of ocean and making us all look good. Tal always looked good, especially when she rested her chin on her palm and gazed at me with a small, knowing smile. She looked like a woman who knew my every secret, my every vice and weakness—she looked beautiful—and I thought, perhaps, she wanted me to kiss her.

But I was drunk.

And could not be trusted on something as dire and recklessly sober as *perhaps*.

"*So I'll sing you a song, but I'm no piano man,*" I sang on, catching the rough end of the chorus. "*I'll sing this song every night. Because we're all in the mood for a drink, and this place has got a few bottles of that, alright.*" I took a sip and chuckled. The lyrics were awful, my singing voice worse. "That'll do me, ladies and gentlemen. Lady in the front row, your dress is lovely. Gentleman on my right, you going to cuddle that glass all evening? You're letting the bubbles escape, my friend."

I cast aside my fake microphone to a round of subdued applause and a few looks of confusion that may or may not have been disdain. Or bemused merriment. Drunk before nightfall in a bar of strangers, but not yet slurring my words—about as well behaved as any Knight who had lived through the Tome Wars.

And there weren't many of us who could claim that.

A strange thought that most of those who had died and died hard in the hundred-year conflict wouldn't be born for ten thousand or so years. I hadn't quite pinned down the exact date or location of Atlantis in relation to my personal timeline. We were on True Earth, the real world, that much I could feel, somewhere mildly tropical, but all I knew growing up was that Atlantis had disappeared—and then been lost into myth—around ten millenniums before I was born. So the current date, the sky above my head, may have been ten thousand years, give or take a century or two, too early for me.

Or three centuries. Or four.

Either way, the history books and even the sacred texts of the Knights Infernal had civilisation during this time period on Earth absurdly, confoundedly, somewhat haphazardly, wrong.

"Hey there, sweet thing," I said to Tal and pulled one of the empty chairs at the table closer to her so we were sitting almost side by side. I gave her a kiss on the cheek and took one of her hands in mine. She was warm and carried a scent somewhere between strawberries and rainfall.

"Sweet thing, is it?" Tal ruffled my hair and straightened my dishevelled eye patch, which masked my dead eye. "You think you're charming when you're drunk."

"I'm not drunk," I lied. "Sober as a fox." In truth, while I was most definitely over the legal limit—if Atlantis had such a thing, what with most of the transport autonomous flying cars, carriages, and shuttles—I didn't feel too drunk. A little tipsy, perhaps. "And I'm charming either way. Where'd you get that nice dress?"

I'd drunk enough to fell bigger men than my good self, but long practice had awarded me the gold medal at the Scotch Games. The old liver had to pull an extra shift if I wanted the same buzz a lone bottle used to give me, and often I got the hangover in the morning without the warm buzz the night before.

Tal raised a single eyebrow and stared at me. "It was a gift."

I thought about kissing her again.

"Okay, I am drunk, Tal. You got me. But you are beautiful, you are lovely angles and olive skin. Where are our minders at the moment?" We were escorted at all times in and around this great city. Wardens, they were called. Will users, perhaps proficient—I had yet to push my bounds and find out—who had graduated from some academy whose name escaped me. A lot of new names and concepts had piled up over the last few weeks. *Vale… something or other*, I thought. The Atlanteans liked to attach the word 'Vale' to certain places. I hadn't figured out why yet, and hadn't really cared to ask.

"They are outside," she said and grinned. "My two are chatting with your two. I think the tall one has a thing for the blonde one. Lucky girl, he's gorgeous. Your two don't come in here anymore?"

"Gorgeous? Sure, if you like the tall and handsome thing. And no they don't come in. I think they've gone and figured me out. I'm not about to sneak out the back door with all this booze in the way." I waved at the bar, at the bartender Galus. He held up a bottle of something blue, Tal's favourite sip from the one or two nights we'd spent here together, and I gave her a look. She shook her head. "No, thank you, Galus," I said with a sigh. I could read body language as well as the best of 'em, and Tal was not in a drinking mood—a drinking with *me* mood. She was in a 'we need to talk' mood. "We're leaving."

"*Leeving*," he said and gestured to the glass doors and the street beyond. "*Do'sad weel'io*, Declan?"

I nodded. The enchantments I'd cast on my mind to understand the Atlantean language had worn thin. Time to recast those in the morning, as I really couldn't be bothered with the groundwork required to complete the enchantment right now, although the subtle stuff like Healing and Augmentation Will was always a little finicky for me. I was more likely to set myself on fire than heal a wound. Dozens of healers far more proficient than me had patched me up and kept me going over the years. I was stuffed if something ruptured internally, as it so often did in my line of work.

And what work is that, Declan? a voice that sounded a lot like Emily Grace, one of the Everlasting—Fair Astoria, the only member of that gang with a soul— whispered in my head. *Are you a Knight? An exile? Hero or villain?* She paused, or I paused, or perhaps the booze paused. *A father?*

"Take me to the gardens," Tal said. "We need to talk."

Called it.

~~*~*

So we went to the gardens, just a few streets over from the bar. Wildflower beds and lush, green grass under canopies of cherry blossom trees, or something akin to cherry blossom trees with bushels of bursting pink petals, bordered a winding path scattered with old leaves across the small park. We walked past splashes of colour mixed with green stems and vines, and water clearer than cut glass in a little trickling river, six feet wide, crisscrossed with white marble bridges. Our minders, four of the best and brightest Will Wardens in the city, kept their distance. Close but not too close.

I strolled hand in hand with Tal through the Elysium Gardens of fabled Atlantis, which surrounded the enormous spire of the Vale Atlantia, stretching a mile above, piercing the clouds, and glinting darkly in the half-light. Creatures akin to fireflies danced around us, small flakes of snow that had been set on fire. I recalled seeing something similar on Voraskel, in the glade where Emily Grace, Fair Astoria, had died in my arms. The tiny sparks passed through our skin, warm and harmless, as if either they weren't real or we weren't. Tal smiled as if she'd spent the last six years as host to an Elder God monstrosity and still thought on those days often.

"I can't go back, Declan." And she didn't say it nervously, or as if she were worried how I would react. Tal spoke simply, a soft, gentle fact that drove a spike of ice into my chest. "I know we've only been here two weeks, but there's a calm to Atlantis. A…

sense of wellness. And no one knows us here. You feel it, too, I know you do. This is the world before it ended. As close to paradise as anything I've seen across the Story Thread. We were born and lived in the ruins of this civilisation."

"What about Sophie?" *What about me?* Tal knew I couldn't stay here. Not forever. Technically I had all the time in the world, years to spare, but the pull to return was strong. A compass in my mind, something I'd shared only with Tal, pointed the way home. We weren't lost in the past, if we didn't want to be, because I was anchored to the future. The petals of the Infernal Clock, which had resurrected both me and Annie Brie, my police detective from Perth who had faced the Everlasting and sort of lived to tell the tale, connected us across time, it seemed. And, if I were brave and true, that connection lit a path through the Void *back* to the present day.

More and more I was beginning to sense that the Infernal Clock was, perhaps, the most powerful object in existence. Time, space, even death were rendered null by its power. And a piece of it, a single crystal petal, rested in my heart. It felt like a Sheriff's badge pinned to my waistcoat, allowing me to traverse the dusty Void at high noon without fear.

So long as I was carrying a six shooter. And the bad guys knew I was more than willing to shoot first.

"Sophie has thought me dead for six years. Tell her I didn't survive the trip here with you. She'll never know any different."

"Lie to her?" I chuckled, somewhat grimly. "She'll blame me again for losing you. That's hardly fair, sweetheart."

Tal looked at me sideways. "You deserve some

measure of blame for what happened to us, Declan Hale. You can take her ire… for me."

"You know the fate of this city, Tal." I gestured at the gardens, at the mighty skyscrapers beyond them and the Vale Atlantia, at the very sky. "The Everlasting are going to attack and this entire city is going to be swept into the Void. That's history. That's what happened and what will happen. I saw it painted on the walls of the Tomb of the Sleeping Goddess— so did you. History to us. We can't change events we know are set. Broken quill, even trying will probably cause it to happen. True Earth will be less one entire *landmass*. You can live here with these people, knowing their fate?"

"They haven't even heard of the Everlasting yet! That future could be hundreds, even thousands, of years away. I won't go back to *your* future and fight the Knights, or the Renegades, or face Oblivion again." Tal clenched her jaw and a tear cut down her cheek. "Call it cowardice if you will, but Declan, I love you. I've always loved you. And if I go back with you, I'm going to have to share you with a war that is going to, at best, decimate the Story Thread. At worst, unravel the whole damn thing. And, at the last, tear you apart."

"Tal—"

"A war that is going to destroy you!" Tal wrapped her arms around me and pressed her cheek into my shoulder. She shook, fighting tears. The twilit air was warm and so was she, like a good fleece blanket. "I can't see that. I won't. You'll fight this war, because that's what you do. When it comes to conflict and battle, war and chaos, the universe seems to spin around your head. You attract the absurd. I won't go back to watch you be consumed by it. Because that's the worst part, you know?" She pulled away and laughed bitterly, grasping my hands. "They won't be able to kill you. You survive, Declan. You always, *always* survive. Even when you die, you live. No, you won't die. But you'll change. I can see it. The war will take you and you'll become hard, harder than you've ever been. You'll sacrifice entire worlds for one inch of an advantage against the Everlasting. Don't tell me you won't, because I know you, and you *have*."

"I'm an Arbiter of the Knights Infernal," I said, hating the dark edge to my voice. "Once commander of the Cascade Fleet and, fuck it all, it should be me on the Dragon Throne and not Jon Faraday. But I am not the *boy* who sacrificed Reach City and all those souls. Not anymore. I'll never be able to atone for that, but I won't make such a mistake again. You're right, of course, I will fight. It's my place, my role in the universe. I'm a soldier. I'm... good at it. It's also the right thing to do. The Everlasting must be fought."

I'm no longer the genocidal librarian. No longer the exile growing fat and slow... just drunk. This is my game, and I play it well.

"You could stay with me." Tal pressed her hand to my chest. I fought a shiver. "We could live out our lives here and let the Void consume us both when the time comes, if that end is within our lifetimes. We'd at least be together."

I met her eyes and, just for a moment, thought about staying, thought about blackberry farms and distant memories. For just I moment, I considered the impossible. I shook my head and Tal pulled her hand from mine.

"You damn yourself, Declan Hale," she whispered. "And millions are going to suffer and die because you don't know *how* to quit."

"It will be worse if I don't fight. We don't belong here, Tal." My time lag headache pounded against my skull. Without drink to subdue the incessant drumming, a hurricane was a'brewing in my mind. I thought maybe I'd drunk enough to sleep tonight. Not well, of course. Never sleep well on the sauce, and my liver never gets a chance to sleep. But enough to put me down and forget for a few hours. Let Tomorrow Declan deal with Yesterday Declan's avarice.

And the nagging thought, the stirring shame, that I was too weak to stop. *The demon's name is Alcohol,* I thought, and the voice in my head sounded unfamiliar, young, *and it will kill me to get a drink.*

"You don't belong here," Tal said, shivering despite the warmth and pleasantness of the evening. "But I may."

~~*~*

I dreamt of the future that night, in the suite shared by me and Tal toward the higher levels of the Vale Atlantia. The High Lords of Atlantis, after several days of something approaching interrogation, had agreed to let us roam the city. Our arrival, in the crown of the Atlantia itself, the plateau that would one day imprison Lord Oblivion of the Everlasting, had caused something of a ruckus. We had appeared beaten, bloody, and bearing the remnants of a sword that was still whole during this time period—the Roseblade.

The ruins of that blade, more than anything, had

convinced those that needed convincing that Tal and I were from a distant future. Especially given that their sword, whole and unbroken, had been resting in its pedestal next to us up in the crown. The alloy used to create the sword, celestial illusion, was perhaps the rarest element in all known existences. It couldn't be created by the Willful—by us magic users, although I hate the word magic. Magic by its definition was inexplicable, defied explanation, whereas Will was the ascending fire at the heart of creation powering the universe. Those who were Willful could write entire worlds into reality, add realms to the Story Thread. All it took was ink and paper. But celestial illusion was rare and precious and one of the very few things of which the Knights Infernal had a finite supply.

Or, rather, no supply, in my time period. Only what could be found and scavenged.

Celestial illusion was also, supposedly, unbreakable once forged. I think the fact I'd somehow melted the sword frightened the High Lords more than my dismal predictions of the future.

The Roseblade itself could unmake worlds. An absurdly powerful weapon, cast with white rose petals in the crystal blade, to maximise and exceed the wielder's Willful talent. I'd wielded it before, more than once, and always to dire effect. As a kid, barely nineteen, I'd destroyed the Reach—a city world home to millions—and more recently I'd unleashed the Peace Arsenal. Lord Oblivion of the Everlasting had manipulated me, had outplayed me masterfully, but in the end I'd done it for Tal. Some poor bastard back in real time would have been possessed by Oblivion in her place. My fault. One sin to right another. I'm not sure morality worked like that, but it was the best I could do.

And I'd no doubt pay for that one day. We always pay for our choices, better to own it now and expect the sword to fall instead of hoping for the best and ending up half blind and owning a dark, dreary bookshop haunted by characters from the novels you read as a kid. Annie had been able to see Roper Hartley in my bookshop back in Perth. For years I'd thought I'd lost my mind, but no, Annie and I had lost it together. Better than drinking alone.

The suite we'd been given, Tal and I, was opulent and polished. The floor was graceful marble tile, and reflected the high ceilings above as clearly as a still blue lake mirrored snow-capped mountains. Chandeliers of soft, flickering flame hung in the common area, a living space overlooking the city about three quarters of a mile up in the Vale Atlantia. Much like the palace in Ascension City back home, a lot of Will had been expended to make the structure bigger on the inside. It had been TARDIS'd to all hell. Weaving enchantments and crossing space in parallel realms of the Story Thread, creating permanent gateways, allowed for violations of basic physics. Well, not so much violations, but most definitely bending the laws of the universe. Sort of bending it back on itself, so to speak. More is less and left is often right when two unique pieces of the cloth canvas are forced together.

The suite had two bedrooms, two bathrooms. Tal and I were not sharing the same bedroom.

I slept alone. And my mind fell into the future.

In my dream that night, I walked the endless fields of the World Cemetery—a planet roughly the size of True Earth that held nothing but grass and trees and graves. The cemetery was the final resting place of all Knights Infernal. Over the long centuries, the graves and memorials had spilled across continents. Even if a Knight was lost in an unknown battle, or to the Void, a memorial was erected here in the hallowed soil. Charged with guarding, policing, and maintaining the countless worlds of the Story Thread was grisly work.

The dead had numbered enough to need their own world, in the end.

My grandfather, Aloysius Hale, walked at my side. He had been, once upon a time, the Chief Librarian of the Forgetful Library, which contained every book *never* written, among other treasures. One of the most highly regarded positions in the entirety of the known Story Thread. He had been imprisoned by my half-brother, King Jon Faraday, for supporting me as rightful king after I ended the Tome Wars. Starhold had addled his mind, last we spoke. A touch of the Void about the orbital prison ensured very few of its inmates escaped time spent there unscathed.

Still, he strolled at my side now. A tall man, my father's father, bespectacled and wearing a tailored suit befitting his new station as caretaker of this particular section of the World Cemetery. His black shoes were polished to a fine point, his lapel smooth, and his jacket held no loose threads. I knew I was dreaming. Knights were trained to not only lucid dream but to assess and *feel* for reality at all times, like a sixth sense. To tune our Will to the right beat. There were a lot of worlds and universes out there, a lot of heavens and hells, and countless copies of True Earth itself. We needed to be able to tell reality from fiction.

Which was the leading theory as to why so many of us were unhappy and turned to drink and worse than drink. Fiction was often kinder than true reality.

"We're going to see her, aren't we?" I asked.

My grandfather nodded. He consulted a fine silver pocket watch, glared up at the sun, and adjusted the dial by a few minutes. I couldn't read the time, but I could see that his eyes were as black as coal. That troubled me, somewhat. Black eyes were also a touch of the Void. Possession, corruption, a failure to stand and be true.

What is happening back home?

"She's missed you," he said, and his voice was a deep rumble, almost a hiss, that shook the dream around us. The creature wearing my grandfather's face wanted me to know it was there.

We walked in silence after that, winding up a hill littered with ivy and moss soaked headstones. At the top, under the shade of a copse of trees, sat Clare Valentine—my friend and lover, once upon a time. She sat on the earth where I knew, in the real World Cemetery, her tombstone stood white and new. I'd lost her half a year ago on the Plains of Perdition. Morpheus, King of the Renegades, had killed her. To slow me down. She had died for me.

A lot of people have died for me. *Because* of me.

"Hello, Declan," Clare said. She was twisting small sunflowers into a crown. Her eyes, which had always raged through a storm of colour, a quirk of the Willful, were as blue as glacial water.

"Hey there, Clare. You look… well." *Alive.* I sat down in front of her, crossing my legs beneath me. The day was bright and I could taste spring on the air, fresh and vital. If this were a dream, it was a darn good one.

"You're running out of time," she said and plucked another sunflower from the soil around her grave. "And you're not paying attention. You're missing the obvious." She showed me the flower. "Nine petals. Well, eight now, after Astoria's death."

I've got nothing but time... I nodded. "Sounds like me. Business as usual."

Clare smiled but it didn't reach her eyes. She stood and pressed the head of the sunflower into my palm, over the scars of promises made a long time ago. Wicked marks from the Tome Wars. "The game is more dangerous than ever. Why can't you see it?"

"I'm tired, Clare." And, seeing as this was a dream, I told the truth. "I could have brought you back with a petal of the Infernal Clock. I didn't. Annie, she... I didn't."

"The dead should stay that way." Clare cupped my cheek. "You're a bleeding wound on the face of the world, Declan. You wonder why you attract such chaos? You died and were resurrected in violence. It's all you know."

"Are you asking me not to fight?" I managed half a smirk. "Because I've already had that conversation today, Miss Valentine."

"No, you must fight."

"I know."

"I'm asking you to *see*." She stressed the word, thumped me on the chest, and threw up her hands as if I were beyond salvation. "To wake up and *see*!"

Clare kissed me then—and I woke up.

A cool sweat prickled at my skin. I lay shirtless, tangled in bed sheets, gazing out at the night sky of Atlantis through the tall windows along the edge of the room. Thousands of stars and a plump blue moon about to sink over the distant mountains to the west. It must have been about halfway between midnight and dawn. I could hear shuffling in the next room. Tal. And gentle weeping.

With a sigh I sat up and rubbed at my face. Something fell from my hand and landed between my legs. The head of a sunflower, squished and… *pulled from a dream.*

A cold, sinking sensation settled in my gut— something between weary resignation and actual fear. *What the hell?* I'd seen enough in my twenty six years to know I knew next to nothing of the universe. But this was strange. This was… troublesome.

I stared at the flower and gently plucked a single yellow petal from the seeds. "She loves me," I said, as Tal wept in the next room. "But, oh dear, she loves me not."

My mouth was hangover-dry and my head a little fuzzy. I stumbled to the bathroom, sat down to pee as I wasn't in any condition to operate heavy machinery, and when I was done stuck my head under the tap in the sink and drank about two litres of water. Sated for now, I fell back into bed, brushed the nightmare flower from the sheets, and returned to a fitful, dreamless sleep.

~~*~*

The next morning I fiddled with my eye patch, placing it down gently over my hard boiled left eye, which had been cooked during a firebomb attack on Tia Moreau's bar in Meadow Gate. The eye wasn't entirely useless, and my body's natural resistance and healing factor as a Willful Knight seemed to be slowly repairing the damage. I could make out sort of a white haze, which was an improvement over red nothing. Still, the eye and the skin around it was ugly, scarred, and the patch hid the damage while adding a certain level of piracy and intimidation to my demeanour.

I shrugged into my pants, shirt, and waistcoat, which had been mended since my arrival and were enchanted against dust, dirt, and sweat. Blood was a bit trickier, as Will light flowed in my veins. Blood resisted enchantment, spells and charms of all kinds, which came in handy against enemy practitioners, but not so much with dry-cleaning. I'd been offered clothes in the local fashion, somewhat tropical getups in the streets and more formal robes and suits in the style of the Vale Atlantia itself, but declined.

The shabby waistcoat was kind of my thing.

Tal was at the table in the living area when I emerged, wearing a silk nightgown and white woolly socks. She was eating fruit from a platter of breakfast that had appeared as if by magic sometime in the early morning. Arrayed on the table were all manner of decadent pastries, sourced no doubt from a dozen different worlds, as well as breakfast meats, fried and poached eggs, milk, breads, and freshly chopped fruit of an exotic nature. *A glass of Tia's honeyberry juice would go down a treat right about now...* The honeyberries that grew around Meadow Gate were unrivalled when it came to curing hangovers. At a glance, Tal and I were guests of the High Lords, and kept in comfort. I think they didn't quite know what to do with us, and were perhaps a touch afraid of what our very presence meant for their future.

The future was grim, and I'd told them as much.

In my short time here in Atlantis, I'd seen that the society lived in something approaching peace. At least, as far as I had been able to tell, True Earth was peaceful in this time period. If they knew anything of the Everlasting, my enemies, then they weren't telling. I hadn't seen any signs of war, which I knew all too well. The skies were clear, free of battleships, and I'd only ever seen handfuls of Wardens patrolling in the streets. Local police, more than a military, and most of the folk I'd met, the general population, had been kind and generous with their time and liquor.

The city was at peace.

I'm asking you to see.

Asking or telling? Requesting or demanding, sweet Clare? What was I missing? Were my dreams trying to tell me something? Every instinct I had was nudging me into action, but there was no enemy. No one had died. Hell, no one had even tried to kill me in two weeks. Save for my time in exile, that was a new record. Had it just become my nature to expect a knife in the back?

"Good morning, Declan," Tal said and smiled. She looked lovely when she smiled. Lovelier. *Loveliest.* Beams of sunlight through the open windows turned her hair to glossy gold. "How did you sleep?"

"Time lag is an awful thing," I said. "It's like a constant hangover."

"Half a crate of that gin-wine doesn't help matters, I'm sure," she replied. "Lay off the drink a few days and you may feel better. Your liver will thank you." Her smile turned distant. "Try six years as slave to Oblivion and then we'll talk headaches, Shadowless."

I joined her at the table and squeezed her hand.

Talk of her unmaking, the fierce bands shackled to her very soul at the hands of Lord Oblivion, nastiest of the four Everlasting I had met, was best avoided. I'd discovered that the hard way. She'd chewed me out quite severely last week when I'd suggested we talk about it. Worse, she had cried.

I was powerless against tears.

"What are we doing today then?" I asked. "Pub?"

Tal rolled her eyes. "Need you showered and shaved. We're meeting the High Lords again, according to Trey. They wish to discuss… matters."

"Who's Trey?"

She grinned. "Vatrey. My tall and handsome minder."

"Oh, he was here earlier, was he?" Not that it bothered me.

"Yes, yes he was. Showered and shaved, Hale."

I mumbled a rough agreement and helped myself to a plate of warm lean ham, toast, fried eggs, and some mango pieces. Always best to feed a hangover. As I ate, I let my mind drift along the connection I felt to Annie Brie—ten thousand years away. I wondered if she could feel me, if she knew that I was still alive, but was unable to reach or talk to me. More than likely, which meant the future knew to expect me. The link wasn't anything I could physically see or touch. Instead I simply focused my thoughts on Annie, her straight black hair and jade-green eyes. Although the image in my mind was hazy, I saw her strolling along a beach in a black bikini, her toes digging into the sand and the warm West Australian sun shining on her skin.

Diablo Beach on True Earth, not a five-minute walk from my haunted old bookshop. I missed that little shop and all its drunken corners. We had fought and defeated Scion on Diablo beach—and beheaded an Emissary dragon. Annie had been killed for her part, her trouble, in saving the world. I'd brought her back with a petal of the Infernal Clock, gifted from lost Emily Grace, the mother of my infant son. I'd given the child to Annie, to make the boy disappear into a normal life, where his father wasn't the Shadowless Arbiter, infamous across a million worlds and considered something of a douchebag on a million more.

In my vision from the link, Annie held hands with a young man, tanned, wearing a pair of Oakley wraparound sunglasses. Her fiancé, I guessed, although I'd never met the fellow. He was talking fast, gesturing fiercely with his free hand. I couldn't hear what was being said, but he was certainly trying to get his point across. Annie bit her lip as he spoke and shook her head. I snapped out of the vision to find my hand in the air, drawing slow circles. A point of soft light hovered around my index finger and I realised, with a start, that I'd almost carved a path into the Void.

A path to follow back to Annie and find my way home.

Could I follow it back here, to Atlantis? Could I forge a path through time that could be traversed both ways? That would be useful. I thought, perhaps, I could. Getting home was easy, getting back to Atlantis... maybe possible.

There was a war to be fought, after all, and I'd unleashed an arsenal in the ruins of this city for the Everlasting to use. I wasn't certain just what advantage Oblivion had gained, but I imagined legions of warships, ancient artefacts and weapons from, well, the age I found myself in now. At the very least, the Knights were in the dark. Many of them did not even accept the Everlasting as real. Myths and fancy, the whole debacle, but I knew better.

They'd been pulling my strings since before I was born. Any victory, such as releasing Tal from Oblivion's grasp, had only come at a cost so high that it may as well have been defeat. No war's end without the Degradation. Happiness without sadness. Day without night. Scotch without hangover.

"Nothing's free except for you and me," I muttered and Tal looked at me sharply. I shook my head, cleared away the future prospect, and bit into a slice of toast and a perfectly fried egg—panacea to the regretful dregs at the bottom of far too many bottles.

Half an hour later found me showered and kind of shaved. I'd used a fine razor but done a bit of a hack job around the chin and sideburns. What with the one eye, I sometimes messed up close quarter jobs—also I didn't care. A bit of stubble worked for my dangerous and Knightly image, I supposed.

"Showered and somewhat shaved," I told Tal. She rolled her eyes but held my hand, which mattered a great deal to me.

Tal and I were led up the Vale Atlantia by our minders, three women and one man—that unlikable handsome bastard Trey— wearing silver robes with charcoal grey lapels, towards the seat of power and governance in Atlantis. From the way our minders carried themselves, I guessed they carried short swords or plasma weapons under the robes, though I'd never seen either. I'd first been in the spire of the Vale Atlantia six years ago and ten thousand years from now. Back then I'd noted the resemblance to the Fae Palace in Ascension City, even though the Voidflood had decimated and disintegrated a lot of the finery. The design had to be more than coincidence. Ascension, my old stomping ground and home of the Knights Infernal, had been modelled on Atlantis.

We walked past hundreds of workers and staff, most of whom offered us curious glances.

We were known, of course, as word of our arrival had spread like wildfire. Some, a handful, knew the full truth, most others knew only pieces. The rumours were far more useful than the truth, to be honest. However peaceful this utopian city looked on the surface, people were people. I'm sure Tal and I were already a part of games and schemes, political and otherwise, of which we knew nothing.

We were also Will users, *magic* folk, of unknown strength and talent. I could wrestle with the best of them, heavyweight and then some, and Tal had been no lightweight back in her day. She may have picked up a few tricks from Oblivion, as well. But we weren't talking about that. No, not at all. *That bastard will bleed for her one day.*

As far as Tal's talents and capabilities went, however, her father had been Admiral Mathias Levy—he had adopted both Tal and Sophie with his wife, Serah, from the slew of urchins and refugees in Ascension City during the Tome Wars. Most enlisted families were ordered to take in at least two orphans. I'd never known my mother and my father had died young, but the Infernal Academy had cared for me. Mathias Levy had been a kind man, but firm and not to be crossed. He had awarded me with my command, the *Dawnstar*, after King Morrow was lost to the Void during the final months of the war. I would have become king, not long after, but instead I'd walked away… having lost Tal to Oblivion.

Sophie lost her mother, an Arbiter of the Knights Infernal, not long before she lost her father, to a skirmish in the outer territories defending the peace accords, and then her sister, all within the year. All of it I'd had a hand in, one indirect way or another. All save Tal, where I may as well have pulled the trigger myself and damned her to Oblivion's service.

A few months ago, lost in the Dream Worlds with Annie, I'd been shown a memory of my time on the *Dawnstar*. Admiral Levy had learnt of my… association with Tal, and had demanded a high price from me in return. The memory was of a skirmish above the alien world of Adena, against a contingent of Marauders—against the mercenary forces for the mercenary nation of Renegades.

"It looks pretty real," Annie said, squinting against the snow-glare and the sun streaming in through the windows of the Dawnstar.

"Engage the eastern quadrant," my younger self said from his chair, watching the battle on a heads-up display that tracked ships and weapons fire and generated tactical advantages. "Targets marked on my visor in order of priority."

The Dawnstar *swerved through the sky, and the display reeled through more mountains and turned up. We hung to the edge of space, as the Marauder ships tried to get behind us. I grinned as my young self grinned, dressed in his battle uniform—the enchanted armour of a Knight Infernal.*

"Oh my," Annie said. "Those are spaceships."

"Yes."

The Marauder vessels were pirate ships, scrapped together

from a thousand bastardized cruisers. No match for the Dawnstar *or the rest of the fleet. Overhead, static burst through the communications speakers, and a familiar, lost voice spoke directly to me.*

"Commander Hale," Admiral Levy said. "There's a tradition in my homeland, no longer greatly observed, but nevertheless… When a young man wanted his prospective father-in-law's blessing, he would go out into the wild and return with the biggest buck he could find as a gesture of respect. The larger the horns, the greater the respect."

"Yes, sir."

"Commander Hale, I see a mighty big pair of horns on that enemy ship." The radio fell into static for a long moment. "Bring me those horns."

Admiral Mathias Levy had been a kind-hearted son of a bitch, and he'd passed his talent and resolve onto his daughter. Daughters. Tal and Sophie were both forces to be reckoned with because of the Admiral's influence, their hard hours put in at the Academy, and the Tome Wars.

"Who were they?" Annie asked. "Flying those ugly ships?"

"Renegades, but of a different sort—more like pirates. Men and women who sail the seas of the Story Thread, looting other worlds and running a trade in stolen and illegal goods across Forget. They're rich and ruthless, and it was the blow you just saw me about to strike, more than anything, that undermined their entire structure and allowed the Knights to get a foothold on Voraskel—the Renegade home world."

Annie shook her head. "You've led an… interesting life, Declan."

A grand staircase, white and shining, rose in a wide, lazy spiral through the heart of the top floors of the Vale Atlantia. As we walked the thousand or so steps, my hangover fighting every step, I worked the translation charm as best I could. It was a mix of augmented hearing and mind magic—although I hated the word 'magic', quite often nothing else seemed to fit. The weaves and bands of invisible Will settled on my mind and translated Atlantean into sort of English. Tal did the same, doing a much better job than me. Her charm was like spinning the dial on the radio and landing on a station. Mine was a few clicks short, picking up a bit of static.

It was a rough translation enchantment. By no means was it perfect, and it skipped the odd word even when tuned to perfection, but it was functional over stylish, which was all I needed. *Function over style has been your modus operandi for years.* The languages were close, anyway, from what I'd seen and heard. Some words were the same in English, or Latin and Ascensionish, or the myriad variants thereof. Rather incestuous, the Story Thread, when you thought about it. We could be understood, which was the important thing. In terms of language, I guess time didn't dilute the pool that much. It gave me hope that if certain words and traditions had survived into my future, to real time as I knew it, then perhaps a great deal of people in this city survived the cataclysm to come.

Our minders led us into the council chambers just below the final few floors and the throne room of the Vale Atlantia. In another life, another time, I'd walked these abandoned halls, caked with millenniums of dust, all alone and found the Infernal Clock abandoned alongside the Roseblade. If we kept heading up a few more levels, I'd find the same again now, though far better protected.

Not so much abandoned, but those two pieces of

celestial illusion, crafted for entirely different purposes, were mighty tempting for an ambitious young chap like myself. The crystal petals of the Clock could grant life, the sword could unmake worlds. Absolute power over life and death. *Been down that road before, boss,* Ethan Reilly, my wayward apprentice whispered in the back of my mind. *How'd it work out for ya?*

Recklessly.

The council chambers were opulent and vast, tiered seating rising to the cheap seats, and centred around a circular table in the heart of the room. At this table sat just three of the Atlantean ruling class. It seemed a full session of the council, as had been gathered upon our arrival, was no longer needed. Apart from the council folk, the chamber was empty. We were old news, apparently, this far up the chain of command.

Or perhaps so they wanted us to think.

"Welcome, Tal Levy," High Lord Visios said, with a genuine smile for the prettiest girl in this or any millennium. He was a tall man, complete with a white braided beard, long enough so he tucked the tail into his belt. His face was lined, wrinkled, but his cheeks were red as if he'd been laughing not too long ago— or sipping something sweet from a hipflask. Half Gandalf, half Father Christmas. "And welcome, Declan Hale."

Visios carried a worn staff of twisted oak, about a foot taller than he was at seven feet. Will users of this time seemed to rely on staffs and wands, on unique channels to focus their talent. There was a magical university in Switzerland, in my time, that taught the same. We'd been taught such use in the Infernal

Academy as children, of course, but a more hands on approach dominated the curriculum during war time. We were taught how to burn and kill with our hands wrapped around a Renegade's throat. Schools and academies that didn't make soldiers were a nice idea. Perhaps one day, many years from now, when I'd ground the Everlasting into dust and the Story Thread was at peace, the Infernal Academy could become something more… civil.

"Howdy, Vis," I said and offered the man a quick salute. "You guys make good breakfast. My thanks."

"Good morning," Tal said. "You have enchantments in place to understand us?"

"Indeed," Visios said and gestured to the man and woman on his left, as we took seats at the round table and our minders gathered to chat amongst themselves across the chamber. "You remember High Lords Adanor and Shuri?"

Adanor disliked me. It was all in the glower. He was a tall, rake-thin man with a chin as sharp as twice cut glass. Atop his old, grey head he wore a black fez with a golden crest stitched into the fabric. A crest of no relevance to me, two circles overlapping and crossed with something that looked like three pyramids side by side. Shuri was a monument to indifference, a regal woman of middle age and greying hair. Her eyes were alight, however, and knowing.

Tal and I shared greetings with the gentry and I thought on how quick I could get away and back to the bar.

"When we spoke one week ago," Visios said, taking his seat next to Tal, "you made mention of your past as soldiers… Knights Infernal, yes? Of which you were an Arbiter, Declan, highly ranked and well trained. We would like to offer you both an opportunity to work at the Vale Celestia—our centre for learning and studying Will. Our students are most eager to learn your unique method of Will control. Without a focus, that is."

"You want me to teach?" I asked with a snort. Of all I had been expecting, from imprisonment to conscription, teaching was way down the list.

"Our student groups are split between experience, potential, and desire to learn. The groups you would be responsible for would be small, our best and brightest, eager to study your unique methods." Visios held up his hand. "Five, six students at the most. And an opportunity to learn about us, as we learn about you."

The translation on that one came through a little formal. I glanced at Tal, who watched me thoughtfully. "We'd teach a team of students each?" I asked. "Tal and myself?"

"That could be fun," she said and squeezed my hand. "Is there any real need to run back to the future so soon, Declan?"

"If it is your desire to stay, we ask you make yourself beneficial to our society. To share more of your knowledge from the future. To help us avert any catastrophe you claim to have seen." Adanor clasped his hands together and smirked. He didn't buy the end of the world tale I was selling, not with the Infernal Clock above and the grand city prospering below. "To that end, we would ask you and Miss Levy to accept a position in the Vale Celestia of Atlantis as warfare instructors, alongside the current staff. You would teach our students in Willful offence and defence, a select team of five or six who will be tested in, say, four months. Where the skills you have taught them—among others—will be put to the test."

Four months... I could do four months. Did I want to? I met Tal's gaze, saw the look in her eyes and the smile playing at the corners of mouth. If she wanted to stay, I wanted to stay. I loved her. Perhaps in a few months I could convince her to return with me. And, if I were being honest, I wanted some time to collect myself. To try and ween myself off the bottle again. I'd managed a few months sober earlier this year, then the loss of Emily and forfeiting my son had seemed like a good reason to have a drink.

What is that demon's name? my mind whispered. *Alcohol!*

And if I were being honest-er, then I never really needed a reason to drink. It's Tuesday, better have a bottle of breakfast wine. Oh, look, a bumblebee. Some honey mead for me. What's that? Steak at the pub? Ten pints of Guinness and a few nips of single malt should see us through, mate. By the Everlasting, I missed Paddy's. Emissary had blown it up a few months back, during the misadventure where I'd met Annie Brie—who was now my link back to the future. My DeLorean if I ever hit eighty-eight miles an hour.

Funny how people could come into our lives and plant their flags in our souls. In Annie's case, the soul binding had been quite literal, thanks to the Infernal Clock. I missed her more than Paddy's.

"I accept," Tal told the High Lords of Atlantis. "Declan?"

"I..." What was I in a hurry to run back to, anyway? War against the Everlasting? I could use the time away to prepare myself—mind, body, and soul.

Train myself as much as the bunch of kids theses all-important and dignified lords chose to saddle me with. *Was there a bar on campus?*

"Yeah, okay, let's go back to school."

CHAPTER TWO

Annie's Concern

"Make it seem worthwhile"

"So what I'm getting from this," Annie said, as the evening hour stretched toward nine o'clock, still early, and a handful of love-struck young couples walked about Riverwood Plaza outside of my shop, dinner and drinks and all things nice planned. "What I'm getting is that you were following Tal around like a poor lost puppy. Worse, a drunken lost puppy. Declan, women just love it when men can't handle their problems. Granted, your problems are generally somewhat more significant than most, but still. Whether it's stop drinking and get a job or stop drinking and save the world, it's the same old hurt. Tal sees it that way, I bet. Sees you... broken."

A barbed ripple of anger shivered up my spine, but I caught it before I said something stupid. "I may not be explaining things too well, but it wasn't as pathetic as you seem to be... understanding."

Annie gave me a frank and piercing look, a look all women seem capable of giving, that saw right to the heart of me and my particular style, Hale's own brand, of delusional bullshit.

I grinned. "Well, I don't remember a lot of the early drunken nights, so perhaps I've a twisted perspective on just how romantic I may or may not have appeared. In contrast to my problems, that's why I'm asking your advice, Annie. You've been a voice of reason as long as I've known you."

"She loves you, that much is clear," Annie said. "Is she... is Tal here? Upstairs?"

I shook my head.

"Is she... OK?"

I shrugged and tilted my hand back and forth in the air. "Depends. Where this story is heading, Annie, means I may have to make a choice that will hurt her. Almost as much as Lord Oblivion hurt her when he crushed her soul and consumed her body for nearly six damn years. There's a plan, you see, my terribly clever plan that went terribly wrong for Tal."

"And what happens if you don't make that choice?" Annie asked softly. "If you don't betray the women you claim to love all over again?"

Another flash of anger gripped me, but I caught it a second time, settled on saying nothing for a long moment, and reminded myself I still had a lot of story to tell.

"Too early in the tale to give away the raised stakes scene, Miss Brie. I—"

Something... malignant stepped into the ward scheme, the net of intent, I'd cast around the shop. A taste like congealed blood flooded the back of my throat, the same scent caught in my nostrils. Annie saw the look on my face and stood with me, our respective firearms in hand. For the second time that night we stepped across my shop, through a thin layer of ash and scorch marks in the *Thriller* section, and headed for the plaza. The much more occupied and busy plaza, which was a concern if fighting were needed.

"What is it?" Annie asked.

I paused at the door, ready to chime the old bell, and stared out of the broken window at a man-shaped thing, something wearing human skin and a top hat, sitting on the rim of the marble fountain. It, he, whatever, trailed long fingers in the water and grinned at me from across the distance.

"Not human," I said. "Close, but not. Maybe once… huh, it's a deadling."

"You're mumbling," Annie said. "Is this trouble?"

I nodded, counting the variables—the honest lives in the plaza—watching the shadows, sensing something akin to the sickness of the Void, but not quite. A first cousin, perhaps, to the Voidlings. That taste of blood, the rough but not quite right shape, the outlandish top hat and cloak wrapped around its thin, almost skeletal form. This was a thing trying to pass for normal, and thus stood out all the more for missing the point entirely.

The creature on the rim of the fountain tapped three fingers across its heart and then waved at me.

"Oh," I said. "OK, then."

"What does that mean?"

"Well," I lowered my shotgun against my leg and reached for the door. "For the Willful, tapping three fingers of the left hand across the heart is a sign of… entreaty? Is that the right word? A truce, I suppose. A chance to talk."

Annie gripped her revolver all the harder. "I'm not Willful, Declan, but even I can sense that the… thing… over there isn't right."

"If it comes to shooting, shoot it between the eyes," I said. "Or in the heart. It's a deadling, one of the lower dead. A reanimated corpse—an emissary, you might say, being controlled from afar by a necromancer."

"That's horrific," Annie said.

I nodded. "Let's go see what it has to say. Stay on my right, would you?"

Annie swallowed, took a deep breath, and then nodded once on the exhale.

Given the civilians, the gentle folk enjoying dinner in the plaza, and the sign of entreaty, I left the shotgun leaning against the wall of books under the broken window. Annie concealed her revolver just inside her leather jacket, and together we stepped out into the warm night and approached the undead creature fouling the water of the fountain.

"Greetings, Shadowless Arbiter," the creature said as we drew level. I stood just on it—his—left, Annie to the right. The deadling inclined its head in a nod of respect that was, perhaps, meant to be mocking.

The lights from the shops, the streetlamps, shone down on us, but although the deadling cast a shadow onto the cobblestones, as did the lovely Detective Brie, I did not. I had sold my shadow long ago to end the Tome Wars, force the end. At the time, the bargain had been easy to make. I had been young, dumb. Tal had paid a far heavier prize in that bargain.

My fault. Always my fault. Consigned to the Void, my shadow had taken on a life of its own. It was me, a darker version, if that were possible. Me without consequence, without... guilt. Last we met, my shadow had escaped, kidnapped the Historian—a teenager who could see the future—and seized control of the greatest battleship in Ascension City's fleet. I felt partly responsible.

"Hey there," I said. "You know necromancy is forbidden on all civilised worlds."

The creature before me grinned, a grin stretched wide through split cheeks revealing yellowed teeth and rotten, grey gums. Dead eyes, pale cataracts, rolled in the sunken flesh of its face. Up close, the deadling wasn't even close to alive. It wore an aged tuxedo, worm-eaten and dusty.

"What on this or any other world makes you think True Earth is civilised?" the deadling asked. The voice was a rasp, vocal cords strained, as if scraped across jagged metal, and although the creature had once been a man, the voice behind the puppet, mingled with that of the necromancer, sounded mildly feminine.

My necromancer was a woman. And, unfortunately, could be on the other side of the world, for all the good that knowledge did me. Using a corpse as messenger like this was intricate, complex Will power.

"Be that as it may," I said, and crossed my arms over my chest. "Speak your piece and be gone."

"We need your help," the deadling said, surprisingly honest. Not a *request for assistance* or a *I require your aid, oh Knight*, just a simple statement.

"I don't help corpse defilers. The dead," and here

I was a hypocrite, "should stay that way."

"You, who have defiled entire worlds, have little authority on the matter."

"I am an Arbiter of the Knights Infernal," I said, "I have the only authority."

The deadling frowned. "I—"

"Why did you firebomb my shop?" I asked, and readjusted the patch covering my eye. The eye was healing, slowly but surely, vague colours and shapes, a perk of being Willful, but the creature before me still had more life in its eyes than my damaged one under the patch. Best to keep it covered.

"I'm sorry?" the deadling said.

"You will be."

"No," Annie said. "I think he… it… meant that it didn't throw the cocktail."

I nodded. "You expect me to believe that? A coincidence for you to show up only an hour or so later."

"I do not intend you harm this night," the deadling said.

"How about tomorrow night?"

It grinned again, gaunt cheek skin splitting almost to the ear.

I raised a single finger and spoke very clearly, allowing a trickle of my power to ignite in my hand, white light flowing through veins of red. "What you say next will determine the remainder of this conversation. Speak your purpose, I command it, or be destroyed."

The deadling considered, then nodded, shrugging a bony shoulder beneath the ruined tux. "The Atlas Lexicon formerly requests the aid of the Knights Infernal. We are besieged, the 'ways between worlds have been severed. This... creature was the only way we could get a message out to the world."

I crossed my arms over my chest again and gave the deadling a deep and surly frown. *The Atlas Lexicon...*

As far as I knew, there were two places in existence with that name. One I had visited not too long ago and promptly watched it be destroyed by an Emissary Dragon, a servant of the Everlasting, and the other...

The Knights Infernal used a nexus of worlds, a convergence point, to afford individuals without Will power, without magic, to cross the Story Thread, to travel to other worlds. A man named Thomas Atkinson had created a grand crossroads, an interdimensional train station, and called it the Atlas Lexicon. An apt name in many ways, but I feared—knew—the deadling wasn't talking about the ruined old train station. No, no.

Thomas Atkinson had named his creation in honour of the original Atlas Lexicon—a school, an academy, a hidden city here on True Earth, tucked away in an enchanted valley in the Swiss Alps. During the Tome Wars, the Knights had almost come to blows with the scholars, students, and practitioners of the Atlas Lexicon in Switzerland. The city was a centre of power, a necessary institution. The lords and ladies that ruled the Atlas Lexicon were not of the Knights, disagreed with our authority and policing of the Story Thread. A mind-set close to that of the Renegades, who had sparked the hundred years of war I had ended at the end of a bloody sword point.

"To whom am I speaking?" I asked the deadling. "Name yourself."

"I am Lady Evelyn Waterwood, Chief Librarian of the Atlas Lexicon."

The boss. "Why on earth would you come to *me* for help?"

"The Atlas Lexicon is cut off from the rest of the world, from *all* worlds. We are trapped in a dome of invisible magic, a source of malicious intent. The Restless Cemetery is stirring, the children are scared. And you, Declan Hale, are the only Knight Infernal we trust in this matter."

"You know who I am," I whispered. "What I've done."

"You forged and broke the shield of degradation that surrounded Atlantis, Arbiter Hale. Who else would we ask in our hour of need?"

"A lot of folks won't be happy if I show up on your doorstep."

The deadling chuckled. "No, not in the least, but we are under attack. The source of which… I believe it to be one of the Everlasting."

Now *that* got my attention. The shield around the ruins of Atlantis, which I had been responsible for in my youth, had been made by one of the Everlasting—one of the cruellest beings in existence. I knew what Lady Evelyn would say next before she even said it.

"I believe Lord Oblivion intends to destroy the Atlas Lexicon."

Oh, now the game got interesting. Yes, indeed. The Everlasting were… a complex lot. Gods, cruel and old, timeless, ageless, imprisoned and not. As children in Ascension City, we're taught an old rhyme that warns of the Nine. Over the centuries-turned-millennia the elder gods fell into myth, but I had met them, I knew them:

'Ware the Nine Forgetful Tomes
Storied names carved of old bone.
For the Nine see you as clear rose-light
Etched to stand against their blight.

Bitter Child craves his father's throne,
Yet Younger Scion sits all alone.

Dark travesty surrounds the Age Flood,
Lord Oblivion drowned in fire and blood.

The Sleeping Goddess can never forget
Fair Astoria, lost in time's tangled net.

Mind the snare of the Nightmare Sea—
Madness, the realm of Iced Banshee.

Distant threads tie the Ancient Bane
Pained Hail and his forever game.

Hear the wrath of the Marked Fear—
Harbinger Chronos is drawn near.

Starless paths through the Lost Sight
Dread Ash turns cold day to night.

Watch Fated Legion be destroyed
Scarred Axis fears the rampant Void.

The World-Eater, last in shadow's husk
The Never-Was King—Lord Hallowed Dusk.

So 'ware the Nine Forgetful Tomes
'Ware the Elder Gods from your home
Ageless, hateful, dull blight-flame—
The Everlasting know your name.

If the Everlasting had truly attacked the Atlas Lexicon—the original Lexicon, not the train station—then it was my duty to attend. Hell, who needed duty? I had lost my life to the Everlasting, an eye, countless friends and more. I'd gladly do my best to put them in the ground, if such a thing could be done. I had won, in the past, with the help of ancient weapons, the Roseblade and Myth, the world-dagger. Both were gone now beyond my reach...

Thoughts of the Everlasting inevitably led to thoughts of lost Emily Grace, my friend, the mother of my spirited away son, and revealed not so long ago as Fair Astoria—one of the Everlasting, perhaps the only decent being in the whole sordid group. She had given her grace, her immortality, in order to birth a child... I didn't know to what end yet. Thinking on Emily confused me something fierce, myriad emotions ranging from fear to anger to love and loss.

Oh, well.

"What say you, Arbiter Hale?" the deadling asked.

I fell from my thoughts and sighed. "It's not Oblivion, no." The terribly awful plan shivered through my mind. *Tal...* Story time with Annie would have to wait, unless I could convince her to come with me. "I'll be there in a few hours."

"Be wary of the shield that surrounds the city. It is... cruel. We lost three Dawn Mercenaries to its malice. Nothing may pass through it one way or the other."

"I've dealt with such before," I said. "But you know that."

The deadling nodded, pardon the pun, gravely. "Which, despite our lack of options, is why we called you."

"Not everyone will welcome my presence at the Lexicon," I said.

"You'll be accorded full guest rights and honours, as all Knights Infernal are granted during this time of... peace."

A smile touched my face at that. "My peace. How that rankles, does it not?"

The deadling said nothing.

I glanced at Annie. "We'll be there soon, within a few hours. Hopefully it will be a small matter to disable whatever malignant energy is powering the shield." It wouldn't be a small matter. It would be a salvage operation. The game was afoot.

"It cannot be disabled from the inside, that much is certain."

I had my thoughts on that. Indeed, such things often could only be broken from within. That's what made them so instrumental, so useful, to *prevent* attack. If Lady Evelyn Waterwood was to be believed, and I had my thoughts on *that*, too, then someone had cut-off the Atlas Lexicon on purpose. To starve it? To stop the librarians and soldiers there from conducting their duty? Or... to distract and escape? I guess we'd find out.

"Ensure this poor corpse is returned to whatever cemetery you dug it up from," I said. "We'll chat soon."

CHAPTER THREE

Road's Fire

"Down… down… down…"

I strode away from the necromanced corpse, turning my back on the marble fountain. Annie fell into step at my side and we headed back into my shop. More and more, I wanted that first drink. Just a sip. Take the edge off. The world was pushing at me, making me mighty thirsty.

"A lot of that conversation I didn't understand," Annie said.

I collected my shotgun and moved through the maze of shelves, brushing towering stacks of old hardcovers, dog-eared paperbacks, the occasional pile of loose parchment—an awesome fire hazard. The dull chandelier light, dim and perfect, cast everything in a timeless filter. Behind the counter, I retrieved a simple black duffel bag.

"No, sorry, I forget sometimes that there's a lot you need to know," I said and leaned over the counter to gently touch Annie's shoulder. "So, want to come to Switzerland with me?"

"Tonight?"

"You've travelled further—a lot further—on less notice."

"Well, that's certainly true."

She looked at the sparkling engagement ring on her finger, wondering no doubt on her fiancé, Brian, and what to tell him this time. Safe to say I had feelings for Annie, genuinely feelings, a lustful sort of love. How much of that was the petal of the Infernal Clock linking our hearts, I didn't know, but if I looked at the situation through the right sort of lens then I could almost believe I wanted her to come with me solely for the job, the support. She was a crack shot, and no rookie.

But in our secret hearts, buried deep where the lies can't reach, we all know the worth of such belief. I wanted Annie with me because I liked her close *and* because she was good with that revolver. If not for her, I'd have died a second time when we faced the Everlasting Scion on Diablo Beach.

As Annie gave the offer of monsters, mayhem, and magic the due consideration it deserved, I loaded the duffel bag with the shotgun, a few cases of shells, a gnarled rune-encrusted half-staff, a handful of useful tomes, a long-barrelled revolver of my own design, and a simple, silver-grey sword that was far more than it seemed. The sword, the result of a night of dark, stolen forging in Atlantis, was as close as I had to my knightly blade. Technically, the sword stripped from me at the end of the Tome Wars, just before my five years of exile began, should have long since been returned. My reinstatement to the Knights granted me such. I was owed.

"Grist for another day's mill…" I muttered and zipped up the duffel bag, hefted it onto one shoulder. It was heavy, but tight, manageable. I put it back on the counter. "Annie?"

"What's the Atlas Lexicon?" she asked. "That station we visited?"

"No, same name, but this one is different. A mini-city, hidden in the Swiss Alps a few hundred miles from the coast. Closest major civilian population would be Zurich, but the Lexicon is fairly isolated."

"I've never heard…" She shook her head. "Hidden. With magic? Enchantment?"

"Yep. True Earth holds many secrets, Annie."

"What do you think we'll find there?"

I retrieved an old book from the shelf behind me. The spine creaked as I opened it, half a decade of dust fell on my wine-stained, coffee-burnt mahogany countertop.

"Well," I said, scanning the index of the book and flipping to somewhere in the middle, "the Atlas Lexicon is sort of a… haven, I suppose. A school, or university. An academy. Its purpose is rather noble, actually. Which is why the Knights haven't bothered with it in centuries, not really. They were a little less than neutral during the Tome Wars, at the Lexicon, which almost led to their destruction." I chuckled. "It was a near thing. Long ago now."

"You're rambling, Declan."

I nodded. "The Atlas Lexicon houses and schools the children, usually teenagers, though much younger isn't out of the ordinary, that return from other worlds. Which is to say, you've read the books, Annie. Narnia, Peter Pan, all those stories of kids going off to other worlds and having adventures. A lot of them are true. What the books leave out, though, is when those kids come back to *this* world, and they almost always do, they come back a little messed up."

"How so?"

I scanned the book, the old maps that didn't quite reflect contemporary coastlines. The book was last updated during Roman rule. Only a few millennia, granted, but enough for much to have changed.

"Well, there are so many paths through the Void, hidden ways between this world and the impossibly infinite number of other worlds. Picture a kid, usually an orphan—I don't know why, but these hidden paths are easy to find for the little bastards—who goes off to another world. Talking lions, adventures... darkness and murder. Then they're thrust back into this world, the real world, and time has passed not always at the *same* time. They could have been gone years in the fantasy world, only to come back a few days after they left here, or decades, or no time at all. What do you think happens?"

Annie pursed her lips and nodded slowly. "They go home, if they have one, they try and fit back in…"

I nodded along. "They talk. Before you know it, they're in with therapists and caregivers who think the other world nonsense is some sort of mental break. The kids grow resentful, doubt themselves. Suicide rates among those that travel to other worlds and come back alone are almost four times that of any other poor soul left here on True Earth."

"So the Atlas Lexicon takes them in. It's like an interdimensional orphanage. I like that."

"That they do. They find these kids and offer them a place to learn, to live and study with hundreds of other kids who are going through the same thing. Often, the kids come back more than mentally changed, too. They come back Willful, or possessed of unique... talents. The Lexicon is the only place for them."

I ran a finger along the coast of Western Australia in the old book and found what I was looking for. "Here we go."

Annie stared at the page. "What is that?"

"The nearest portal point." I tapped the small island just off the coast, about twenty kilometres out to sea if the scale was right. "Rottnest Island. That's where we need to go tonight. This book, Annie, is *Road's Fire*. An ancient and spooky grimoire that lists all the known portal access points not between worlds, but between points on *this* world. They don't get much use anymore, but there's a line of convergence on Rottnest Island that links to the forests just outside of the Atlas Lexicon. We can be there in a few hours."

Annie frowned, considered, then shrugged. "Little convenient, isn't it?"

"How so?"

"Doorway exactly where we need to go only an hour or so away from here."

I chuckled. "There's doorways everywhere, if you know what you're looking for, and I do. Hell, the mirror in my bathroom upstairs is a portal directly into the Void. You've been through the stone archway under McSorley's in town—*that* one leads to thousands of other worlds."

Annie slipped her phone out of her pocket and

waved it at me. "Let me just make a quick call and we'll head out then. We're going to need a boat to get to Rottnest Island."

"I know a guy. You know him, too."

~~*~*

Ethan Reilly, my wayward apprentice and Sophie's boyfriend, stood at the helm of the small four-metre boat. The sea air whipped his long, shoulder-length brown hair about his head as he navigated through the portside markers toward Rottnest Island.

"Sophie still not talking to you then?" he had asked me, when Annie and I met him in the carpark at Hillarys Boat Harbour a half hour ago. "She's been off-world, you know. Not talking to me much, either."

I nodded. "Ascension City, last I heard, doing some advanced healer training courses. Keeping herself busy."

Ethan turned into the swell, the boat bobbing up and down a little too roughly for my liking. I was more at home in zero gravity, on the command bridge of an interdimensional battleship. The ocean was another game entirely. One I didn't have the stomach for.

"We're on the rocks, I think," Ethan said. "Sophie. Not the boat. It's your fault mostly, boss."

Annie gripped the aft railing for support. She held my duffel bag full of toys between her legs, gripped at the ankles. The rough crossing looked like it was making her feel a little unwell, too. She focused on the dark horizon, taking slow, deep breaths.

"A lot of things are my fault," I said. "She blames

me for Tal."

Ethan glanced at me sideways. "She should. You know that."

"I miss when you were scared of upsetting me," I said.

"That ended when I broke you out of space prison two or three adventures ago."

I grunted.

"Is Tal really not coming back?" he asked. "You'd think—"

"Think what?" I said, my tone low, careful. Dangerous. Tal was always a sore subject, now more than ever. I dwelled on the sword in my bag, the linchpin of my terribly awful plan.

"That she'd want to see her sister."

I can't go back, Declan.

I thought on Tal, left ten-thousand years in the past, in old Atlantis. She loved that city, loved the peace. *You'll fight this war, because that's what you do. When it comes to conflict and battle, war and chaos, the universe seems to spin around your head. You attract the absurd. I won't go back to watch you be consumed by it. Because that's the worst part, you know? They won't be able to kill you. You survive, Declan. You always, always survive. Even when you die, you live. No, you won't die. But you'll change. I can see it. The war will take you and you'll become hard, harder than you've ever been. You'll sacrifice entire worlds for one inch of an advantage against the Everlasting. Don't tell me you won't, because I know you, and you have.*

And here I was off to tangle with the Everlasting again, barely a week back from Atlantis myself. The Atlas Lexicon—of all my dark and difficult choices, involving that city had been among the worst.

"Where you off to this time?" Ethan asked.

"Rottnest is a tourist destination. Sandy beaches, old chalets, a decent bakery. Home to the quokka."

"What in the seven hells is a quokka?"

Ethan exchanged a look with Annie. *Can you believe this guy?* the look said. "Cute and furry marsupial. Rottnest is the only place in the world they live. Think like a cross between a squirrel and a kangaroo."

"Right, not relevant, but thanks."

Ethan rolled his eyes. "You're a miserable bastard, you know."

"Yeah."

"There's a mini fridge of beer in the bow storage if you want a drink," he said. "It's my uncle's, but he won't mind. Coopers Pale Ale, if I know him at all."

I was sorely tempted, but knew enough of that temptation to know that anytime I wanted a drink was the worst time to have one. "No, thanks," I said.

Ethan gave me another funny look and then a shrug. "OK, we're nearly there. About fifteen minutes out from the main jetty on the island. What's the caper this time, boss?"

"One of the Everlasting causing some havoc up north in Switzerland."

"Need a hand?"

"Don't know yet. For now, no, we'll be fine. I've got a plan. If you could, keep an eye on the shop for me. Someone tried to burn it down earlier tonight. Be careful, but I'd like to know who."

"You got it."

~~*~*

We said farewell to Ethan on Rottnest Island's main jetty. A cool sea breeze scented with salt whistled across the island. Lights from the nearby settlement, the beachfront villas, and the old white stone hotel and bar guided our way.

The hour wasn't yet midnight, and a few souls were out and about on push bikes, having dinner at the string of restaurants, drinking in the expansive courtyard of the Hotel Rottnest overlooking the water. Dozens of expensive boats bobbed on the calm water in the bay. And, as promised, dozens of little marsupials—quokkas—dotted the pathways and buildings, hiding under shrubs and trees. They looked like tiny kangaroos crossed with possums.

"I haven't been back here in years," Annie said. "Ten or more. It doesn't seem to have changed much."

"It's quiet, I like that."

Annie rolled her eyes. "You'd be bored inside a week, stuck here."

I thought about it and had to agree. Tal had been right about one thing—well, most things—I needed to be part of the fight. I liked to take names, bust heads, save the world. At least, that was always the idea. Reality was rarely so kind, and some days I was tired.

I muttered a quick incantation and a small marble of light, blue hue, appeared in the air. It hovered lazily, cast a small circle of light on the ground, and then floated east, away from the settlement and the hotel—toward the centre of the island.

"Follow the light?" Annie asked.

I nodded. "It'll take us straight to the edge of the Road's Fire portal. Won't be more than an easy mile, I'd say. I can feel it ahead somewhere close."

The tracking enchantment led us over hills, passed

the island's police station, small cemetery, and round a bend in the road. We sauntered past another block of accommodation, the Lodge, and a smaller bar full of drinking and merriment, and came to a vast, pinkish salt lake in the interior of the island. The water stank of algae, the light from the settlement barely reached the water's edge, but the night was warm.

My sphere of light came to a stop on the edge of the lake above a thin ribbon of sea foam stretching around the shore.

"Huh," Annie said. "I was expecting an archway or a stone circle or something."

"Road's Fire portals are more… points of convergence, of meeting. We can twist and bend reality here, touch this point to the one in Switzerland. I could have tried to force it from my shop, would have definitely made an opening, but the chance of catastrophic failure was too high."

"Catastrophic?"

I shrugged. "Reality stretched too thin… it's how we access the Void. Tear a hole through the canvas. Remember Myth, the Creation Dagger, made of celestial illusion? The fact that the knife could create points *anywhere* was perhaps its most valuable function."

Annie considered all that while I got to work with a few enchantments. In most of Europe and the old world, at points of convergence like this there *would* be an archway, a stone circle, or something to mark the portal-way. Stonehenge, for example, was perhaps the most concentrated source of Road's Fire on the face of True Earth. From there, almost all points on the globe could be accessed. Here though, on little old Rottnest Island in the cold and lonely Indian Ocean, we'd have to go in raw.

But I'd been trained by the best. I was the best.

Two minutes of silly hand waving, enchanted intent, and my Will forged a doorway in the air, eight feet tall by four feet wide. At first it was just a curtain of white light, reflected on the salt lake as a glowing rectangle, but then like a slide fixed on a microscope the portal came into stark, clear focus.

My Will snapped into place and the doorway opened. It was late afternoon in Switzerland, bright sunlight poured through the breach, along with the scent of wet, old forests—something foreign to this part of Australia. A quokka hopped along the shoreline, gave us very little notice, and bounced through the portal. The little creature looked around, surprised to find himself so suddenly in Switzerland, and disappeared from view around the edge of the doorway.

"I guess it's safe then," Annie said.

I sent one of my trusty mind webs out from Rottnest, through the doorway, and into the immediate area surrounding the portal in the forest. Nothing seemed out of place. Strong currents of magic in the air—untamed Will—but that was to be expected, given the nature of the Atlas Lexicon. It was, perhaps, the largest centre and concentration of power on True Earth. I knew that for fact. That concentration would get the Lexicon in trouble one day... and perhaps it already had.

Just on the edge of my senses, through the fairy-tale-looking forest, I felt something wrong. Something *malignant*. It was a shimmer, a pale reflection, of the Degradation I'd used to end the

Tome Wars. But whatever it was—a shield, a dome, a chokepoint—it was first cousin to my dark work all those years ago. And that work had been possible only with the help of the Everlasting.

"Not looking good?" Annie asked, reading my face.

"It's definitely our usual caper, which means death and demons and old gods. You still in?"

Annie grinned. "Never a dull moment."

I offered my hand, she placed hers in mine firmly, and we stepped as one through the portal, travelling several thousand miles in a single step. We left behind the warm night air, the stink of the pink algae on Rottnest, and entered the forests surrounding the Atlas Lexicon.

"What a nice day," Annie said. "That portal beats the hell out of ten hours on a plane and jetlag."

Moss and brambles, tall trees forming a canopy pierced by beams of warm light, and a meandering network of trails and pathways made up the nearby forest. I glanced over my shoulder, found an old worn stone archway holding my portal in place, and snapped my fingers. The portal vanished, the way cut off.

From my duffel bag I retrieved the sword and belt forged in Atlantis and strapped the weapon to my waist, and the gleaming shotgun. As before, I loaded my pockets—jeans and waistcoat—with extra shells. A little dell disappeared behind the portal archway, and I stashed the duffel bag down there. Nothing I couldn't replace in the bag, but it was best to have a few secrets. Especially if a hasty retreat were required. I loved a good hasty retreat.

"Which way?" Annie asked. She had drawn her

revolver. We were alike in many ways, almost reading each other's minds. If the connection through the petals in our hearts kept strengthening, mind reading wouldn't be far behind. I needed to sit Annie down and explain. She already suspected something, that much I knew.

I pointed northwest through the trees. The little quokka, thousands of miles from home, chewed quite happily on some leafy foliage atop a small mound of dirt.

"Guard my bag," I told him, as Annie and I set a quick march along a well-worn path through the trees.

"I think we're about two miles out from the main city," I said. "It's hard to judge. There's definitely something up ahead that's wrong. Dark magic, corrupted Will, that sort of thing."

"Any bad guys?"

"I'd wager yes."

Annie nodded and double-checked the load of her revolver.

Five minutes of walking and the trees thinned, the dirt path became a wide cobblestone lane, and we got our first proper look at the majesty of the Atlas Lexicon.

We were at the southern end of a massive valley, surrounded on all sides by towering mountains, the peaks and granite faces snow-capped and distant. Rolling green fields to the east, dotted with dozens— hundreds—of wild horses. To the west, something I'd only read about—the Restless Cemetery. A city, sacked and destroyed in Roman times, that now housed hundreds of thousands of tombs, surrounded by a sixty-foot high enchanted wall. To keep the dead inside. Much like the necromancy back in Perth that had summoned me here, the Restless Cemetery wasn't quite dead.

Annie and I glanced south, back along the cobblestone road toward a town—perhaps a mile away—of quaint little cottages, smoky chimneys, and a few odd farmers working in tilled fields. One of the fields held a contingent of tents, emergency vehicles, and dozens of people dotted to and fro within the mess. A mobile military command centre I could hazard a guess as to why it was needed.

The Atlas Lexicon sat at the north end of the valley. A solid mile north from where Annie and I had emerged from the forest. A mini-city of silver spires and towers, connected by crystal skybridges— and at its heart, as with all cities designed by the Vale, like Atlantis before and Ascension City after, the tallest tower, a skyscraper. The placement of such a tower granted the Atlas Lexicon legitimacy, power. Only a handful of places in all creation could claim a Vale-constructed tower. A sign of nobility, of the right to rule.

The one in Ascension City, where my brother sat on the Dragon Throne, was far cooler.

The Atlas Lexicon was impressive, but endangered.

A horrid purple-black shield of light, a dome like a snow globe, covered the entire city. It pulsed with ugly sourness, near-transparent, allowing us to see the towers within. Around that shield, creatures shambled and shuffled—things that looked vaguely human, things that didn't even bother. I knew, at least in part, what I was looking at.

"It's a breach."

"Sorry?" Annie said.

"A breach. Someone, something—our bad guy—has opened a breach to one of the dead worlds. They call them Wastewheres here at the Atlas Lexicon, if I remember that right. The worlds along the Story Thread that house nothing but monsters and darkness. Something cut a path through, letting all those creatures in. As for the shield… that's a different problem entirely."

"Declan, what's that over there?" Annie pointed not to the north, but more toward the west, across the cobblestone lane, to something moving through a copse of trees not too far away.

I threw a detection net in that direction and felt it ping against something cruel, old, dangerous. Something held together by ancient magic and pure cussedness. Surprisingly, I felt it sense me back, so it was at least mildly Willful.

I hefted my shotgun onto my shoulder. "Target practice," I said. "Come on!"

Knowing it was sighted, the beast burst from the trees, uprooting them, blasting the trunks into splinters as if tearing through tissue paper. What emerged was a skeletal thing, about twelve feet tall, with burning red coals for eyes in a skull elongated, stretched, to look like something you might see on a dragon.

Black leathery wings, rotten and useless, hung from its back. It stood on two legs and carried shackles, chains, in its bony arms. The beast roared, a sound that echoed across the whole valley, shook snow from distant peaks, and snapped the chains like whips. Blue fire erupted along the cold steel.

We closed the distance fast.

I was barely across the cobblestone lane when the

beast leapt—a deadling, I was sure, but of a kind I was unfamiliar—and covered the ground between us in three seconds. My shotgun was already raised as I cut to the side, a great mass of burning chain links gouging the earth where I'd been standing a half-second before. Cold air rushed past me, leaving a rime of blue frost on my arm.

I pulled the trigger on the shotgun, aiming for the pulsating black heart in the beast's chest. The heart ran slick with black, congealed blood—blood like oil.

A torrent of magenta and red flame roared from the barrel of my shotgun, six feet of fire, and a storm of pellets slammed into the beast. The deadling shrieked in pain and surprise, as it was thrown twenty feet back through the air, landing hard on its back, coils of its chains wrapped around its legs.

I was thrown back a few feet as well, the shotgun braced against the groove in my shoulder. Less than perfect form, but need's must and all that tosh, I hit the ground hard.

Annie offered me her hand and pulled me to my feet.

"That hurt?" she asked.

I grunted. The beast still howled in pain, desperately yanking at the knot of chains around its thin, skeletal legs—each of which, I noticed, ended in four razor-sharp claws.

"Want to kill it?" I asked.

"Yes, please," Annie said.

"I hit it pretty good. When it gets up, aim for the heart, Annie. Destroy the heart or the brain, that's how you put down a deadling. The shotgun blast should have opened up a nice hole in its ribcage."

Annie swallowed—myriad emotions warred across

her face: fear, doubt, resolved into tempered anger, righteous fury. I felt the moment she decided to put the beast down and raised her revolver.

The beast tore itself free of the chains and stumbled to one knee, red burning eyes focused on me with hate rarely seen in this world, and struggled to pull itself up. The shotgun had torn a good chunk of its hipbone away. One leg hung useless.

It reared back, arm and chain whipped up into the air, and exposed its chest.

The ribcage had shattered—but not nearly enough for Annie to make her shot. I could see its pulsing heart, bleeding more oil light from the few shotgun pellets that had pierced its armour, not enough to put it down, but enough to slow it down.

"Detective Brie—" I began.

"Shut up, Hale," she replied.

Being Hale, I shut up.

Annie rolled her shoulders and gazed down the sight of her revolver. She pulled back on the hammer for a hair trigger. The dark silver barrel wobbled, held, and then grew perfectly still. The breeze whipped Annie's dark hair about her face, but she didn't flinch. She breathed in once, exhaled slowly, as the beast leapt from the torn earth with a tremendous snarl—a fetid gust of decay washed over us, made me crinkle my nose.

Annie sighed, a gentle sound, and her revolver roared.

It happened almost in slow motion—at least for me. For a perfect few seconds, I saw the future clearer than the Historian. The silver bullet spiralled through the air, the beast fell into its path, and the lance of lead took the space between two of its ribs. A space no wider than a deck of playing cards.

The bullet punched the beast's heart, exploding that pulsating black mess, and time sped back up.

It's shrieks—of pain, of anger—stopped abruptly. As it fell through the air, truly dead, its entire form burst into pure white flame. By the time the beast struck the ground only five feet from us, it was already so much ash in the wind.

Annie gasped and took a step back. I put a hand on her shoulder and grinned.

"Nice shot," I said, knowing full well such a shot was impossible, and not of this world. Again, I thought of the petal in her heart. What was the Infernal Clock doing to her? The conversation would have to wait until our business at the Lexicon was concluded, but I feared even that much time may have been pushing my luck now. My hand was going to be forced, one way or another.

"Why did it burst into flame?" Annie asked. "Cold… flame?"

"Destroying the heart, you severed its connection to the magic keeping it 'alive'. Centuries of decay and death caught up with it all at once."

Annie took a deep breath and chuckled. "Cool."

"Agreed."

We turned to the sound of a convoy of vehicles roaring down the road from the town in the distance—or more likely the field command tents. A sleek set of four green Land Rovers, accompanied by a detail of military jeeps with rear-mounted machine guns. *M240's*, I thought, though hard to tell at this distance.

I retrieved my shotgun, the barrel red hot, but kept it pointed at the ground.

"Holster your weapon," I told Annie. "We're about to be arrested."

We walked back to the cobblestone road as the trucks pulled up level with us. I placed my shotgun down on the ground. My sword belt joined the weapon as the mounted machine guns swivelled in my direction. The grim-faced soldiers behind the machine guns looked young, far too young, but then in the grand scheme of things, I was young, too.

A tall man emerged from the first Land Rover, toting a blue crystal staff. He was classically handsome, dressed in a fine suit, and carried the air of a leader—of the big swingin' dick in charge.

"You are under arrest…" he began and trailed away. The colour drained from his face. His mouth moved soundlessly for a few seconds and he used his staff to steady himself. "By the Everlasting, Declan Hale!"

"Howdy," I said. "And this is my friend Annie."

My name spread like poisoned wildfire through the convoy. All four weapon mounts swung solely to point at me. Annie took a clever step to the side, distancing herself from the infamous Shadowless Arbiter and the potential hail of hot lead.

The tall man with the staff recovered enough to hold up a hand. "Nobody move. Nobody fire." He met my gaze, though it pained him. "I am Lord Towré Winter, the Seat of Neverwhere, of the Atlas Lexicon. The Knights Infernal are not to visit the Atlas Lexicon without invitation, Arbiter Hale."

"The Knights Infernal," I said, "don't know I'm here. It's just me, Winter, and I go where I damn well please." The sharpest knife in existence—a knife I used to own—would have struggled to cut through the tension in the air. "That said, I am here at the invite of Lady Evelyn Waterwood. She requested my assistance to deal with the... well, you know. Your infestation." I gestured vaguely to the north, at the horrid purple shield strangling the city.

"Lady Evelyn is trapped in the Lexicon," Lord Winter said. "We've had no communication with any of the governing body in two days."

"She used... alternative means to contact me," I said. "Means best discussed in private, Lord Winter."

Lord Winter considered, then nodded.

"Guest rights," he said. "For you and... Annie."

"So not under arrest?" I lowered my hands.

"Maybe later," Winter said. "Once we've had a chat. Avery, collect Arbiter Hale's weaponry. If you'd like to ride with me?" He gestured to his Land Rover.

I dropped Annie a wink. "Splendid. Let's go."

CHAPTER FOUR

The Twilight Hour

"So I never went back"

An armed escort... escorted... us through the encampment in the green fields just north of the quaint little town in the southern valley, which I learned from Lord Winter was known as Spire-Brunnen, the Fountain Spear—a bastardised translation from the old Germanic, but fit to purpose, I was assured. Whatever that meant.

The sleepy cottages, old churches, winding cobblestone lanes and markets, made the town look like somewhere worth living. I'd put a pretty penny on there being a damn good tavern. A tavern hoarding wooden-barrelled kegs bulging with delicious, foamy German beer. Bah, I shook my head to clear it. Sober and lovin' it, that was me.

I'd been in my fair share of military encampments,

emergency management centres, triage tents, and the operation in the field outside of Spire-Brunnen commanded by Lord Winter was a professional job. We marched past mess halls, armouries, barracks, vehicle depots, alongside communication tents and armaments pointed toward the Restless Cemetery and the Atlas Lexicon beyond. Lord Winter saw me inspecting his camp and I gave him a respectful nod.

The command tent had been constructed at the heart of the camp, a wide and white pavilion of reinforced steel frame and, at a wager, enchanted cloth to repel the most common—and a few uncommon—methods of attack, of eavesdropping, and intrusion.

Annie and I were led under the flaps at the entrance and entered a modern space, panels on the floor over the grassy field, and rows of desks holding computers. A large screen on the far wall held dozens of conflicting images—aerial views of the valley and the Lexicon, mostly. Dozens of people manned the desk, spoke into headsets, through tablets attached to their wrists. None of them spared us a glance. I saw attack parties in the fields to the north, battling with the deadlings and creatures surrounding the Lexicon at checkpoints and in trenches. They weren't idle, I'd give them that much. Hell, I was impressed.

Lord Winter led us to a glass cube of an office on the western wall of the tent. We sat down on a fine leather sofa, Annie and I, and were brought cups of steaming hot coffee, which given the hour stretching toward midnight for us, on Perth time, was most welcome. We had no worry about jetlag, as Annie had said, but it was still going to be a very long day.

The doors to the glass cube closed with a

whispered hiss on pneumatic rails, sealing Annie and myself in with Lord Towré Winter. He walked with a limp, I noticed, masked by his impressive dark obsidian and blue staff, which he now racked against one of the glass walls.

Winter, perhaps the most handsome man I'd ever seen, sat opposite us in a leather armchair and smiled. I noticed the canine teeth on either side of his upper jaw were diamond, or something like diamond. The man had crystal teeth. Sure.

A long moment stretched toward uncomfortable. Annie fidgeted next to me. I took a polite sip of rather decent coffee, though I was no real judge of such things.

"I never thought to actually meet you," Lord Winter broke the silence. "You're more myth than man. More legend than legit."

"True Earth is under my protection," I said mildly. "That includes the Atlas Lexicon." Winter frowned and opened his mouth to protest. "Whether you want that protection or not." My tone brooked no argument. "Though I've no intentions to dismantle your leadership or upset the sovereignty of the Lexicon. I admire the work you do here. I would like to see it continue once we clear up the unpleasantness to the north."

"Thank you for your candour," Winter replied with half a smile. Ever the diplomat, it would appear. "Unpleasantness, indeed. That's putting it mildly. Deadlings roaming outside the Restless Cemetery. That hasn't happened in centuries."

"They're not from your cemetery, if that helps," I said. "You've been world-breached. That shield encasing the city is more than just a barrier—it's a doorway, a path, through the Void. Whoever put it in place, and there's only a handful of suspects there, linked it to a dead world."

Winter scratched his chin and nodded. "That answers a few questions we had, yes. I see." His gaze flicked to Annie. "Annie," he said. "Detective Annie Brie of the Western Australia Police. I'd ask what you're doing here, but glimmers of your reputation precede you. Your work with Declan Hale, for one. Repelling the invasion of the Everlasting Scion. And that shot on the forest outskirts was nothing short of miraculous."

I tensed, then reminded myself of the guest rights, that for all that mattered Winter and I were on the same side. Still, he was remarkably, and swiftly, well informed.

Annie smiled and it was beautiful. She elbowed me in the ribs. "Well, sir, I have to be sharp to keep this one out of trouble. Can you tell us more about what happened to your city?"

Winter nodded. "Just under two days ago the cancerous shield you see around the Lexicon fell, cutting off the city. All lines of communication were severed. I was off-world at the time, but returned to lead the counterattack."

"How many enemies do you estimate?" I asked.

"Between nine hundred and nine hundred fifty visible targets lurking outside of the shield."

"How many people in the city?" Annie asked.

Winter heaved a heavy sigh. "Some thousand. Mostly children, teenagers. We've only just commenced our summer term. Plenty of people and soldiers in there who know how to look after themselves, of course, but we have no real idea what's going on. We can't penetrate the shield at all. Our drones have some visual, but the image grows hazier the closer you get to the city. It is… maddening." He clenched and unclenched his fists. "How did Lady Waterwood contact you?"

"You won't like it," I said. He held my eyes. "Necromancy."

Lord Winter inhaled sharply and cursed in a very unlordly way. "She would never. Edicts as old as the Lexicon itself forbid such dark magic."

"It was used to good purpose," I said. "With me here, you've a chance of saving the city."

Winter scowled and cut his hand down through the air. "Please. The Shadowless Arbiter, the genocidal librarian—the boy who destroyed the Reach, who split the sky above Voraskel and Avalon, who used the Roseblade to slaughter countless innocents. The most infamous Knight Infernal to ever blight the Story Thread. You'll do more harm than good."

I took another sip of coffee. "Hey now. A man could take that all personal."

Lord Winter stood and paced his office. He took a moment, hands clasped behind his back, before turning to face me. "That was… unseemly," he conceded. "I hope no offence was taken."

Not an apology. I shrugged.

"Did Lady Waterwood report on conditions in the city?"

I frowned. "Actually, no. She was… almost happy. Perhaps an effect of the necromancy, but the corpse she used kept grinning like an idiot at me."

Pensiveness stole across Annie's face. "Slightly mocking, I thought. Arrogant."

"Has it occurred to either of you," Winter said carefully, "that perhaps Lady Waterwood was not the person to summon you here. That, perhaps, you've been brought here by someone—or something—with less than good intentions."

"It's occurring a bit now," I said. *But you would have ended up here eventually, Declan, sooner rather than later.*

Winter grunted. "You said the pool of suspects for the shield would be small?"

I ran a finger along my eyebrow, skirting the edge of the patch over my dead eye. "Can you not guess?"

"All too well," he muttered. "I'd still have you say it."

I looked to Annie.

"One of the Everlasting," she said. "An Elder God."

"Or so they like to think." I scoffed and crushed my empty coffee cup. "They bleed, they can die." Emily Grace, Fair Astoria, laughed softly in the back of my mind. "They're more human than they care to admit, sometimes."

"The Everlasting…" Lord Winter shook his head, face pale, despaired. "Thousands of years without a whisper from them, just scatterings of old rhymes, half lost myths, and now ever since you recovered the Lost City of Atlantis, Arbiter Hale, and the Roseblade, we seem to have to contend with the Everlasting every year."

"Sometimes twice a year," I said. "It'd make a damn good series of urban fantasy books one day, all these hijinks. Maybe I'll write them."

Lord Winter moved behind his desk and scrawled a few words on a notebook. He spared a look at me, paused, and then signed his name with a flourish on the paper. "Official request for aid from the Knights Infernal," he said. "Whether you spoke to Lady Waterwood or not, you are now officially here, Arbiter Hale. I formally request, by the old accords, your services in dealing with the matter to the north."

I cracked my knuckles and grinned. "Cheer up, mate. This could be fun."

"I do not see how this can end without greater loss of life."

My grin faded. "Yeah, that's usually cover charge at the door for these parties." I shook my head. "Anyway, let's hear it then. What's your plan?"

Lord Winter cast aside his pen and crossed his arms. "We're launching our major assault in three hours, just before sunset. If you know the lore, you'll know deadlings are at the weakest during the twilight hour. The corruption holding them together more susceptible to attack."

I nodded. "Zombie Fighting 101, chief. I would like to assist."

Lord Winter considered, then his façade broke and he gave a nervous laugh. "I have no idea what to do with you, Arbiter Hale. Or where to place you on the battlefield."

I threw him a lifeline. "Front and centre. I wanna take a shot at that shield. If I can get through, and I have a sneaking suspicion I can, then I'll have this nonsense sorted by dawn. And call me Declan, Winter. My friends call me Declan."

I said that idly, but there was a weight behind my words, an implication. I was here, officially, as a requested representative of the Knights Infernal. To offer my friendship alongside that messed with the accords—in the best way, in my favour. Lord Winter, who would not have risen to the title of Lord of the Atlas Lexicon, in the Seat of Neverwhere, without being at least marginally intelligent, would understand the ramifications.

He took a deep breath and exhaled. "You… bastard."

I grinned.

Annie looked lost, then masked it. She was my wild card, and knew it.

"Very well," Winter said. "If you want to charge headfirst into an army of deadlings, who am I to stop you?"

"Could you stop me?" I said quietly. Then winked.

Lord Winter found a wry grin. "You might be surprised by what we're capable of here."

"I hope so."

That felt like the end of the meeting. Annie and I stood and shook hands with Lord Winter.

"The camp is at your disposal. Food, sleep for a few hours, whatever you need from the armoury. I intend to wipe that undead mess from my pretty mountain valley before nightfall. I trust we're on the same page there."

We said goodbye and stepped out of the command tent, back into the late afternoon sunlight. I was a little hungry, thinking about it. It was long since dinner time back in Perth. Annie and I walked over to the mess tent, following the scent of roasting meat, exotic spices, and all things delicious.

We helped ourselves to the buffet and I pointedly ignored the stares, the looks—some careful, some fearful, most assessing—I got from the other soldiers and support staff. Word had spread, it seemed, that the Shadowless Arbiter was in town. Annie and I found a quiet table on the edge of the mess, overlooking the mountains and the forest to the east.

"Three hours to kill," Annie said. "I'm going to need some more ammunition."

"They'll have all sorts of cool stuff here, Brie." I took a bite of roast beef dolloped in mashed spuds and gravy. "We'll be like kids in a candy store."

"Apart from the demons, this is a nice part of the world." Annie held another cup of coffee warmly between her hands, gazing out at the picturesque landscape.

"They're not actually demons," I began, then saw her look and waved my words away. "Want to hear more of my time in Atlantis with Tal while we wait? Two hours should get us through most of the next bit."

Annie blinked. "Oh, I'd almost forgotten. The dark and brooding choice you have to make, the lost love Tal, all the drama that is your life."

"If I didn't know any better, I'd say you were poking fun."

Annie stuck her tongue out at me. "Tell your story, Declan. Tell it well."

REMINISCENCE THE SECOND

(Back in Atlantis, may it do ya fine)

The Vale Celestia

The Vale Celestia School for Gifted Youngsters was off-world, which was the way of things back home at the Infernal Academy in Ascension City, as well. A pocket world had been written into existence, kept secret and safe and tailored to the needs of the Atlantean Willful. If they were doing this business right, only a handful of access points to the world would have been created and known. Hiding worlds away like this was like hiding a needle in a stack of needles the size of a planet... that shifted and changed dimensions. Rather effective.

Still need to figure out why they stick 'Vale' in front of everything important.

The Vale Atlantia in the city of Atlantis held a portal chamber, much like the interdimensional train station (also called the Atlas Lexicon, just to keep things confusing) of my time, only smaller, which led to a few dozen such pocket worlds. The bustling floor of the spire was packed with people, Willful and otherwise, flipping between worlds like the pages of a book. Grand archways of archaic brown stone, small doorways of dark glass, and simple tunnels disappeared into the walls of the portal chamber. Glimpses of other worlds, from snowy landscapes to busy cities, to wide open fields littered with wildflowers and oceans of tranquil blue water, filled the portals.

The largest of these portals, in the very heart of the room, framed by twin curved pillars of white stone, led to the Atlantean academy—to the Vale Celestia. Or so my minders told me, as we were escorted through the VIP lines. A familiar tingle rushed down my spine as we crossed the threshold, stepping from smooth marble floors to a stone pathway, and left True Earth behind. My Knightly senses tingling again, sensing the change in worlds.

We stood in a field above a wide valley full of buildings, some nestled against the slopes of mountains that stretched toward the sky, a half ring of distant peaks running in a horseshoe around the valley. The marble stone path wound down toward the various buildings, some of which looked as old as time itself while others as shiny and new as most of Atlantis. The valley was strewn with small forests and rivers, and a warm, crystal blue light bathed the entire world.

We went from daylight, morning, to night in a matter of footsteps.

I took one look at the sky and figured out why they'd given this place a name as pretentious and ethereal as *Celestia*.

The heavens here were, in a word, beautiful. I use that word an awful lot, often with vague romantic ideals, but here, in this place, it was the truth.

I'd seen some sights in my life, walked a few paths unknown, unseen, and unfound. Wonders enough to marvel the mind, abuse the senses, and horrors all too imaginable. I have flown starships through the fiery crucibles of distant stars, I've wandered in worlds where the oceans are made of diamonds, and the mountains ruby fire. Worlds of pure thought, written into existence by the Willful. Madmen and geniuses alike.

I've seen some shit, you could say.

But the sky above the Vale Celestia was something else again.

The source of the blue light bathing the world was a band of what I assumed were asteroids of pure gemstone, or ice, caught in interstellar cloud. The asteroids, some large enough to be rightfully called planetoids, haloed the Vale Celestia, diluting the black of the night and obscuring the starry arms of the galaxy. Twin moons hung in the sky, close and large, one just above the other. The larger one seemed near enough to reach out and touch. I could see the shadows in the craters, darker lunar soil in deep canyons, and veins of manmade light that I guessed was a small city on its surface.

The sky reminded me of the Voidflood that had forced the Renegades to abandon Voraskel and destroyed Avalon. Dark days in the Tome Wars, when I was rising to prominence and just before my fall from grace. Those two worlds had collided, two points of reality that should never had touched had *slammed* into one another. The result had been, in a word, apocalyptic. A victory, the Knights had called it, at the time. Destabilising the entire Renegade regime and eventually forcing their surrender after I'd bargained for the Degradation in the ruins of Atlantis. *Everything came back to that city, one way or another, and now I'm actually here.* I'd visited Voraskel a handful of weeks ago, to watch Emily die and retrieve the Roseblade from the Tomb of the Sleeping Goddess. From Emily's tomb. The world of Voraskel was crumbling, home now to nothing but Forgetful spawn and prone to the Void leaking through the immense cracks. Voraskel would be consumed before the decade's end.

Tal wasn't watching the sky. She was watching me. I felt her gaze, met her eyes, to see the glowing belt of gemstones reflected in those deep, green pools.

"For a moment," she said and smiled. "Just for a moment. You wanted to stay." She kissed me on the cheek. I considered turning to try and catch her lips but thought better of it. "Love at first sight, this place."

"Come. This way," Trey said. "You are expected for the feast."

"Hey," I said and took Tal's hand. "Feast. Cool. Will there be rum, my good man?"

"It's technically not even ten in the morning," Tal said. "No drink for you."

"You know that saying 'It's five o'clock somewhere'." I gestured to the new world, swept my hand across the Vale Celestia as we began the slow, winding descent toward the main streets and thoroughfares in the valley below. "Yeah. This is what it means. Plus how many time zones do you think we crossed travelling back in time ten thousand years? We're not on any sort of normal time, Tal."

She bristled. "You want a drink, then have a drink."

I nodded. "I do. But... I probably won't."

"Probably?"

"Well, if there's dark rum we're doomed."

Tal let go of my hand. "Please take this entirely as

it sounds, Declan, but at a certain point your need for a drink turns from charming to desperate. Pathetic, even. You crossed that point some time ago."

And you used to be a lot more fun, I thought but didn't—could never—say. Not only was it mean and unfair, but six years of rape, torture, and murder at the hands of Oblivion was enough to destroy the heart and hopes of any soul. Tal had, for all that mattered, clung to the essence of who she was—the girl I had known and loved.

And that was incredible.

I would have buckled long ago.

I hated myself for thinking she used to be more fun. We'd all been through hell and back, more than once, some of us even had a platinum membership card. One more trip and I got a free spicy kebab. Yes, sir, right this way. Welcome back, Mr. Hale. We've prepared your usual seat at the bar. Shall I open a bottle of the '89 or the '72 Regret Pomerol? But Tal... Tal had given herself to Oblivion willingly, sacrificed herself so the entire Story Thread could be brought to peace.

A peace that, given the events of that night, atop of the ruins of what I now knew was called the Vale Atlantia, had only lasted six years. The Everlasting were free—by my hand, although it had been manipulated well. For that reason alone I couldn't stay in this world and grow old with Tal. I had work to do.

But perhaps a few weeks or even months wouldn't hurt.

I won't bore you with the details—we feasted well, that night, though it felt like mid-morning for me and Tal. Decadent plates in a banquet hall fit to burst with students, teachers, and the rich and powerful. All come to see the two time travellers, who had arrived bloodied and beaten, bearing portends and prophecies of doom. I felt like something of a jester, a novelty, but resisted the drink, and instead gorged myself on pork belly and plum sauce, and a few honeyed apples.

I shook many hands, met many professors, craftsman, engineers, guards, the sort of folk that kept a university—particularly one that trained people to harness the power of creation—spinning along. Another reason these sorts of places were built in pocket worlds alongside main cities was because if the students lost control, the damage was contained.

I learnt that the amazing, interstellar sky here was permanent—we were moored in space, not orbiting a star. A nifty piece of Will enchantment. The sky was eternal night, and I liked that. It removed the element of time, made it easier to forget my responsibilities back home.

Of most importance that night, I met a cute, pixie-faced woman named Fix. She was lithe, bubbly, standing at just five feet and change. One of the vice chancellors introduced her as my caretaker here at the Vale Celestia. Fix's hair was cut short, bounced over her ears, and changed colour depending on the light, but favoured lilac. Her eyes with bright, sparkling purple, and her smile was contagious.

"I think we're going to be great friends," she said, and pulled me onto the dance floor for a bit of a shuffle. "We've had many applications for your course, Arbiter Hale."

"Declan, please," I said, finding her face fascinating. "Just Declan."

"What's the future like, Just Declan?"

"There's a lot less dancing."

"Oh no." She laughed. "If you've time later, we can go over the applications together."

I nodded, and a few hours later found myself in a tiny little office of one of the central buildings surrounding the Vale Celestia. It was a quaint little space, quite academic, full of books, and a desk, and no weapon racks. To be honest, having an office made me uncomfortable. But Fix made the experience more than pleasant.

I sat down at my desk and surveyed the applicant files before me with a critical eye, tapping my chin thoughtfully, as if I knew what I was doing. Opening the first one, I was met with an image of a pretty girl with silver-grey eyes and blue skin that made me think of Clare Valentine. The file was written in a runic script I didn't understand. With a sigh, I handed the documents to Fix.

"Read this to me twice, please," I said.

"Would you like a tablet to take notes? This girl's name is Tylia Vuleta Vale."

Vale again.

I shook my head. "Read it twice and I'll remember the important bits. Come on, let's get started. We've a dozen more to go after this one."

~~*~*

The next morning, though it was still eternal night outside, I gave my first lecture in a small theatre within the heart of the Vale Celestia. Yeah, I know, I had a job, a normal job, and I could see myself being good at it. Wouldn't be too long before some monster or demon showed up to ruin things, I'm sure, or an Everlasting jumped out of the shadows, but until then.

Training. Teaching. Learning.

"Good morning, ladies and gentlemen," I said. "Can you all hear me? Can you all… understand me?"

A general murmur of assent rippled through the ranks. I nodded to my assigned translator. Fix stood and said, in what I assumed to the rest of the class was fluent Atlantean, "Do you all understand this man? Raise your hand if you do not."

No hands went up so I clapped my hands together and rubbed them in anticipation—all the translation enchantments were in place.

"Very good. Then welcome to Infernal Training 101, my friends. My name is Declan Hale. My rank as your commander is Arbiter. You may call me Arbiter, or Arbiter Hale. Or Declan. Hell, I'm not too fazed."

A hand went up in the front row. A young man who reminded me of Ethan, Sophie's boyfriend, although he had darker skin and more laughter in his eyes, cleared his throat. From the files I'd read last night, his name was Elan. He was eighteen and useless at the subtler Will enchantments, like healing, much like my good self, but a lot of raw power pooled unseen behind those merry eyes.

"Question at the front?"

"Arbiter… Is that a title? A designation? I am unfamiliar with this rank."

"So you are—so you should be. Where I'm from, a very long way from here, I belong to an order of knights. Men and women of Willful inclination who are devoted to the cause of protecting the Story Thread from the enemies of humanity." *And protecting it from humanity itself, more often than not.* "In this room you will be graded accordingly and in line with the ranking system of the Knights Infernal. If you are here today, it is because *I* wanted you to be here. I intend to turn you into delicious, soldier milkshakes, because the high lords didn't really understand what they were doing when they put me in charge of you lot—who I am or what I'm capable of teaching you." I laughed. "We have something approaching the element of surprise there."

The files I'd read—translated by pixie-faced Fix—had not been encouraging. My selection of students had been what was left after the other commanders, teachers really, had formed their squads. Which was fine. Which was all good and well. Because I didn't need the best or the brightest—I just needed the eager and the willing. If these kids, and I did think of them as kids despite some of them being in their twenties and only a handful of years younger than me, wanted it badly enough, I could show them how to command Will beyond their wildest imaginations.

"Arbiter… Declan," Kara Denitae said, seated next to Elan. She was nineteen, blonde, nimble and fast. Some of the best Knights I'd ever trained alongside had been short but swift. Size didn't matter when you could shoot fire from the palms of your hands. I could use her.

"Yo," I said.

"We heard you and another… visitor have been put in charge of the last two teams of students. Could you tell us more about yourself?"

Kara glanced at one of her fellow teammates, a redhead named Sardi, according to the files. Sardi was the oldest kid in my squad at twenty-two. She had a face of severe angles and wore a necklace of fine gold which travelled under her shirt and down her bare arm to become a bracelet. I hazarded a guess that the golden contraption was the focus for her Willful talent.

"Who are you?" Sardi asked. "Where do you come from?"

"All in good time. Someone tell me about the Vale Celestia," I said with a grin and leaned back against my desk. "Pretend I've never heard of this place before, never seen a single team of students work together. What should I expect?"

The class exchanged looks, shrugs, and it was Tylia Vuleta, the youngest in the group at seventeen, who spoke up first. She was of a race I didn't recognise, most likely from some world that didn't exist in ten thousand years, or had mingled with the rest of the Story Thread so much to dilute the culture into something else. Her skin was sapphire blue and her hair, tied up in a bun atop her head and held in place with white chopsticks, was as dark as shadow on a moonless night. Her eyes were mesmerising, the iris' cut with a grey spiral through pale green pupils.

"Well, once you have trained us, Declan, we are to compete in a tournament designed to test our understanding of the several avenues of Will studied here at the Vale Celestia," Tylia said, and her voice was a soft whisper that somehow echoed in the small room. She carried her focus, her magical wand, on a brace strapped to her arm. A piece of gnarled oak wrapped around a rod of obsidian glass about eight inches long. "The stages of the competition will include duelling, Willful artistry including practical demonstrations, forging Will-infused artefacts, and team skirmishes designed to test our nerve."

"Duelling, is it?" I nodded. "One on one?"

"Not necessarily," Tylia continued. "We are each gifted a cosmic sphere before the assessment begins. One for each team member and one for our team leader, Arbiter Hale." She glanced at her companions. "Six spheres, small crystal orbs about the size of an egg. We can wager these spheres against our competitors. If we want to enter the duel with two members of our team, we must gamble two spheres. Three members, three spheres, you see? You, as our team leader, are meant to be kept only for the more difficult challenges. Some of the duellists on rival teams are quite adept. It may take two or three of us to best one of them."

Not by the time I'm done with you. "And if we lose all our spheres?" I asked.

"Elimination," Tylia said simply, and as if she expected this as the most logical outcome. "Expulsion from the Vale Celestia. I imagine you, too, will lose your employment."

Elan scoffed. "I will win all our duels," he said to Tylia and gestured to the room at large. "You may bet your spheres on that, *castri'l.*"

Tylia bristled as if stung and I looked to Fix, who chuckled softly. *What does that mean?* I asked with a raised eyebrow.

Fix shrugged. *"Castri'l,"* she said, twirling her finger in the air. "Hmm… perhaps 'sweet of heart', is the closest translation. A term of endearment or affection. Elan is being flirtatious."

Tylia turned a deeper shade of blue and glared daggers at Elan. He let those daggers stab him and smiled.

"Moving on, Elan," I said. "I've got a few months to whip you lot into shape then. I expect my squad to decimate the competition, you understand. We will win the trophy or the cup or the whatever the devil is on offer here. Gold medals all round, you hear me?"

They heard me, but the translation didn't seem to go over too well.

"We're going to win," I clarified. "You have a problem with that, Nemin?"

The last member of my ragtag group of no-hopers was a young man of eighteen. He had heavily augmented himself with Will enchantments that had altered his physical appearance. He was human, unlike Tylia, but his eyes had been modified to resemble those of something feline, like a jungle cat—narrow slits and a haunting glow. He had a mane of long purple hair pulled back in a ponytail. He wasn't burdened with muscle, but his chest and arms visible around the tight black vest he wore looked strong and corded. His ears tapered to a fine point, like shark fins.

"No problem," he said. "Unlikely we win, but no problem."

"We'll see. Training starts tomorrow morning, ladies and gentlemen. Be here an hour before first light—dressed to run five miles."

"There is no first light, Declan!" Fix said brightly. "It's always sparkling night here at the Vale Celestia."

"Right, of course. Five a.m., ladies and gentlemen. Nice and early."

With my instructions known and clear, I walked out of the room and went exploring my home for the next four months.

~~*~*

I spent most of that day exploring the grounds of the Vale Celestia on my own. Fix looked like she had somewhere to be. "Have to see my sister," she said. "Always a family emergency with her."

But she wanted to meet me for lunch, which was nice, so I wished her well and went for a stroll across the campus. Of the minders that had tailed me everywhere in Atlantis, there was no sign. Perhaps I was trusted enough to meander through the forests under the crystal night sky alone now that I was gainfully employed.

More likely I was being watched through subtler means. Enchantments and the like. I could have cast a few diagnostic incantations, but with the myriad charms already clinging to my waistcoat and the translator enchantment running pretty much night and day, I'd be hard pressed to sense any unique trackers through the maelstrom. I was drenched in Will.

It was the sky that amazed me the most about this school. The gemstone asteroids and the city built on the surface of the moon. Perhaps when I made it back to Ascension City, to the Knights Infernal and the Academy, I'd suggest some changes. We could have used an obstacle course like the one above to train pilots during the war. Most of the recruits had been baptised in fire, given the supply versus demand in the Tome Wars.

I'd been a pretty decent pilot. An even better commander.

A could-be king?

"Bah," I said, following a dusty trail between two

buildings covered in old vines. "Too nice a day to think on such things."

The students of the Vale Celestia, colourful and quiet, in groups and alone, did give me curious glances as I made my way around their campus. Word had already spread ahead of me, as word was wont to do. I was beginning to see that my arrival and my job here was something of a big deal. Olympics-style big deal. To have two new teams of students enter the fray a few months after the initial selections had created some buzz.

Part of me, and not a small part, was looking for a bar. I knew the road back to the portal which would take me to Atlantis would be open. I could slip back to the city for a few hours, get nicely toasted, and stumble back. But every time the thought crossed my mind I also thought of Tal's sad eyes, her almost entreaty for me to lay off the sauce.

Don't do it for her, do it for you.

Hell, that voice sounded far too much like personal growth for my tastes. I squashed that vector for change swiftly and sat down on a grassy hill, sparsely populated with spruce saplings, and lay back with my head resting on my hands so I could spend a lazy hour staring at the pale night sky.

Ten thousand years, I thought. As far as running away from your problems went, I'd run a marathon or two. The Roseblade inserted into the melted and warped devastation of the Infernal Clock had sent me back here—Tal had hitched a ride at the last minute—and I couldn't help but wonder if there was some reason for me to be here. I wasn't arrogant enough to think the universe revolved around me— okay, yes I was, sometimes, and indeed, sometimes it had—but most of my life had been manipulated and guided by some purpose. Some sort of... divine destiny.

Now *that* was arrogance on par with the Elder Gods.

But I always found myself in the wrong place at the wrong time. Time and place enough to make some sort of difference on global, even universal, scales. For good or ill, my choices had ended wars, saved or ruined millions, and made a lot of people cry. I was an Arbiter of the Knights Infernal.

We made a mess, that's what we did.

But *by the Everlasting*, we cleaned it up.

~~*~*

The next morning, as the moon rose and diluted the dark blue asteroid belt to a sort of azure haze, I had my recruits—sorry, my students—out running laps around the Vale Celestia. A light rain had fallen in the night, soaking the ground, and a humid mist clung to the air like an annoying shower curtain to the leg. I ran at the head of the group, surprisingly somewhat in shape after a few weeks of heavy drinking.

I'd made a promise to myself last night, all alone in my chambers up in the staff quarters on the eastern slopes of the valley, that I'd get back into the routine I'd followed during my time at the Infernal Academy and the Tome Wars. Tried, tested, and true, a daily routine had seen me at my best, most productive— and most dangerous. Even back then, though, I'd been able to enjoy a drink and still get up and run in the morning.

These days... bones old before their time ached from past fractures, joints torn and shredded sang the song of their people, and scar tissue ropy and tight pulled at my side, along my stomach. One scar in particular, where Morpheus Renegade had gutted me in the ruins of Atlantis close a year ago. I couldn't get up in the morning with a hangover as well as those aches and expect to run at my best.

I was older. Not old. Just older. Wiser? I understood the need to stop drinking. I also understood that one drink with dinner couldn't hurt, right? *Bullshit.* When a train hits you, it's not the third carriage you need to worry about. There's a certain sort of wisdom in self-awareness, and I was aware that when it came to alcohol, for me, one drink was too many and ten was not enough.

Hi, my name's Declan. Declan Hale. I'm the Shadowless Arbiter, the Never-Was King, architect of the Degradation and wielder of the Roseblade. I walk between universes, I've seen civilisations burn, I've burned them, and I commanded the Cascade Fleet against the Eternity-class battleships of the Renegades during the Tome Wars. Oh, and I'm an alcoholic.

I didn't think there was a meeting anonymous enough to hide my particular brand of bullshit.

So I'd made a promise. To Tal, because I couldn't trust myself to keep it otherwise. Commit to the routine. Just for the days, weeks, or months I called this time and place home. Atlantis and the Vale Celestia... it was like checking into rehab. I had time to *breathe*, away from the dregs of the Tome Wars and the Everlasting. If I didn't feel better after a few months of sobriety then I could go back to killing myself one drink at a time once all this Atlantis nonsense was said and done.

"How... much longer... do we have... have to run?" Elan asked. He drew in deep, desperate gasps of air.

"Two more minutes," I said, breathing a little heavier than I would have liked myself. "Oh, and look, Elan, it's all up hill."

Tylia gave him a disdainful look over her shoulder. "Hurry along, *castri'l,*" she said sweetly.

I laughed and so did Fix, who had decided to train with the six of us, even though it was outside her job description. I liked Fix, she was pretty and fun, so I was certain we were heading for heartbreak.

A few minutes later I called a halt to the run on a small rise overlooking the northern bend in the valley. Most of the Vale Celestia stretched out behind us, and some impressive snow-capped mountains rose up in front. A cool breeze rolled down those mountains, fighting the humid mist which hid most of the buildings and trees.

"Okay, good hustle," I said. "Now we're going to do it again. On three!"

Groans and desperate gasps for mercy burst from my small little group of hopefuls. I started to jog back down the hill and all save Elan and Sardi made a half-hearted effort to follow me. A few paces down the hill I raised a hand to stop.

"You two," I said to Elan and Sardi. "Need to pick up your game."

Elan gulped in a lungful of air and scowled. "That was a test?"

I nodded. "And you failed. Never surrender, my little soldiers." Sardi's glare turned into a rough nod.

"Why... why are we out here so early?" Kara asked. "What is the point, Arbiter Declan? The examinations are a contest of Will, not physical endurance. Not that I don't enjoy a good run, but this is not how we will be tested."

"Strong mind and body, strong Will," I said. "They don't teach that here? Blimey, that's encouraging." I took a deep breath. "Now, who's really ready to run again?"

Another chorus of groans and a few muttered curses emanated from my group.

"Move," I said, and dashed down the rise. "If you don't hate me then I'm not doing my job."

Only Tylia and Nemin ran after me this time, and ten seconds later when we reached the bottom of the hill I called a halt and clapped them both on the shoulder. "That's enough. Good work you two."

"We are not to keep running?" Nemin asked.

"No, we're done for the day. I just wanted to see who would keep going when it got tough. You two just became my favourites."

I waved to the rest of the gang, my three stragglers and Fix, to catch up. Once we were all together again, and just as the sun began to peek over the mountains to the east, I ended the exercise session. All said and done, my crew had kept pace over three miles, which was something to work with. By the time the examination rolled around in four months, they'd be running ten miles and liking it.

"Showers then breakfast—nothing greasy, you hear, eat some avocado and boiled eggs—and then get to the classroom when that first bell goes off and the rest of the school is just getting out of bed."

"What are we to learn today?" Sardi asked.

"I need to know your strengths," I said. *Your weaknesses.* "You're all going to duel me with the intent to incapacitate and render me helpless."

My soldiers, my recruits, my students, my crew, my protégés and misfits shared a mildly distasteful look. I cracked my knuckles, had a good laugh, and thought about how far of a run it was to the nearest bar.

~~*~*

"So, who's first?"

I'd shoved the desks aside and cleared some space in the classroom. The room was about fifty feet by thirty, which left plenty of space to get creative. I'd also taken the time to soundproof and tint the windows, as well as add a bunch of minor enchantments which would serve to deter prying eyes and protect me and the recruits from any serious damage.

Unless any of them were Elder Gods in disguise or genuinely harboured me some ill will.

Ill… Will. A strange feeling, like I'd forgotten something, tried to bury itself in the back of my mind. I shook the thought away.

All puns aside, it had been far too long since someone or something had tried to kill me. I was ten thousand years out of my comfort zone but, damn it all, I was a shade bored and looking to stretch my legs a little. Taking it out on these students would help.

"Are you aware of the duelling standards?" Kara asked. She carried her staff, a thin rod of petrified wood about three feet in length, inlaid with veins of silver, against her shoulder. "What do you use to focus your Will?"

"Standards?" I was not familiar with no stinkin' standards. "No punching in the back of the head –

that kind of thing? – and I don't bother with a focus, Miss Denitae. My game is very hands on."

"So what's the point of this then?" Nemin asked.

"The point, my good fellow, is to bind me at your mercy. I want you to consider me an enemy, one with vital information to the war effort. Wrap me in lashings of Will light so I no longer present a threat. Fair warning, I've had some practice at this over the years." I'd sent more than one Willful fool hurtling across the Void during the Tome Wars. "Call it street duelling for now. Never mind the standards. I want to see how creative you can be, how clever."

"You don't think we can best you, do you?" Elan asked. He crossed his arms over his chest and leaned back against my desk. "You may be surprised by what they teach us here, Arbiter Declan. And without a focus, your intent will be sloppy."

"I'm very much hoping I will be surprised, Elan. Now, for the second and last time, which one of you would like to go first?"

Elan stared me down for a moment and then shrugged. His smile was confident, assured, as only the young can be. He couldn't help himself from glancing at Tylia, who sat with her legs crossed on one of the chairs pushed to the side, and flashing her his charming smile. She rolled her eyes and gestured for him to pay attention.

We duelled.

His style was graceful, despite his use of brute force and rather obvious patterns of strength. Elan wanted to bloody my nose, knock my defences aside, and bind me as directed in lashings of Will as quickly and as forcefully as he could.

It was a valid tactic. Overwhelm, force me to

defend, and then shatter my shields as if they were glass and his enchantments a sledgehammer.

He was playing by the standards I hadn't read, though, which made his style oddly formal, predictable. The best swordsman in the world didn't worry about the second best, because measures of talent suggested certain proficiency, certain rules and codes of behaviour—expected styles and flourishes and point scoring. No, the best swordsman in the world worried about a young, dumb kid picking up a blade for the first time and swinging it wildly, without knowing the rules or the codes.

Someone who didn't play by the expected standards became unpredictable.

And if you became unpredictable, you won. In war as in anything, the unknown would always hold an advantage.

I'd spent most of my life in grudge matches, from the Academy to the Tome Wars to my exiled adventures in the last year—I was good at fighting. A soldier, born and bred.

I allowed Elan's barrage to crack my shields, to reverberate across the air and force liquid light to bleed from the cracks. He barked a rough laugh, happy to have scored some points, I'm sure. I flicked my wrist and summoned a single lashing of Will, a thin whip as fine as cotton but as strong as steel. With another twist of my wrist the whip cracked through the air, under his protective barriers, and wrapped around his left leg.

He looked down, cursed, and then up again with a snarl as I moved my fingers just ever so slightly towards me.

The whip recoiled and Elan was hurled up into the

air, spinning wildly, before landing with a thump on the hard stone floors. I heard the breath leave his lungs and almost winced in sympathy. He rolled over, gasping and defeated, and I surveyed my four remaining Knights in training.

"So, who's second?"

The next four duels went much the way of the first. I was a lot more experienced, a lot more willing to hurt, which was not necessarily a good thing, but it was useful. I knocked Sardi out in round two, Nemin in round three. Kara had adapted a little bit to my style when it came to round four, but that only meant she fell harder in the end as I encased her hands in heavy blocks of ice.

Tylia was lucky last, her pales eyes narrowed and her dark blue skin shining with Will light. She was fast, running circles around me and casting varied and slightly dangerous elemental enchantments my way. She'd been reading the right books for battle magic, learning useful invocations, but I was better.

And by the time I was through training this bunch, they'd be formidable on the field.

I caught Tylia with a net of Will light, thrown into the air and designed to use her speed against her. The light latched on to the fastest thing in the room, which was her, and wrapped around her knees like a belt cinched tight. She stumbled to the floor and slammed her palm against the stone, ready to keep invoking, but I raised my hand and called an end to the duel.

"Some improvisation towards the end there," I said, once we'd pulled the desks and chairs into a rough circle around my larger desk at the front of the room. "By the third round, Nemin, you expected to lose. Bad attitude to have, but sometimes unavoidable. You weren't wrong. By the fourth, Kara had noted a bit of the technique I was using—a battle stance known as Ass Kickery—and tried to adapt. Tylia, in the last round, your speed is your advantage. But it can be used against you."

My students rubbed at their bruises and nodded along. Some of them looked thoughtful. Elan had a face full of scowl. He scratched at his desk and wouldn't meet my eye.

"Did we pass whatever test this was, Arbiter?" Sardi asked.

"Just watch, learn, and keep improving. That's how you stay alive. Be smart and think as many steps ahead as you can. Sideways, if not forward, you know." I ran a hand back through my hair and sighed. "We need to start back at some basics. Will Light for Beginners, Volume One."

As with many things, the 'magic' came down to a matter of will over Will: self-control, determination, and resolve, infused with the ascending oils that burn at the heart of creation. Young Knights, apprentices at the Academy, are taught to do this until they can dive into a book, in whole or in part, and draw forth whatever they needed. Weapons, food, clothing—safe passage through the Void—anything and everything. Intent and imagination, *desire*, could make fiction a reality. The lie that whispered truth.

After training and lessons, my recruits—*students*—shuffled from the room sore but satisfied. I asked Tylia Vale to hang back and answer a few questions for me. Who she was, what was the deal with that word 'Vale'.

"I am the last of my kind, Declan," Tylia said, after

considering my questions for a good half minute. "My world was claimed by nothingness, borne on the wings of an immortal monstrosity."

That piqued my interest. I knew three short of a dozen 'immortal monstrosities'. The Everlasting. "What happened?"

"My race, the Vale, built the Vale Atlantia in Atlantis, where the city found its name. We shaped the earth of this world, and built the Vale Celestia here at the university. You are human and can control Will light. I am Vale—and I am Will light. We are bonded to the unseen rivers that turn the universe."

"And you're the last."

"I am the last. Darkness ate my world. I was just a child of five and remember little." She brushed a loose strand of hair back behind her ear. Her blue skin seemed to shimmer in the light of the gemstone planetoids far above. "The stars went out, Declan. The land simple disintegrated. I was torn from my mother's arms and when I awoke all were dead and I was here, alone in the Vale Celestia."

"A Voidflood," I said quietly and cursed the word. A Voidflood could happen when the Willful, the rare few strong enough, tore open a hole into the space between universes. We did that all the time, travelling between worlds, but if control were lost… severed… if the intent turned malicious. Well, I'd seen what happened to Tylia's people, the Vale, first-hand. Hell, I'd been responsible for minor floods—recently in the storm clouds of Jupiter to cast Scarred Axis and the Shadowman, my rebellious shadow, into the Void.

"I have been a ward of the Vale Celestia ever since," Tylia said simply. "Alone, but alive, I carry the legacy of my people."

"If you survived, perhaps more of your race did," I said, not with much in the way of hope or enthusiasm in my voice. Surviving a Voidflood was impossible. Tylia was merely the exception to prove the rule. And the look she gave me said she thought the same.

"Our world shared trade with Atlantis, with your True Earth, as you call it. We were not of the worlds written into existence by the Willful. We existed before humans started to shape the universe with their words. If any had survived, they would have travelled here by now."

"You don't remember how you made it through the Void?"

Tylia shook her head and gestured at the awesome sky. "I felt the darkness, I blinked, and then I woke here in this forest under the sky. I remember staring at the moons for so long, before Forge Master Alexas found me."

The Void spat her out. The odds of surviving being cast into the Void were so small as to be non-existent. The odds were better on firing an arrow, blindfolded and dizzy, from one end of the solar system to the other and hitting a target smaller than the head of a pin. No, the odds were worse than that. She had spun through the Void and somehow hit a target. A living, breathing world.

~~*~*

The peace and quiet lasted about a week before I saw my first ghost in the Vale Celestia. And it was one helluva ghost. An unfair spirit.

A week. A generous, easy week before I realised I was already caught up in perhaps the most dangerous scheme I'd ever had the misfortune to stumble ass backwards into, in this or any time.

The Everlasting were in Atlantis.

I met the first of them in a fancy cocktail bar along the market quarter of the Vale Celestia. There was a plan to meet Tal for dinner, and show her how cool I was with my not-drinking, even in a bar full of booze. True will power.

I was at the bar early, seated on a fine leather couch and wearing something resembling a suit—a bit of the local fashion—that resembled more of a tight-fitting robe. It was black and severe, and made me look somewhat dark and menacing. I sipped from a tall glass of bubbly water and lime. Saving on the empty calories by quitting the booze, if nothing else.

A lady in a black-green dress sat down next to me, an older woman, grey at the temples, beautiful, her light brown eyes knowing and large. Her hair fell in gentle curls over her strapless shoulders.

We spoke politely for a few minutes, passing the time, her casual demeanour putting me at ease.

"You can't be any older than thirty," she said.

"Oh," I replied, ever the suffering charmer, "but I feel a lot older."

"Nonsense. You've too many enemies to die old," she said.

I sighed and placed my tall glass on the coffee table, as the cocktail bar hustled and bustled around us. "Not just a pretty face then. Who are you?" I eyed her perfect curves, her sparkling eyes, and realised she was everything I found desirable. A woman tailored to my particular tastes. "*What* are you?"

"My name is Saturnia." She grinned. "I want you to look over at the bar, Declan."

I glanced that way, marking the bartender, the bottles of strange and alien liquor on glass shelves, and the patrons standing at the marble bar. An old man and woman, a couple of kids, a lady dressed in red—

"Oh," I whispered. "Oh my."

The lady in red.

I met the eyes of my new companion. "What in all the worlds is she doing here? I watched her die."

My perfect woman nodded once. "Emily Grace," she said. "Otherwise known as Fair Astoria of the Everlasting."

"That's her… ten thousand years before I met her, isn't it? She doesn't know me yet."

"Quite so," my companion said. "Ageless and yet so young."

"She'll learn."

"I wasn't talking about Astoria."

I finished my soda and lime. "You know about me and my future. Are you a time-traveller as well? Which of the Everlasting does that make you, eh?"

I was fairly certain I was sitting with a god.

"None," she said. "My name, for all that it matters, is Saturnia."

I rolled the name along my tongue. "That is a nice name."

"I've always liked yours, Declan. So much… potential. You're a storybook hero."

"What are you, Saturnia?"

Saturnia smiled. It was, perhaps, the saddest smile I've ever seen. "Their mother," she said. "The Everlasting are my children."

"Ah."

Saturnia smiled and offered me her glass of red

wine. I declined, though it was a struggle.

"Are you my enemy?" I asked.

"Perhaps one day. Not now."

"I butchered one of your sons."

"Scion was always too eager to please."

"I intend to unmake Lord Oblivion."

"You may succeed."

"I loved your daughter." My gaze stumbled back to the bar. "Emily Grace... Astoria."

"I know. She loved you, too."

"Should I... should I talk to her?"

Saturnia's eyes flashed. "You're many things, Declan, but never a coward. Of course you should talk to her."

I heaved another heavy sigh and ran a hand over my eyes. "What's your end game?" I asked. "Is it too much to hope this doesn't end in fire and blood?"

Saturnia leaned in and kissed me on the cheek. "You're at war with my children. You're mortal, for the most part, and have the backing of the Knights Infernal, of factions of men and women who will fight and die for you... but in the end it's you, Declan. It's you alone against them all. Fire and blood is all you can expect."

"I will destroy the Everlasting," I said. "I... they are everything that is wrong with creation."

"They are immortally flawed."

"Can I save Atlantis?"

Saturnia blinked in surprise. "Declan," she said, "you are the reason it burns."

She disappeared. Faded away. I sat staring at a seat as empty as my soda and lime glass.

I thought about it, considered Tal, then shrugged. *Fuck it.*

I sauntered over to the bar and bought the pretty lade in red—Fair Astoria of the Everlasting, a ghost to me—a drink.

"One for the lady, and a soda water and lime for me," I said.

Astoria met my gaze, that old knowing look, and smiled. "You're the mysterious traveller from the future," she said, her voice sending a shiver through me. "Declan Hale."

"That I am," I said. "What should I call you?"

Not 'who are you', but 'what'? What are you pretending to be? I didn't dare ask aloud.

"My name is Astoria," she said and took a sip of an Atlantean martini. "A pleasure to meet you."

Well, real names, then. I was already out of my depth. And I'd held this woman as she died not too long ago.

"Not drinking tonight?" she asked.

"Trying to maintain a sober streak," I said, sipping at my fresh glass of soda and lime.

I'm bar folk. I'm the guy you see drinking alone and lamenting. Not something to be proud of, I know, but one is too many and ten is not enough. Cheaper to drink alone at home, I know, but I think the white noise—the ambience of the right dimly lit bar—makes all the dark and dreary thoughts seem that much deeper.

I can begin to take myself seriously after enough drink. To believe that my deep thoughts may have some sort of... deeper meaning. Or at least make it feel less like I'm alone in a crowded room.

Some of us are better in the dim light. Justified. Alone but not alone. Caught between the glass and the crimson wine, we're somewhat alive. Justified isn't the right word. I'm not sure if I have the right word, or the right excuse, for what amounts to a supreme lack of self-control and an addiction to the haze of alcohol. Bring on the haze. Days without the haze are like being lost in a maze.

"I tried quitting earlier this year," I said. "Even managed to last a few months, but the weight of the world got to me in the end. I suppose it comes down to self-discipline, at some level, but addiction is an ugly thing. No excuses—no one is putting the bottle in my hand. I pick it up every time… but I don't want to stop, not really."

"Do you consider yourself addicted?"

I shrugged. "Have you ever drunk scotch in a public washroom before eight o'clock in the morning, Astoria? I think that qualifies for addiction somewhere on the scale. Thing about alcoholism, though, is it does it best to convince you otherwise. That toilet scotch is normal."

"Think how much better you could be without it," she said. "What could you do if you got your life in order? Stopped drinking, studied your craft, put your sheer talent and strength to good use. You could be great. You could be magnificent."

"Oh, Emily Grace," I said. "You're far too kind to me."

Astoria frowned. "Emily Grace? Who is Emily Grace?"

I frowned and put my glass on the bar. "Sorry. Got confused for a moment there. You remind me of someone I used to know."

Her eyes shone. "Someone from the future?"

"My past," I said. "So, yes. A woman named Emily Grace."

"I like that name."

"Thought you might."

"But you say it with such a depth of sadness. What happened to her?"

I knocked back the rest of my drink in one swallow. "She died," I said. "We all do, in the end, at least once."

"Oh, now there's a story to be told there, I would wager."

"Are you a writer?" In my world, such a question was a subtle, polite way of asking if someone had the talent—if they were Willful. I already knew Astoria was more than she claimed to be here. Did she know that I knew? Emily had always been several steps ahead of me. But in this timeline, this point of history, she had yet to meet the true Declan Hale. I knew more about her than she about me.

Still, I felt plans in motion about my head that I couldn't grasp—knowing Emily, plans I wouldn't grasp until it was too late and my part had been played. I needed to know why the Everlasting were in Atlantis, though I could hazard a dark and terrible guess.

"I dabble in short stories," Astoria replied. "Romantic pieces, mostly."

I rolled my eyes—not unkindly.

"What do you write, Declan?"

I tapped my glass on the bar and like magic the bartender appeared to refill it with soda and lime. No matter the time, place, or culture tapping your glass against the bar was a universal sign for yes, I'll have another. The Story Thread could fray to a single, solitary strand and the last men standing would still clink their glasses, drink their poison, and watch the world end alone.

"Me? I write stories about gods and demons. Knights and angels. One man against the whole world, who always gets the girl."

Astoria laughed. "And are these stories based on you? Does the hero wear a waistcoat, an eye patch, and spend his time in bars talking to strange women?"

"You've read my story before, eh?"

She tilted her head and offered me an enigmatic grin. "No, no I don't believe I have. But I'd like to… one day."

When I'd first met Astoria—as Emily—she had pretended to be a non-Willful customer in my bookshop. Just someone who lived and worked around Perth and liked to read. Well, pretended wasn't the right word—she had never lied. I had just never asked the right questions. She had been playing a game, at the time, to get me *back* in the game. I'd killed her husband, by her design, and she had killed me so the Infernal Clock could be infused into my soul.

Why?

Why any of that? Because of who I was in the Tome Wars? I was infamous, certainly, and good at my job as a solider and commander of the Cascade Fleet. But to a creature like Fair Astoria, an ageless god who had lived when Atlantis was young, was I really that important? Emily had thought so—was it because of my words now, here in this bar, or because of something I'd yet to do?

Was I laying the groundwork for our sordid future? One that saw her giving birth to our son on the dying world of Voraskel under a ruined sky. A child I would abandon to Annie Brie.

Hell, had my slip up a moment ago, when I'd used the name I'd known her best by—Emily Grace—was that where she found the name, too? Had I named her *for* the future? What came first: the drunk or the fool?

"May I ask you a question?" I asked.

"I would very much like that, yes," she replied and pressed her red lips together in a smile that was far too knowing.

"If you knew something was going to happen, say," and I smiled softly, "because you've seen the future. And then you had a chance to maybe change things, perhaps right some wrongs before they become wrongs. Wrong some rights, even." *Like the Degradation.* Better a hundred more years of the Tome Wars than the Everlasting unleashed from their prisons. Alas, for the could-have-beens. "No, forget that. Let me try again. If you cared for someone, someone special and lovely, and you had the chance to spare them hurt, real hurt, but at a cost you can't foresee, would you do that?"

Astoria shrugged a single porcelain shoulder and took a sip of her drink. Her lipstick left a pink mark on the rim of the glass. "Would you not?"

"I…" I shook my head and then held her gaze on mine. "Let me ask that question another way then. Tell me, what comes first, the drunk or the fool?"

The reason I spend so much time in the dimly lit bars is because under that light, that dull half-yellow light, no one really casts a shadow. The gentle hue, the faint, subdued colour of almost-light was a space not in the real world, and not of the Void. Far removed from that anti-existence. It was the other way, something of genuine magic, of goodness and –

dare I say it – close to happiness. Perhaps the only piece of true magic left to the world hid in that ambience.

But I loved it for a different reason, a simpler reason.

In the dim light, we were all shadowless.

And in the end, all of us, even the Everlasting, were nothing but mere dust forged in the impossible furnaces of distant stars.

Distant memories, one day.

A few days later, Astoria sought me out in my private quarters. Her knock on the door was light, delicate, and when I saw her standing there in a white dress, a soft smile, eyes that knew the true turning of the world, I invited her in.

Whether it was enchantment or just plain foolishness, a desire to unload some of the weight I carried on my shoulders, or the guilt of her death, I told Astoria everything of the future to come. I told her I knew she was Everlasting, I told her that we knew each other a long time from now, that her name to me was Emily, and that's how I liked to remember her. I told her she had given birth to a son—our son—and sacrificed her grace to do so.

At that, Emily/Astoria grasped my arm. "Truly?" she asked, her eyes blazing. "I can conceive a son?" Tears brimmed on her lashes. "You are not entirely a herald of doom, after all."

"I love you, Emily. By the *Everlasting*, I love you." I felt like a thrice-damned fool for saying that last bit, but I wanted her to know.

And as always, Astoria showed nothing but her surreal calm. She knew that I knew that she was one of the Nine. In this time, they had yet to be known by their true name—the Everlasting. I had named her, and names were powerful things.

"Oh my, Declan Hale," she said. "You are no longer interesting."

"No?"

"No." She kissed me gently on the lips. "You just became *fascinating*."

No fate. No destiny. Wake early, work with your hands, and in the evening light a candle to keep the darkness of an indifferent universe at bay.

THE SECOND RESOLVE

Scotch, Lies, and Distasteful Pornography

"That's the problem with drinking, I thought,
as I poured myself a drink. If something bad happens
you drink in an attempt to forget; if something
good happens you drink in order to celebrate; and
if nothing happens you drink to make something
happen."

~Charles Bukowski

CHAPTER FIVE

Attack on the Atlas Lexicon

"You used to be Hale. The Declan Hale. Who are you now?"

The same convoy that had driven us to the field command centre formed part of the assault party for the attack on the Atlas Lexicon.

"I'll try and finish the story later," I told Annie as we loaded up in the back of a roofless dark-grey military jeep. My weapons had been returned, and I strapped on my sword, the barrel of my shotgun resting in the comfortable nook below my shoulder. "Some exciting, world-ending nonsense coming up."

"It seems no matter where you go—other worlds, other times—your life is tangled with Emily's. With... Fair Astoria's."

"Yeah, don't think that doesn't worry me." The jeep sat on idle in the motor pool, our driver getting his marching orders from Lord Winter and his generals. A cool breeze rolled down the mountains, and the first can of purple paint—twilight—fell spilt across the sky, turning azure to mauve. "There's a long game being played here, and not all of it is by my design. Time travel really... it really complicates matters."

"Oh, you have a design?" Annie quipped. "Here it looks to me like you make things up as you go along."

I grinned and nudged her knee with my own. "I put a lot of effort and planning into making it look like I don't know what I'm doing."

"Then I am very impressed."

"Thank you."

An old hard case, gristly grey stubble, shaved head, sleeveless Kevlar vest, hopped into the driver's seat of the jeep and winked at us over his shoulder. "Thought you'd be taller, Hale," he said. "Sergeant Arlon Grenn."

"What's the word, Arlon?" I asked.

"Direct assault for us poor bastards in the jeeps. Winter and the handful of Dawn Mercenaries here will flank left around the biggest nest of deadlings and hostiles, draw them off us if they can. I've been tasked with getting you to the shield surrounding the city, above all else."

I grunted. "So we're basically not part of the main attack."

"Near as I can figure it you two are Plan B," Arlon said. "And are to be kept out of the way. Think you can get through that shield, Hale?"

My heart beat a little faster in my chest. "Yes

indeedy."

Arlon squinted at me and nodded once. "Well, you believe it if nothing else. Ma'am," he said to Annie. "I hear you're a sniper with that cannon on your hip. I'd request you target anything on the left side of the jeep as we ride in through the deadling lines."

Annie drew her revolver and placed it on her lap. Her pockets held bands of sixes—ammunition pre-stacked for quick reloads—as did the small table between us. Hundreds of rounds, if hundreds were going to be needed.

"The heart or the brain," Annie said.

"Aye, right you are." Arlon knocked the jeep into gear as the rest of the convoy began to filter out onto the charming, antiquated cobblestone roads that snaked across the valley.

Nothing about the location, the postcard-pretty mountains, forests and rivers, the enveloping twilight, made it feel like we were about to go into battle.

I felt the cold excitement of the fight to come anyway. Tal had been right about that, too. I not only wanted the fight, I *liked* it.

At a rough count, as Arlon peeled out onto the road—a quarter of the way along the length of the convoy—about twenty vehicles were taking part in the assault. Primarily jeeps and troop carriers like we rode in, but also Winter and his no-doubt Willfull allies in the sleek SUVs.

Lord Winter rolled up alongside us, young and handsome, and flashed us such a charming grin that even I wanted to blush. "Luck, Declan!" he cried. His staff shone with pale blue light, the top two feet poking out of the window. "Luck, Detective Brie!" His car peeled away, splitting the convoy in half along a separate road to the west—the left flank—of where our fight would take place.

"Good god, that man is pretty," Annie said. Her hands shook, her cheeks were flushed. She was nervous, but not in a bad way. I knew she could hold her own on this—or, indeed—any battlefield. I'd served with Knights who had less courage, who couldn't play the hand they were dealt. Annie was good people.

I snorted. "Yeah, but do you really think he knows how to use that staff?"

Annie flashed me a grin. "Oh yes. I think he does."

"Concentrate on shooting something dead, please."

The jeep roared over cobblestones, the road widened, flat green fields on either side. To the east, herds of wild horses disappeared over the rising foothills, away from the noise and the Lexicon. Four other jeeps, one troop carrier, and two armoured units with mounted machine guns kept pace with Sergeant Arlon, smashing through wooden fences and spreading out along the fields.

We drove into a dell, arced around some outer buildings—cottages and such, a little village—and turned north on the road for a straight shot at the city trapped within the purple shield.

Alongside the road, and in our path, the landscape was strewn with slag, scorch marks from explosions, small trenches and the signs of struggle. A cheer went up from the complement of soldiers on duty, grimy—armed with swords and guns—as we thundered past the front checkpoint. They'd held the outer lines, and their work spoke for itself. Husks, bodies, the semblance of things no longer living littered the road, alongside piles of ash that had once been deadlings, burst into white flame upon being put out of their misery.

Up ahead, things not so dead lurked. We were about half a mile out from the city, from the edge of the shield. At this distance, the gleaming red-purple dome, the monstrosity of dark intent and corruption, didn't look so transparent. It swirled with power, *oozed* with dark radiance. Perhaps it was my imagination, but as we drove closer, Arlon expertly navigating the debris through coiling clouds of smoke and the stink of expended copper, I saw a face form in the mile-high shield. A flash of sharp teeth, the wink of a narrowed eye. A promise of horror yet to come.

Everlasting, I thought, and flipped the shield my middle finger.

Annie gave me a curious look. I shook my head and pointed out to her left, raising my shotgun to the right as I did so. She nodded and readied her weapon.

Up ahead, seconds away, the fight would begin.

The armoured trucks sped past us as we got within a quarter mile and opened fire on the deadlings and monsters blocking the road. A hail of gunfire, rocket-propelled missiles, burst from the trucks, a wall of firepower, and shredded the creatures where they shambled. The deadlings didn't even have time to fall before they burst into white flame, fireworks, lamplight, to guide our way.

The troop carrier, six men and women in the tray at the back, drew level alongside us, blocking my sight to the right. No matter, the soldiers aboard began blasting away, covering my flank. Annie started picking off corpses on the left.

We made it another few hundred feet before the road became impassable for the jeep. Great gouges had been forged through the stone, boulders the size of horses blocked the way. Arlon came to a screeching halt, as did the troop carrier and the other vehicles.

"Right," he said, hopping out of the jeep. He focused for a moment, eyes distant, and then twin blades of hard light flowed down from his elbows, wrapped his wrists in cords of power, and formed twin swords of yellow energy three feet long. "Close-quarters work. We've got maybe two, three hundred metres to cover and reach the shield, Hale. You ready?"

I was already out of the jeep, shotgun pumped. Annie reloaded and joined me.

Off to the east, I heard the sound of explosions, men and women shouting, and *felt* the powers being thrown around at the left flank. Lord Winter and his team. The ground shook and, I realised, my head was pounding.

"Declan," Annie said, rubbing her temple. "I feel funny."

I nodded. "It's the shield around the city. It'll get worse the closer we get. You're brushing against the Void here, Annie. Try and concentrate on something else, and if you need to be sick, do it quickly."

Arlon and the squad of six soldiers from the troop carrier formed a phalanx in front of us. "Right," he said again. "You lot know the deal. Shoot anything dead, and protect Hale and Annie. Our mission is to get them to the shield and then fall back. Any questions?"

Grim nods and the sound of rounds being

chambered, swords being drawn, were the only answers to the questions not asked.

Something the size of a minivan—thick tentacles, a heft of heavy grey flesh—slammed into the cab of the troop carrier and sent the entire vehicle flying over our heads.

The soldiers guarding us unloaded on the beast. I ducked to the side and got off one blast from the shotgun, severing a fat tentacle and casting a spray of yellow ichor and grey meat into the air.

Arlon swept in through the gap I'd created and drove his light sword through the nest of bulging black eyes in the creature's face. It bucked tremendously, the energy of Arlon's sword slipping through tough hide like butter, and reared back before falling to the ground—dead.

"Bloody hell," Annie breathed. "What on earth was that?"

"Nothing that should be on Earth," I said darkly. "Ladies and gentlemen, we need to hurry. We're attracting to much attention."

Arlon nodded and we set off for the shield. The ground was ash and broken stone, dirt and debris, but our going was quick. Deadlings stumbled out from behind boulders, other monsters, too, but we made short work of them. In slow numbers, we would make it. If not for Lord Winter's assault to the east, we would have already been overrun.

On the outskirts of the city now, the enemy had made short work of defiling the parks, fouling the streams, and breaking the buildings outside of the shield. The zone between the fields and the city was a ruin, which was a shame, as only a few days ago it would have been lovely. The Atlas Lexicon was an academy, a great university, and the campus was meant to be picturesque, enlightened. This attack had violated that to the extreme.

An eel of guilt squirmed in the pit of my stomach. The Everlasting were loose because of me, and this shield was my… well, I would do what needed to be done to fight them. To destroy them all.

A bone-beast, like the thing Annie and I had destroyed near the forest, erupted from beneath the ground. An arm of razor sharp claws tore through the outer guard on our phalanx, cutting through a young woman and an older man, shearing them in half.

Annie was first off the mark to put the deadling down—and again, she moved with such speed, such precise aim, that I don't think she knew just how impressive her shot looked. The deadling flew back, white flame engulfed its form. Annie reloaded with a wild grin.

The rest of our guard spread out to cover the losses, Arlon grim-faced and on point. The ruins of the cobblestone road became more of a lane. To the right, a pack of about thirty deadlings—fleshy, once-human things—cut a line straight for us.

I dispensed with the shotgun and fired a blast of pure, raw Will at the pack, blasting half a dozen of them into the air. Destroy the heart or the brain, sure, but both at once was better. From over the small rise to the east, about sixty feet away, poured another pack of the bastards. A rough count of fifty, and more behind them.

Without it needing to be said, we broke into a sprint. The mission was the shield. Lord Winter's attack force, or the other contingent of jeeps in our assault, would hopefully deal with the packs from the front while we swept around their back. If not, we'd be in all sorts of trouble if the shield proved impassable.

The stink of the dead filled the air, as did the not unpleasant smell of burning stone, ignited wood, and the spent shells—a coppery, primal tang. I felt a rush, eager to be alive and on the ground in a fight. Bracing the shotgun against my shoulder, I spun and dropped to one knee, firing once—twice—thrice—into the pack of deadlings behind us. The shotgun bucked in my hands, slammed into my shoulder painfully, but the curtain of enchanted pellets cutting through the rank and file deadlings was immensely satisfying.

"*Ha!*" I cried, and found myself laughing as the barrel of my shotgun blazed hot.

Annie's revolver pounded in my ear, smoke curling from the barrel, felling deadlings one after the other. She couldn't miss. Her grin matched my own.

We ran some more, the shield within a few hundred feet now.

Great beasts, massive goliaths, shaped like bears but nastier, hairless, pale-skinned, bruised purple flesh, red glowing eyes—you know, the usual monster fare—sprung in on us from the east. Two more of our soldiers went down under the assault before we could tear the bear-beasts apart. That left a final two soldiers plus Arlon.

"Come on!" he growled.

Nothing for it but a final sprint.

We moved against the breeze at speed, Annie's revolver roaring, picking off deadlings in the air as they leapt toward us. A rain of white-flame ash and bone fell around us, sparks caught by the wind. We were death and firepower at the heart of a tornado of fire. Only minutes, perhaps two, perhaps nearly three, had ticked by since our assault began.

As we drew within sixty feet of the shield we were bathed in rotten purple light—my headache intensified, a sharp stab of pain behind my useless eye, and Annie went pale. She snarled and reloaded, picking off more of the fell creatures.

At last we reached the shield—within half a dozen feet. The cold coming off the monstrosity, which arced into the sky a mile above our heads, was like midnight in the heart of winter. Arlon and the two remaining soldiers moved from our front to our back, providing a guard between us and the approaching armies of deadlings and monsters.

"Do what you have to do, Hale!" he roared.

I shook my head and looked at the shield, to Annie. She spared me a quick glance and continued to fire at the enemies. If this didn't work, if we couldn't get through, then we'd die here, our backs literally against a wall of dark magic.

"*Thirty seconds!*" I shouted. "*Buy me thirty seconds!*"

I cast a web of Will at the shield, felt sick to my stomach when my power touched the seething mess of energy, and burned through all the diagnostic enchantments I knew, one after the other, as fast as thought. The thing about using Will like this, was that I got the readings and measurements back just as quickly. The shield was pure power, touched by the Void but not *of* the Void. It's source, the on/off switch, was within the city. It stood point-nine of a mile high at its crest and was about ten feet thick in front of me. I saw no way through, no unlatched back door. It was impenetrable... for most.

"*Declan!*" Annie screamed.

I spun, shotgun swinging up. Another of those hideous tentacle monsters spilled into our little glade before the shield, throwing aside debris, slithering over rocks and screeching to high hell. It picked up one of the two remaining soldiers—a woman who laughed as it grabbed her and began unloading her assault rifle into his face. The monster sprung back and threw the soldier through the air—over our heads—and *into* the shield.

I watched her fly, watched her hit, and watched her burst into flame as she struck the shield. Her entire body flared green, I saw her skeleton beneath her flesh, before she fell as less than ash.

"Oh fuck," Arlon spat.

Two, three, a fourth tentacle monster, leaders of the deadling packs, it seemed, emerged over the rise on our backs. The last soldier and Arlon fired and reloaded, fired and reloaded, trying to stem the flood.

"*Hale!*" Arlon cried. "*You have to go!*"

No, I thought.

I'd lost men and women who had served with me before. I'd lost entire battalions, I'd *killed* whole legions, and seen interdimensional ships with crews in the tens of thousands plummet into stars or—worse—fall into the Void. A fate worse than death. War was war, fights were fights, but I hated winning at a cost so high it may as well be defeat.

I tossed the shotgun to Annie and summoned my Will, brought my force to bear against the nightmare hordes—monsters and worse I had spent my whole life fighting against, and never seemed to get any closer to defeating. I stepped forward, placing myself ahead of Arlon and the last soldier.

"*What are you doing?*" the grizzled old man yelled.

"Get thee the fuck out of the way—"

I slammed my glowing fist into the ground with a tremendous shout. My Will, my power, I directed outwards in a half-circle of raw strength. The ground shook, split, and a concussive wave of shock-force tore into the lines of monsters and deadlings.

Several dozen tonnes of earth, steel, and stone tore up from the ground. I hurled the chaos into the packs of enemies. A hundred deadlings disappeared in the maelstrom, the sound was deafening, the end of the world.

I fell back, utterly spent, a wave of nausea sweeping over me, maximising my headache from the shield. I leaned over and threw up a good deal of my dinner.

All fell silent as the dust settled.

Annie offered me a hand but I made it to my feet by myself.

"You look like you're about to pass out," she whispered.

"I never believed the stories about you," Arlon said, eyeing me. He shook his head. He looked afraid, even... disgusted. "They don't do you justice by half."

A great crescent had been ripped into the earth for about seventy feet, dotted with white fire and twitching tentacles. Howls, screams, rose on the air to fill the awful silence. At the edge of my damage, the deadlings—more deadlings, fresh deadlings, and other evils—began to regroup. They screeched in rage, pure anger, and spilled into the crescent.

"Time to go," I said grimly. "Arlon, you won't get out of here alive. You're coming through the shield with me and Annie. You too," I said to the last soldier standing.

"Fuck," she whispered. Blood trickled into her eye from a cut on her forehead, the gash stuck and sticky with her frizzy blonde hair.

I grinned and tasted blood of my own. "Quickly now. Cancel your energy swords, Arlon. We've got half a minute at best. To the edge of the shield and all of you line up alongside me, with Annie at the far end."

I turned back to the shield and stepped right up to its edge until all I could see was oily purple-red light. I snapped my hand out and gripped Arlon's right hand. The last soldier took his other hand, and she took Annie's with her left.

"Take a deep breath," I said. *Please let me be right about this…* "On three."

At our backs, the deadlings and monsters roared, as if sensing we were about to escape.

"*One!*"

Arlon squeezed my hand hard enough to hurt.

"*Two!*"

This had worked once before, on a shield far more malignant—the Degradation surrounding Atlantis, put in place by Lord Oblivion, my greatest enemy. I hadn't planned on another degradation for this fight, but then not everything could be accounted for, especially when dealing with the Everlasting.

"*Three! Run!*"

I yanked Arlon forward, and he the last soldier. We braced ourselves for fire and death, no doubt deserved for being so foolish, but instead got cold and pain.

My head nearly exploded with the pain, but a soothing light emanated from my chest, from my heart, and the shield couldn't touch me. We moved through the sickly purple light, like trying to run through syrup, but we moved. I couldn't see anything save the dark shield, but I felt Arlon's hand in mine—which was good, as I wasn't sure the protection that allowed me through the shield, and Annie, would pass to him. He'd have been certainly dead, had I left him behind.

What felt like an hour later, but was less than ten seconds, we emerged through the other side of the shield as one group of four. Alive—harmed, pale, shaking—but alive. We collapsed to the ground under a sky blood red and purple before the massive silver towers of the Atlas Lexicon.

I fell utterly spent.

It was Annie that got me back on my feet this time. "Come on," she said. "We need to get away from this thing." She threw a thumb over her shoulder at the shield.

I nodded agreement and we managed to stumble down the road, the four of us supporting one another, and came to a park of green grass full of picnic tables and little huts. We saw no one, nothing. If there were thousands of people here in the city, they were either dead or hidden well. Our footsteps echoed far too loudly.

We made it to one of the three-sided huts in the park, near a statue of bright marble that looked like a war memorial to me, and slumped into the benches around the table. We'd held onto most of our weapons. Annie passed me the shotgun and I began to slowly, painfully, reload the weapon from the shell cache in one of my pockets.

"How did we get through the shield?" the lady soldier asked.

I cleared my throat and nodded. Fair question. "I cast a net of protection," I lied. Well, half-truth. I was certain—certain now it had worked—that the petal of the Infernal Clock in my heart had granted us passage. The petal was pure anti-Everlasting. It could resist their Will.

"Well, OK, so that got you in," Annie said. She was staring at me, and I suspected that she didn't believe me.

Damn. Well, my dear, I am lying, but not for much longer. The petal in your heart helped, too. "Staying close to me got you all through. Few other options that could have helped, perhaps to do with you not being Willful, but I'd wager it was being swept up in my awesomeness."

Annie gave me a wry smile. "Oh yeah, I'm sure that was it."

Arlon grunted. "Now we're here, what do we do?"

"I'm low on ammunition. We need to hit an armoury sooner rather than later." The lady soldier gave us all a look and then half a smile. "I'm Caitlin, by the way. Caitlin Collins. Or C.C."

"Nice to meet you," Annie whispered. "Sorry it's not under better circumstances."

"How well do you know the city?" I asked Arlon and Caitlin.

From one of the pouches on his utility vest, Arlon produced a bandage and pressed it against the ugly cut on Caitlin's forehead. "Fairly well," he said. "If our people are anywhere, I'd say they're in the Vale Crystalis—the big tower in the centre of town—or the accommodation towers on the east side of the city. We should make our way there, try and contact the leadership."

I nodded. "That's one plan." *I've a few others.* "How long to reach the Vale Crystalis?"

"The shuttle craft don't seem to be operating," Caitlin said, scowling out at the city from our hut. "Everything is far too dark, dead. There's no electricity."

"And we don't know what's between us and there," Arlon added.

"If it were a straight shot on a sunny day, we could walk from here to the square outside the Vale Crystalis in about forty minutes. We'll probably have to move a lot slower if we're going to make it, though."

"We don't know what's out there," I mused. "Could be nothing this side of the shield."

Arlon gave me a look only the old seem capable of giving the young and naïve. I was young, but I didn't think I was naïve. "You think there's nothing out there?"

I shook my head. "No, I expect more if not worse than what we fought through to get here."

Annie sighed. "When should we move?"

I gazed out at the city, up at the sick shield over our heads, the blood-red and burnt-purple sky. There would be no night, no day, just the awful light until the shield came down. Again, I thought I saw a monumental face in the barrier, something ancient and old and cruel watching me from above. The Everlasting.

"Ten minutes to rest, recover, reload," I said. "Then we head out."

CHAPTER SIX

Dread Ash on the Wind

"Gotta give up the booze and the one night stands"

"Are we trapped in here with one of the Everlasting?" Caitlin asked. "That was the rumour circling the command centre back in Spire-Brunnen. The real reason you, of all people, Arbiter Hale, were brought in."

I eyed the woman while I considered just what to say, how much of my dark and terrible knowledge to impart. She was tall, and I liked that, blonde frizzy hair and light blue eyes. She wore the standard battle garb of a soldier, military fatigues under an armour plate vest. More than all that, Caitlin had proven her worth on the battlefield. Here was another one I could use, another one I'd most likely get killed.

"I'm curious to know more about this as well, Hale," Arlon said.

I caught half a grin from Annie. She liked to see me bombarded with questions.

"Call me Declan," I told my new allies. "Anyone who fights like we just fought gets to call me Declan."

We'd left the hut in the park behind us about five minutes ago, moving from the outer city and into the wide avenues, the grid-like streets, of the Atlas Lexicon. Large buildings and mighty towers, connected far above by crystal skybridges, rose all around us. No corpses—of students or deadlings—littered the streets, but carts were overturned, small vehicles crashed, a general feeling of menace clung to the air. And it was silent. Deathly silent. The heels of my shoes clicked against the sidewalk and echoed down the deserted city blocks.

"Fine, Declan," Caitlin said, hefting her assault rifle from one shoulder to the other. "You didn't answer my question."

"No, you didn't," Annie agreed.

"If it's one of the Everlasting, then we're fucked," Arlon said simply, scratching at his rough stubble. "Pardon my French."

"Oh, it's definitely one of the Everlasting," I said, glancing up at the ugly shield overhead, to all sides. "But she's trapped in here with us—not the other way around."

"She?" Annie asked. "How do you know that?"

I shook my head and didn't elaborate. "We have to be mindful of... people... listening in to our conversations. I'm playing things close to my chest for now. You'll see why soon, I'm sure."

"And the Everlasting created the shield around the Lexicon?" Caitlin asked. "Mercy."

"Actually, I think the shield is *part* of the

Everlasting," I said and stopped them all in their tracks. "A part of her power, her soul, her essence—whatever you want to call it. I've been seeing faces in the muck."

"How can that be?" Arlon asked. He swallowed hard. A cool breeze swept down the street, trailing dust and stale air. "How can we fight it?"

"I've hurt the Everlasting before," I said. "Even watched one of them die."

Arlon and Caitlin exchanged a worried glance. They didn't quite believe me. Well, proof will out, should they survive the night. And it was night now, the sun—although we couldn't see it—would have descended well beyond the mountains to the west. The valley would be dark. I wondered, in a detached sort of way, whether Lord Winter and his Dawn Mercenaries had survived their assault. Certainly they had not breached the shield, nor could they, if my hunch was correct.

"Three blocks up, about a ten minute walk, and the grid pattern of these streets gives way to a few blocks laid out in concentric circles," Arlon said. He was on point, a few feet ahead of me and Annie. He had renewed one of his energy blades, coating his right arm and three feet beyond his wrist in hot yellow light. "From there, fifteen minutes or so—if we're quick—to reach the piazzas and square out front of the Vale Crystalis."

I could see the tip of that impressive spire, a good mile and a half away, peeking above the buildings and towers directly ahead. Something didn't feel right. Well, none of this felt right, and my head still throbbed dully from the influence of the shield, but something else was nagging at me.

"This feels like a trap," Annie said, voicing the concerns of all in our party.

"It's definitely a trap," I said. "But we're not snared so easily, are we?" I tried for a grin, failed, and clenched my fists to keep them from shaking. I was still a little low on juice after dispelling the army of deadlings before the shield. I needed rest and a good meal. I'd find neither tonight, of that I was sure.

Unseen eyes watched us from the windows on either side of the street, hundreds of pairs of eyes it felt like, glaring down at us. Perhaps it was just the malice from the ugly shield, but I thought not.

"You all feel that, right?" I whispered.

My band of merry warriors exchanged uneasy glances and nodded.

"The city is infested. Whatever madness was set loose outside the shield... it's inside, too." Arlon spat on the ground. "Why don't they attack?"

"We're being led to slaughter," I said. "Which is a nice way of saying the Everlasting needs us." *Needs me.*

Annie caught my eye again and raised a single eyebrow. *What aren't you telling us, telling* me, *Declan,* that eyebrow almost shouted. I gave her a reassuring wink, a reassurance I didn't feel, and we crossed from one block to the next at a set of dead traffic lights. Somewhere in the distance a crow squawked against the silence, shattered the stillness, and a shiver ran down my spine. The shotgun barrel felt heavy, frozen, numbing my fingers.

Up ahead, a sawing sound like rusted chains grating together followed the crow's cry. Like nails on a chalkboard in that deathly quiet city, the *screech-creak-screech* put me on edge.

As Arlon had said, once we walked past the next block the grid-like pattern of the Atlas Lexicon gave way to rings of streets and curved lines of buildings, disappearing east and west around the bend. Wide open spaces sat between the rings, linked through promenades, bridges across quays and rivers, and if not for the deluge of sordid light from above, the area would have been green and vibrant with inner city parks.

...*ssscreeeaakk*...

The parkland was marred grey and black by the mix of purple-red light striking what should have been emerald-green grass. In the heart of the park stood a set of children's play equipment: moulded plastic slides, wooden climbing frames and monkey bars, and in a pit of woodchips just off to the side, a set of swings.

The god-awful noise—...*ssscreeaak*...— emanated from the metal chain links of the swing. A pretty woman, olive skin, dressed in a white blouse, blue jeans, and a pair of killer knee-high leather boots, swung back and forth. She saw us on the edge of the park and waved us over with a wide, beautiful smile. Even from distance, her teeth shone clear and white.

I drew in a sharp breath and felt my heart skip a few nervous beats. I'd been expecting this, or something like it, but it still hurt to be right, to *see*. My allies looked to me, noted my discomfort.

"That doesn't seem right," Caitlin said, frowning at the woman. "Is this the trap we're meant to fall into, Declan?"

"I fell into this one years ago..." I muttered to myself, shaking my head. "Come on, let's go say hello. Stay behind me. That woman will be... cruel."

With soft and spongy grass underfoot, we crossed the park and came to the edge of the play equipment—to the edge of the woodchip pit holding the set of swings. The woman smiled at me, perfect angular features, soft ringlets of hair brushing her shoulders. I knew that face, knew it didn't belong to the creature of ageless hate staring out at me from behind green eyes.

She cocked her head at the spare swing next to her.

"Wait here for me," I told my companions and handed Arlon my shotgun. "I need you not to interfere. This won't take more than a few minutes."

I walked over and sat in the passenger seat, idly kicking my legs back and forth, getting a slow swing going.

"How long has it been for you?" the woman said quietly. She reached out for my hand, wrapped gently around the swing chain, then thought better of it and pulled her hand away.

"For me?" I shook my head. "Just over a week since leaving Atlantis."

Anger flashed in those beautiful eyes. Overhead, arcs of wicked red lightning tore across the surface of the shield surrounding the Lexicon. The woman took a deep breath, visibly calmed herself, and the lightning faded.

"It has been... far longer for me," she whispered. "How dare you have things so easy. Was all of this part of your plan?"

I shook my head. "We're way off book here. None of this," I waved at the shield, the empty city, the tears in my clothing and splashes of blood and ichor from the battle to enter the city, "was what I wanted.

I didn't know she could pull you from your last vessel. No, I didn't want this."

"What did you want?" she hissed, spat. "Give me the pleasure of knowing what you were denied."

I chuckled. "I won't be baited so easily."

Her face changed from hostile to friendly in the blink of an eye. "Can't blame a girl for trying."

"Say that again, it almost makes you sound human, Ash."

Dread Ash of the Everlasting swung sideways into me, giving me a gentle nudge. A wave of cold air, wholly unnatural, battered me to the side as I swung back in a slow figure-eight before righting the swing.

"There were several thousand people in this city," I said.

"They're alive, for the most part, secluded themselves away in the western towers and various levels of the Vale Crystalis. I have no quarrel with them. Do they know all of this mess is your fault?"

I shook my head. "No. Perhaps some suspicions, but then I was here long before this city even existed. If anything, they're getting in my way."

Dread Ash's eyes flashed. She laughed. "Such wonderful arrogance. You would have made a fine Everlasting, Declan Hale."

"Oh perish the thought." Annie and the others watched from a safe distance, forty feet or so away. We were speaking quietly enough not to be overhead. "What's your end game here?"

"You know why I'm here, why now. It is your design."

"You think so, eh?" I ran a hand back through my hair. "Do I look like a man with a plan, Ash?"

She frowned. "No, don't do that. You don't get to

do that anymore. We may not have taken you seriously in the past—or the future, depending on how you look at it—we may have underestimated you to our detriment, but no more. The Everlasting *see* you, Declan Hale. We see you very well."

I tried not to let it show just how much that frightened me. Who was I to fight the gods? To wage the wars? At times I felt my age—twenty seven, young and dumb, and way out of my depth.

"What is *your* end game?" Dread Ash asked.

I shrugged at that. "Stand in your way, I suppose."

"I may just kill you now. If no accord can be reached." Dread Ash shrugged. "Give up True Earth to us, Declan. Stop getting in our way. Most of my family wants you dead, but I'd hate to waste such fire." She bit her lip. "Yes, I may just kill you now. Save the heartache later."

"You know you can't, not yet. Not until you figure out the terribly awful plan." I considered, then nodded. *I'll recover the blade, then all bets are off.*

"And what's to stop me killing your friends over there? You wronged me, Declan. If for no other reason than it pleases me to watch them die, I will kill them."

I nodded. Same old bluster, same old... high stakes. Likelihood and consequence. "Absolutely nothing. I doubt I could stop you. I'd much rather you didn't. If you kill them outside of combat, I will consider it in poor taste and remove myself from the playing field."

Dread Ash's eyes widened. Her mouth dropped open, she gaped, then recovered. "You'd kill yourself?"

"And trap you back where you belong for all

eternity," I said. "No more fun and games in the real world." I offered her half a grin. "Come now, I thought the Everlasting would have jumped at such an opportunity. To have my out of your hair after all these years, all these petty victories, betrayals, defeats…"

"The petal of the Infernal Clock in your heart won't allow you to die," she said. "You are the Immortal King."

"Fair Astoria certainly thought so." I said her name idly, as if it were a minor thing, of no real importance.

Dread Ash began to cry. "My sister is dead and you killed her."

There we would have to disagree. Emily, sweet Emily Grace, had made her own choices—a very long time ago now. My influence may have been responsible for swaying some of those choices, but a woman as remarkable as Emily knew the risk, *chose* the risk.

Ash kicked at the woodchips beneath her, two grooves cut through the mulch with the tips of her boots. "You blinded my brother, defeated Scion, you humiliated Oblivion. How you've survived this long, made such enemies, is perhaps the most absurd thing in all creation. What are you planning this time, Declan?"

"I made my intentions clear to you in Atlantis. Ten thousand years ago, Ash." I stood up from my swing and moved to stand in front of her. Her boots struck my shins gently as I pulled her swing to a stop. Here I knelt on my knees and took her hands in my own. Her fingers were cold, frightfully cold. "I will stand against the Everlasting with everything I have, with every ounce of my strength. I will fight you all. I will kill you all. So make the smart choice, make the only choice, like Fair Astoria did all those years ago. Give up your conquest of the Story Thread."

Dread Ash smiled sadly. She cupped my cheek with one of her hands. I shivered from the cold. "You have no clue just how much Astoria violated when she gave up her grace, do you? What she set in motion? The *attention* she has drawn down upon all the worlds you hold so dear? Once upon a time, Declan, as all good stories should begin," she smiled, "we Everlasting were guardians of the Story Thread. Against the nightmares that lurk in the darkest depths, the forgotten reaches of the Void and beyond."

"There's nothing beyond the Void. Just more Void."

"We will reclaim our guardianship," Dread Ash said. "It's for your own damn good, you know."

A long moment passed between us, and we said more to each other in that moment than in any amount of conversation. There was no middle ground here, no resolution. The fight could not be avoided. The battlefield was chosen, the stakes raised beyond impossible.

I leaned forward, inclined my head up, and placed a delicate kiss, feather-light, on her pink lips.

"That was nice," Dread Ash said, her smile soft, sly, slow.

"It wasn't for you," I said.

She scowled—near snarled—green eyes flared purple with hate, anger, and something that may have been envy. Dread Ash pushed away from me and disappeared from the swing in a rush of white sparks, ash on the wind, she faded away. I sighed and stood, the empty rubber seat striking my knees. So much for diplomacy.

I stared at the empty swing for a good ten seconds before shaking my head and walking away. My allies—my friends, at least Annie—stared at me lost, confused, uncertain.

"Who was that?" Caitlin asked.

"That was the Everlasting Dread Ash," I said. No sense in pretending otherwise. They'd all seen her anger strike the shield, all seen her turn to sparks.

Arlon cursed, Caitlin's eyes bulged so wide I feared they'd pop out of her skull. Only Annie showed no reaction, but I saw her mind working, felt her putting the pieces together.

"Whose body was she possessing?" Annie said quietly, the question not so much a question as a confirmation. "That was Tal, wasn't it? Tal Levy. Oh, Declan, what have you done?"

I tried to meet her gaze but the shame, the ache in my heart and the scar on my very soul, was too much. I fell to my knees overwhelmed with the scope, the loss, and wept from my one good eye.

CHAPTER SEVEN

Across the Square

"You'll break. We all break, eventually"

"You need a drink," Annie said, and hauled me up under my arm with her free hand, her other wrapped around that magnificent revolver. "Dry your eye, princess."

I snorted. Coming from Annie, her words helped me get a hold of myself. "Sorry," I said. "It's been a long year. I never thought we'd be here…"

"Are you going to explain what's going on?" Annie asked. She wasn't demanding, wasn't angry, just asking me if now was the time to confess to the whole sordid affair or not.

I considered, then shook my head. "No, not now. I'm hoping you'll still have some good advice for me, once I finish the Atlantis story."

"Will you have chance to finish it?" she asked.

"Things seem awful grim here, Declan."

I recovered my shotgun, comforted by the familiar weight. Arlon and Caitlin were sending me mixed signals—concern, fear, distrust. I sniffed and did a slow count to five in my head. By four, I was calm, back in the zone.

"Tal is the only person in existence who can do that to me," I said. "She's always been... far more than I deserve. Come on, we have to hurry."

"The Vale Crystalis?" Arlon asked.

I nodded. "Listen, can you hear that?"

I angled my head back down toward the city blocks we'd walked from the edge of the shield. Something on the air, not carried on the wind, but gaining on us nevertheless. From the towers and buildings marking our path, Dread Ash's army of fell creatures and deadlings tumbled onto the street.

"Ah," Caitlin said. "Oh dear."

Dozens became hundreds in a matter of seconds. Now that we'd had our palaver, our intentions made shamefully clear, Ash was playing to win.

"Ahead, too, but not as many," Arlon said. "We can punch through that to the Vale Crystalis if we hurry."

We set off across the park at a steady jog—I was eager to sprint, we all were—but too much chance of something surprising us that way. The parkland gave way to a city street on the inner circle of buildings surrounding the Vale Crystalis. Here were a handful of deadlings and not much else, a few overturned vehicles, and we quickly outpaced the walking dead.

Arlon and Caitlin led us down a back alley between streets and to a row of cafés and restaurants, high balconies, overlooking the square at the very heart of the Atlas Lexicon. Behind us, still some distance away, vicious shrieks, terrible roars, and unpleasant growls filled the air. We were being hunted by things far worse than the rank and file deadlings.

The square, about two hundred feet across and the same wide, leading up to the polished limestone stairs and the entrance to the monumental tower, the Vale Crystalis, was swarming with deadlings and a few of those ragged hound-like creatures. Not with fifty fresh soldiers could we get through that unscathed, if at all.

"Bugger," I said.

"To the east," Caitlin whispered. "We don't actually need to get into the tower directly. See the skybridges up there? Connecting the Vale Crystalis to the accommodation towers? If we can get into one of those buildings and work our way up, we can cross at the bridges into the Crystalis."

"It's a plan," Annie said. "I like it."

We hopped barriers along the row of balconies, two at a time, handing weapons and gear back and forth, already working as a well-oiled machine. Battle did that, as did the constant threat of death. Work together or die. Arlon made short work of the few deadlings in our path, cutting them down silently with his energy blade, and we skirted the edge of the large square, jumping over fountains and pushing our way through hedges and flowerbeds.

It was this quick, careful movement, killing anything in our path, that got us to Apartment Block 12, a shiny glass tower built across the street from the Vale Crystalis. The doors were barricaded, security screens in place, and that was as good sign. Once again tossing my shotgun to Annie, I summoned some Willful light into my hand, grasped the roller door protecting the building, and yanked it up with a grunt of effort.

The thick metal-mesh screen roared in protest, but rose about four feet. Enough to break the glass door beyond and shuffle my allies into the foyer of the apartment block. Once we were in, I forced the security screen back down and melted the broken lock into the floor. Crude, ugly, but secure again.

We took a moment to breathe a collective sigh of relief. Out of the fire, for now, but for how long?

"How do you intend to clear the Lexicon of this filth?" Arlon asked me.

I slumped down in one of the leather couches in the foyer's centre. The ground floor of the apartment block resembled a hotel lobby—comfortable couches, a café and bar, reception desk—though it was empty, abandoned. Where were the residents? Further up, if Ash was to be believed, and I'll say this for the Everlasting, they didn't lie.

Clever with the truth, selective, but never outright deceit.

I carried a sneaking suspicion that they *couldn't* lie.

"We need to bring that shield down," I said. "It'll most likely close the rift, the tear in reality, where the filth, as you say, is crawling through."

"It will also allow Lord Winter to lead a much stronger attack force—the Dawn Mercenaries from the Restless Cemetery, at the very least—into the city," Caitlin said. "Yes, our goal should be the shield."

"How do we bring it down?" Annie asked. "The streets will be crawling with deadlings and worse before too long. We're trapped. Trapped again."

147

They looked to me, as if I had all the answers. Which was fair. I had most of the answers, and none of them were kind. Delaying the inevitable, I checked the load on my shotgun, rechambered a shell, took it out again, put it back in.

"Declan?" Annie said.

"It's simple, really, Annie. Straightforward. We just need to severe the link." I shrugged. "We just need to destroy Dread Ash."

Arlon whistled low between his teeth. "And you can do that? Kill an Everlasting?"

I shrugged again, entirely noncommittal, refusing to commit. Zero commitment.

"Let's make for the Vale Crystalis," I said. "We need reinforcements, more Will casters, soldiers, if we can get them. I sure hope the elevators are working. I don't want to have to climb fifty flights of stairs."

We had to climb fifty flights of stairs.

CHAPTER EIGHT

The Vale Crystalis

"I like my scotch old enough to order its own scotch"

From the roof of the apartment complex stretched a crystal skybridge, forty feet wide, across to the twice as high tower of the Vale Crystalis. We all needed a moment to recover after the drudge march up the stairs, me most of all, having expended a legion's worth of power fighting the deadlings and breaching the shield.

The rooftop of the building, one of the taller towers in the Lexicon, was a wide-open space comprised of coffee carts and a shuttle station. Like the rest of the city, there was no power, all was quiet. The lack of other living souls was beginning to grate. It felt *wrong*. We made for the skybridge, sticking to the middle of the crystal structure, though railings four-feet high guarded against the fall.

From this vantage point, I could see down into the square and some of the streets we had taken to get this far. The ground below crawled with stumbling deadlings, thousands of them, and much faster moving creatures darted among them—a swarm of evil decay.

"Hey! You lot, stop there!" cried a voice on the Vale Crystalis side of the bridge.

The four of us obeyed and came to a stop about three-quarters of the way along the length of the skybridge. Overhead, the purple-red sky weighed down on me, a heaviness I felt on my shoulders as an actual weight.

"What are you doing out here?" an armed young man said. "It's past lockdown!"

Keeping my weapon pointed at the crystal floor, I walked forward slowly, one palm raised. "We're here to rescue you, mate. Sent in by Lord Winter."

The guard waved us over and we crossed entirely into the Vale Crystalis, a similar style balcony and shuttle station on this side of the bridge. Now that we were close, I could see that the guard wasn't only young—he was a teenager. Fifteen, sixteen at the most. He was armed with a short sword on his hip, much like mine. I recognised the craftwork—an enchanted blade.

"You didn't look like deadlings," he said with a grin.

"Soldier," Arlon said. "What's the situation here?"

The guard snapped Arlon a quick salute, either knowing him or his reputation, I gathered, and scratched at his chin. "Haynes, sir. Private Haynes. We're hold up mostly on the upper floors of the Crystalis, sir. About a thousand of us here, some thousands more in the towers to the west. The accommodation block you've just come from was meant to be sealed, which is why it's just me on patrol on this level."

"Is Lady Waterwood available, Corporal Haynes?" I asked politely. "She sent for us."

Haynes nodded. He squinted at me, as if he couldn't quite place my sexy face.

Arlon cleared his throat. "This is Arbiter Declan Hale of the Knights Infernal," he said, and that was enough to make the young corporal take a wide step back. "Best you lead us to where the lords and ladies are sipping their tea, lad."

"What took you so long?" Lady Evelyn Waterwood, Chief Librarian of the Atlas Lexicon, said with a smirk, her silver-blonde hair hung in gentle locks, her blue eyes flashed. We were presented to the seated council of the Atlas Lexicon near the summit of the Vale Crystalis sweaty, tired, and grumpy.

Getting up here had required another thirty flights of stairs, and my knees throbbed. A few hours rest was going to be needed before I started to work my dark schemes on solving this mess. Annie looked ready for a nap, too. For us, on Perth time, it had gone something like three in the morning. We were spent. Food and an hour's rest, that was the plan.

Next to Waterwood was an old man with a long, scruffy beard tucked into his belt. He was bald save for a thin ring of hair circling the sides of his head. "Lord Maerlyn," he muttered, half asleep, resting his chin on his palm. "I was against involving the Knights

Infernal."

The opulent chamber held a horseshoe table of fine dark wood, nine high-back chairs placed around it, one for each lord and lady of the Atlas Lexicon. Only two of the chairs were occupied, by Waterwood and Maerlyn. Winter was locked outside, of course, but I wondered where the other half dozen rulers of this city were hiding.

"Where are the other half dozen rulers of this city hiding?" I asked.

Lady Waterwood leaned back in her chair. "Some are sleeping, some are working on the protection enchantments in the western accommodation towers. Our students' safety is paramount. We've been pulling long shifts to keep the ward schemes in place, which as you know, against such an overwhelming force as the one below, requires constant maintenance. Everyone is pulling their weight, but we cannot last much longer. A day, two at the most, before the wards fail."

"This will be over long before then," I assured her.

"Is that a promise?" she asked. "I trust there will be something left of my city when you're done with it, Arbiter Hale."

I found half a grin. "Oh yes, one or two towers left standing, I promise."

"What is happening outside of the shield?" Lord Maerlyn asked. "And how did you get through?"

"The offensive is being led by Lord Winter." I let them ponder that a moment. "He extended an official envoy for my aid, given that we weren't sure what we would find here in the Lexicon."

Maerlyn grunted. "He had no authority to do that, not without speaking to the rest of us first."

"Which was quite impossible," Lady Waterwood said, trying to keep the peace. "I would know how you breached the shield, Arbiter Hale. If we can evacuate through that monstrous piece of dark magic, then we should."

I was shaking my head before she finished. "No, we're all trapped in here. I can't be certain of even getting myself back through, let alone thousands of children."

"We must bring it down then."

"I agree."

Over the next ten minutes, I filled in my new allies (perhaps) on what I knew (not much), most of which was already public knowledge. I told them of Dread Ash, loose somewhere in the city, and that raised a few eyebrows, I told them the outline of my plan to bring down the shield, and that I would need their aid—supplies, manpower, something to eat, a place to rest for a few hours.

"The shift on the enchantments changes at midnight," Lady Waterwood said. "Just over two hours from now. Arbiter Hale, Detective Brie," Annie, on the edge of the room, perked up, "we can offer you a quiet corner and some food until then."

"Sounds good. I take it you're going to summon the entire council, what's available, and decide whether to act on my plan or not." I adopted a severe frown. "Know that I'll proceed regardless of what you decide, but I hope you'll help me."

That got me a few irate frowns and a long moment of awkward silence.

"Hey, you wanted me here," I said. "Be careful what you wish for."

~~*~*

Sipping bowls of creamy tomato soup, dipping crusty chunks of stale bread, Annie and I had been given a small waiting room a few floors below the grand chambers, with a window overlooking the Atlas Lexicon. The hour had grown late now, true dark beyond the shield, and turned the ugly barrier almost wholly bruised purple.

I sat in a comfortable lounge chair, feet up on the coffee table, shotgun and sword resting on the glass table top. Annie sat next to me, occasionally tapping my boot with hers as we devoured the warm soup.

The waiting room was small, but cosy. Not quite an apartment, but secluded, secret. We were being hidden away until the lords and ladies decided just what to do with us. I felt no worry on that matter— we were, for all intents and purposes, their only option. The lords would bicker, the ladies would argue, but in the end they would fall just short of demanding my help. They would formally ask, as Lord Winter had done.

"Feeling better?" Annie asked.

I laughed softly. "Feeling fine."

"You didn't look it," she commented, ever honest. "Not since punching us through the shield, not since you spoke with… Dread Ash."

"Reserves running a little low, that's all."

Detective Annie Brie rolled her eyes. "You're lying to yourself as much as me, Declan. It's OK to be… drained, emotionally as well as physically."

"Can't afford the weakness," I muttered.

"That's horseshit."

A scoop of soup masked my surly frown.

"How long have you been fighting?" Annie asked. "Most of your life, and not once have you stopped to reflect. Even in your exile, before we met, I'd put good money on you not doing a damn thing to work through the mess of emotion in your head. You're only human, Declan. It's OK to feel it."

"You my therapist now?"

"Someone needs to be—and I'm all you've got. Right now, at least. When we get back to Perth, I'm putting you in touch with the psychologists the police use. And I'll see that you go."

I snorted. "And the first time an elder god or demon attacks during our sessions what do I tell them? That it's not all metaphor and fantasy? That the monsters are real, and after my head? No, Annie, thank you, but no."

She sighed and finished her soup. "Are you going to tell me more of your Atlantis story or not?"

I glared out at the city and into the purple-night. Above, ripples of distant lightning coursed through the shield. Below, armies of dead, dying, and worse. We'd be back out in that mess soon enough.

 "Sure, we've got an hour or two to kill. Get comfy."

REMINISCENCE THE THIRD

(Eight months before soup and scowls and purple skies)

Games in Atlantis

Four months in the Vale Celestia went by faster than I thought it would, but such was the way when you were busy, when you were avoiding something, when you didn't want the time to pass at all.

One afternoon, long after I'd begun to suspect there was more afoot in Atlantis than I'd seen, than I'd been shown, Tylia Vale—the blue-skinned, painfully quiet girl from my squad of students—showed me something that changed everything, that moved the time frame for getting home from worrisome to dire.

We strolled through the hills and dells of the Vale Celestia, speaking about her people, how they had been lost in a Voidflood and remnants, only pieces of remnants, remained.

"We were not just cast from our homeland, our world, but across time, as well. What odds do you think I have of ever seeing a member of my race again?" Her tone was light, light in the way only the very sad can be.

"It's a large multiverse," I said. "But I've seen longer odds on harsher fates, Tylia. Your people really created the central towers in cities like Atlantis?" I shook my head, believing but awed. "They survive, you know. Ten thousand years from now, we still use the towers—the Vale Whatevers."

"My people built three such towers on True Earth. One in Atlantis, one to the north of your world, and one in the far south... they are fine works, fine memorials, I suppose. Other towers are scattered across worlds of power and influence. You have encountered many?"

Three on True Earth... I knew of two—well, one, as the Atlantis tower would be lost to time and the fire before too long, the whole city and a great deal of the land swept into the Void and adrift for ten thousand years, until a dumb kid with everything to prove stumbled across it and started the ball rolling on all this sordid dark work.

The second tower, the Vale Crystalis, sat in the heart of a secret city in Switzerland. A place I had never visited, never had plans to visit. The Knights Infernal were not enemies of that city, but we were not friends, either.

"I've encountered the same tower in different points of time," I said. "But for all that, yes, one or two others. And your people—they are out there, Tylia. You will see them again."

Tylia smiled but her heart wasn't in it. She liked my words, didn't believe them, but liked them. I knew that look well—the look of someone who had seen their entire civilisation come crashing down. Hell, I'd been responsible for that look in hundreds of millions during the Tome Wars.

"What was it you wanted to show me?"

Tylia pulled herself from her thoughts. We crested

a rise under some bent redwoods, the canopy overhead thick and heavy. A scent of burning copper, hot metal, flame and fire, but somewhat ordered, hung in the air. Down below a small collection of buildings surrounded an open courtyard. Mighty furnaces and chimneys, vast forges, metal works, blacksmith anvils and crucibles stood in the courtyard. I hadn't visited this part of the pocket world yet, but I was impressed.

"There's a man here who wants to see you," Tylia said. "I apprentice under him, create enchanted weaponry and armour. He asked me last week if I could bring you along."

A thousand thoughts—and worries—ran through my mind. "Who would want to see me?" I said, with a grin I didn't feel. "I don't know anybody here." *Emily?* Was this her doing?

"Forge Master Alexas," Tylia said. "This is his workshop, all of it. He's a… genius, when it comes to creating things. I'm sure you'll like him."

"I'm sure I will."

I followed Tylia down the hillside and into the courtyard proper, the heat from furnaces and forges almost stifling even in the open air. Playful starlight, those bands of interstellar cloud overhead between here and the broken moons, gave the whole works a midwinter fair vibe. All I needed was a cup of hot chocolate and two feet of snow.

Tylia navigated the maze of iron stores, tool shops, storage sheds, and brought me to the eastern corner of the workshop. Here I saw something wonderful. More furnaces and forges, yes, but infinitely more precious. A wide space, about the size of Riverwood Plaza back home in Joondalup, sixty feet across by a little more wide.

Great troughs, circular pools, had been dug into the stone, and were filled not with molten metal or fire, but with what I could only describe as liquefied starlight. Glittering, molten-black fluid dotted with glowing sparks of light, like the canvas of the heavens cast down into the earth, God's own can of paint. Several of those pools swirled around the central forge, a massive chimney of gleaming silver-blue metal, a metal I recognised as mythril, fed by enormous self-pumping bellows.

Apprentices and staff darted around the courtyard, carrying shining materials, working with foreign, exotic tools I didn't recognise.

A bear of a man, tall and wide, dressed in a simple pair of leather trousers and a sleeveless jerkin, swung a massive hammer into a piece of shining crystal. The chime produced when the hammer struck the crystal was ethereal, soothing. He was a walking stereotype—the original blacksmith.

"There's the Forge Master," Tylia said. The star pools shone in her eyes, cast her blue skin almost purple. "Let me introduce you."

We approached the large man, Forge Master Alexas, as he poured a stone bucket of fluid from the swirling pools into a sword mould and thrust the whole thing into the furnace in front of him. I expected a blast of heat, smoke and sweat, but the air blowing from that glowing furnace was cool, refreshing, like mountain spring water after snowmelt.

"Hello, sir," Tylia said and gave a small curtsey. "I've brought Declan Hale, as you asked."

Forge Master Alexas turned and I got a good look at the man for the first time. Something happened to time then, it slowed, and in the space of about two seconds I had time to recognise his face, tag it well, and knew—*knew*—who I was really about to shake hands with.

The man forging starlight into glass, hammering shadow into substance, was none other than the Everlasting Scarred Axis.

Yet to be scarred, it seemed. His face was unblemished, almost handsome. The creature I had met, chained to a pillar in an abandoned outpost in the storm clouds of Jupiter, had only vaguely resembled something human. In the sense that it had had two arms, two legs, and a head. The rest of Axis had been wasted, elongated grey skin stretched over ruined bone. His eyes had been removed, leaving only twin scars like that on a scarecrow.

I had cast that monstrosity, who had claimed to be responsible for gifting Will to humanity, along with my rebellious shadow, into the Void. It had mangled my hands and nearly killed me, but I had done it. Such a journey into darkness wouldn't kill something as ancient or as vile as an Everlasting. But it would have pissed him off good and proper.

"Ah," Axis… Alexas said and offered me his hand, attached to arm corded with thick muscle and coated in ash from his forge. "You must be our visitor from the future. Tell me, my friend, what of our fair Vale Celestia ten millennia from now? Does my forge still glow hotter than starheart?"

"I… don't know."

That was an interesting question. Although Atlantis had been swept from the map, well and truly annihilated, for all that mattered, the dozens of pocket worlds linked through the portal chamber in the Vale Atlantia wouldn't have been touched. Merely severed from their access point. This world, this school, even this mighty forge and workshop could still exist in my time.

Lost and cut off from the rest of Forget, a bead of the Story Thread almost cast into the Void, but very much whole.

It didn't have its Forge Master, though, that much I knew for certain.

I shook hands with the man, the elder god in disguise, and forced a grin onto my face.

"This is an impressive forge," I said. "What is it you make here?"

Alexas nodded and smiled. He held my gaze for a quiet moment, perhaps trying to read my mind, but I had protections against that, and then let go of my hand. "I am forging the fires of creation," he laughed. "I am creating celestial illusion."

"No you're not," I said, before I could stop myself. Tylia frowned at me. "I mean, that alloy is naturally occurring, and it cannot be recreated."

Alexas gave me a funny look that I read a lot deeper—I knew him as Scarred Axis, I *knew* him under the disguise he wore now, and that funny look was more condescending than confused, more arrogant than confident. "You mean to tell me, millennia from now, the art of my craft has been lost? Say it not, Declan Hale. I would have you say it not."

"I say it not not," I said. "I'm telling you, celestial illusion cannot be… *made*." The very idea offended me. A petal of celestial illusion sat in my heart, I had used the Roseblade to devastate entire worlds, end wars. The alloy was priceless, the shards leftover from creation itself.

161

Alexas grinned, reached into the pouch on his thick leather apron, and handed me a single seed of celestial illusion. "Here is what I have managed to create in the last few years. With enough time and left undisturbed," he said, "this seed will grow an entire grove of alloy. What would that be worth to the future, hmm?"

A piece of celestial illusion the size of a golf ball would be priceless. An entire grove… to be used as I saw fit, to create weapons and defences against the Everlasting. That would level the playing field somewhat. An idea occurred to me, and I saw the look on Axis' face. He had come to the same conclusion.

"Of course, a grove would take thousands upon thousands of years to grow," he said. "And finding a place to leave it undisturbed for so long would be difficult. If only we could know the future." The pointed look he gave me was about as subtle as a train wreck.

But not impossible for a Knight Infernal, for the Willful who could create and travel to their own secret little worlds. *Or…* I thought. *Or even hide it on this world. Somewhere quiet and out of the way.* When I made it home, followed the path through time and space using the petal of the Infernal Clock tying me to Annie, ten thousand years would have blinked past in a heartbeat. I'd be moments older, but my little seed of celestial illusion…

"I need to think about this," I said. *And talk to Tal.*

"Of course, I would hope to see the grove in bloom," Alexas, the immortal Everlasting, said. A clever not-lie. "But knowing my seed is planted, I could die happy." He chuckled, a deep rolling barrel of a laugh. "I would speak with you more, Declan Hale, perhaps over ale?"

He held out his hand for the celestial illusion. I gave a weapon capable of annihilating worlds back to one of my greatest enemies somewhat reluctantly.

~~*~*

I looked for Tal that night, to speak of Axis and the possibility of *growing* a cache of celestial illusion. If I could do such a thing, hide it away, then in the future, back in my own time, the war against the Everlasting would be a lot less... uncertain. I could burn them from creation. Kill them all.

I looked for Tal in the markets, sent a messenger to find her, but she was not to be found. Perhaps she had returned to Atlantis for the day, I didn't know, but I wasn't worried. We'd spent much of the last three months together here in the eternal bright night of the Atlantean academy, the Vale Celestia. Shared dinners, walked hand in hand, rested and relaxed, though events moved around us ever more swiftly.

I wasn't off my guard, never that, and I felt the future tugging at me, the petal in my heart urging me to return to my proper time. But the workings of a very cunning plan had taken seed in my mind, a way to leverage ten thousand years of useless time. Above all, I wanted the war with the Everlasting to be swift, brutal, ended. Ten millennia to prepare for that, given what I knew, what I suspected, felt like more than enough. Generous, even.

I could almost glimpse the whole picture, the years I spent fighting the Tome Wars, the inevitability of releasing Lord Oblivion in the ruins of Atlantis, the battles that followed, my death, my resurrection, my son born to Fair Astoria in the ruins of Voraskel on the outskirts of the Tomb of the Sleeping Goddess. On the tip of my tongue, in the back of my mind, I saw the whole convoluted outline, the story from beginning to end. I wasn't just a character on the page, the Everlasting weren't just the bad guys, we were more of an orchestra, each playing our parts. What I did in the Tome Wars, the years fighting after, would only come about because of what I did now in the past. I created myself, my enemies.

If I was willing to accept my fate, my warmongering, then I had to own it.

But then the glimpse faded, the orchestra fell silent, I lost the bigger picture and felt stupid for thinking anything I did effected events on such a timeless, universal scale. It was all disorder and madness and sheer dumb luck, wasn't it? Perhaps the truth, as it so often did, fell somewhere between the certain and the chaos.

I couldn't find Tal, so I had dinner with pixie-faced Fix instead. My translator for all things I couldn't enchant or bullshit here in the past. In the four months I had been here, Fix had become more than a colleague—we had become friends. At five feet and change, purple spiky hair and bright blue eyes, pale-faced and always smiling, Fix was a tense coil of busy happiness. I enjoyed being near her, basking in some of her reflected light. Where life had crushed me—and I had taken some crushing—she had flourished.

"Always looking so serious," Fix said. "Storm clouds following you around, creased lines in your brow, sad old Declan."

We were in a quaint little tavern, just off the main thoroughfare of markets and on the road to the academy buildings. Warm and cosy and rustic. I pulled a bar stool over to the high table Fix had saved for us and took a seat.

I adopted my most severe frown, deep creases in my surly brow. "You make that dress look good," I said.

Fix grinned and flicked the skirts of her blue, strapless dress. A black shawl covered her shoulders. "And, surprise, surprise, you're in that same black shirt and waistcoat combination. Thanks for making an effort. A girl could think you didn't care."

"Hey, in the future, this get up of mine is all the rage." No, it wasn't, but I was slowly bringing it back.

"No, it isn't," Fix said.

I raised my palms in defeat. "You look nice, anyway. Plans tonight?"

She shrugged a delicate shoulder. "Sometimes it's just nice to dress up and pretend I have a social life, plenty of friends, a dozen invites to parties across the Vale Celestia and Atlantis."

I chuckled and grabbed a menu. "And you don't have that?"

"Not tonight. My sister wants to get together and discuss her latest boyfriend." Fix rolled her eyes. "She'll be here later, if you're still around."

Fix and I chatted the evening away, enjoying food and drink (soda and lime for me, which was enough, these days), and polite conversation. She held my hand across the table a few times, brushed her foot against mine, giving off all the signs that this evening could be far more pleasant, if I wanted. I had to admit, I loved her smile and purple eyes.

Somewhere toward the later hours of that evening, a familiar woman entered the tavern and spied us at our table. I thought, for a moment, she was here for me, but in that I was wrong.

In many things, most things, I was wrong.

Emily Grace—Fair Astoria—put an arm around Fix's shoulders and gave me a polite, oh so polite, smile. Her eyes danced with laughter.

"Declan," Fix said, and shattered my happy little world, "this is my sister, Astoria."

"We've met, briefly," Astoria said. "A few months back. I wanted to talk to the man from the future."

"He's pretty tight-lipped about most of that," Fix said, frowning and wagging her finger at me.

I almost ordered a drink, and tried very hard to keep the shock and surprise from my face. If Emily and Fix were sisters, as she had claimed earlier in the evening and then again to introduce Emily, then Fix... my little pixie-faced Fix, who I thought had quite the crush on me, was *another* of the Everlasting.

Which made the crush dangerous—deceptive. I had a strong feeling I was messing in matters I didn't even begin to understand.

But I would understand. I would outlast them. So I ordered another plate of chicken wings and mozzarella sticks, the Atlantean equivalent, and had a late evening snack with two elder gods.

With two lovely women older than the planet beneath our feet.

~~*~*

"Which one is she?" I asked. "You're all here, aren't you? Every one of the Everlasting. Well, at least three of you."

Emily swung her bare feet back and forth in the cool waters of the Elm River, a trickling stream near the university buildings, more of a bubbling brook in the forest where we'd taken our walk that morning— though the endless galactic night sky overhead gave the word morning only a passing nod. It was ten o'clock, brunch, and we were bathed in interstellar light. My dinner with Fix, where I had learned the truth, had been the night before.

"In one form or another, yes, my brothers and sisters are all here on True Earth, Declan," Fair Astoria/Emily said.

Less and less I could discern between the two, less and less I wanted to make the distinction. Emily Grace was Fair Astoria, infinitely ageless and wise. Fair Astoria was Emily Grace, ruthless and kind.

I ran a hand back through my hair and straightened my eye patch. Playing for time, to think my dark thoughts, I took a deep breath and exhaled slowly. "What is it you all want?"

I feared I knew the answer to that, but better to hear it.

Emily kicked a spray of water droplets at me sideways and said nothing. From where we sat on the edge of a wooden bridge, close enough to embrace, I gazed downstream at the glittering lights and spires of the Vale Celestia.

"You want what you've always wanted," I answered my own question. "Power, dominion over True Earth and by extension, the Story Thread. Every world charted and uncharted in every possible universe under an Everlasting heel."

"We want to protect those worlds," Fair Astoria

said. She wore a lovely white gown, her shoes held by the heels in one hand. "Don't you?"

"I think we've different, *vastly* different, ideas on just what that might look like."

"What am I in your future, Declan?" Astoria asked. "A friend?" She stroked my cheek. "More than a lover?"

"Do you really want to know?"

"I am… curious."

I laughed, but the sound of my laughter wasn't kind. Perhaps I was bitter, more than a little, but what this woman, this fading god, would put me through in years to come and years recently past… Was it fair to blame someone for something they hadn't done yet? Time travel really needed to come with a handbook on morality.

"We are lovers," I said, "although I'm not sure when. We are friends, although you killed me once. We are enemies, for a time, as you marry Morpheus Renegade and become his Immortal Queen. The first time we meet, I help you find a copy of a book called The Illusion of Separateness by Simon Van Booy and you genuinely love his words. I own a small bookshop around that time, because I was exiled from the Order of the Knights Infernal for ending a war I'm not certain you didn't have a hand in starting."

Astoria's lips quirked. "Oh, is that all we are?"

I grinned in kind. "You are one of the Nine, one of the fabled Everlasting. Nine monsters, nine elder gods, that sometime between now and ten thousand years from now became so feared and hated by the peoples of the Story Thread that you descend into nightmarish myth. We sing songs about you and your brothers and sisters, sing *warnings*. We choose to believe you never existed and we forget how to fight you."

"We cannot be fought," Astoria said. "We cannot be killed."

Oh, you're wrong there, sweet thing. I held you in my arms as you died.

"Knight's bite repels the blight, my dear. You give us mortals too little credit." I sighed. "So what are we, Emily, when all's said and done?"

Dead, I thought. *Parents.*

"Distant," I said and waved at the sky. "Like the stars."

She sighed softly. "You always sound so sad."

"And you still haven't answered my question." I met her eyes, which was a conflict of emotions in and of itself. "Fix. Who is she?"

"My little sister. Ashaya D'levaney, seventh born of the Everlasting."

I blinked, honestly surprised Emily had given up that information so easily. Perhaps she had lied, but I didn't think so. I had a sneaking suspicion the Everlasting couldn't lie. Bend the truth, change the subject, refuse to answer, certainly—but purposeful deceit? No. The idea was a dangerous one, an ass of an assumption, and entire worlds may burn for it, but I had my suspicion nevertheless.

"Ashaya..." *Dread Ash.* That old, painful children's rhyme played through my mind:

> *Starless paths through the Lost Sight*
> *Dread Ash turns cold day to night.*

"What do you think of her?" Emily asked, a loaded

question if ever I heard one.

I answered honestly. Capable of terrible lies and deceit, yes I was, but Emily deserved more than that. Still plenty of opportunities for us to be enemies before our dalliance and destruction in the future, I know, but in the end she'd die for me and our son, and her dying would be hard.

"I think she's lovely," I said. "I admire her… happiness. She inspires me to god awful cheerfulness." I tossed a small pebble into the Elm. "I haven't met her in the future, either. She's new to me and not at all what I imagined."

"Oh?" Emily's lips quirked, she raised a delicate eyebrow, auburn hair falling from her shoulder. "What did you imagine?"

"Dread," I said. "Fear… ice." A fitting word slithered across my mind. "Scorn."

Emily leaned against my arm, placed her head on my shoulder. Her hair carried the scent of wildflowers. I tried not to read too much into such easy, absent affection.

~~*~*

The months began to pile up in Atlantis and the Vale Celestia—Tal and I, though we never rekindled our intimate relationship, grew ever closer. Something beyond friends, beyond old lovers.

Our students competed in the tests and trials to hold their place at the Vale Celestia, all the high lords were in attendance, parades and crowds, and both our teams passed with flying colours. Tal and I 'fought' at the end of it, a duel of our powers against one another. We put on a show, shot off a few fireworks, and called it a draw.

Seven months since arriving in Atlantis, some months of time passing not quite concurrently in the future, as I occasionally checked in on Annie through our connection, and I found I didn't want to go home. Not yet.

There was an opportunity here. A dark one, fraught with peril, but also purpose.

Three of the Everlasting were here in Atlantis, at least three, possibly more. One of them, Emily, I could almost consider trusting. I thought, perhaps, she was on my side. After all we'd shared, the memories of the future I'd shared with her, she was on my side.

It seemed a waste to, well, waste such an opportunity.

My sole purpose, all I hoped to achieve in my life, focused around overwhelming and annihilating the Everlasting. The so-called elder gods had caused me nothing but grief, hurt, loss. And here they didn't know me yet, not really. Here in Atlantis I had the advantage.

I didn't want to leave before I'd made full use of that. What I did here, today and now, could echo into the future... possibly as far as ten thousand years away.

I should have known better.

I don't get to win without losing.

I stayed in Atlantis. I stayed with Tal.

I doomed us both.

CHAPTER NINE

Bat Country

"Never let them see you cry"

The meeting with the full council—minus Lord Winter—of the Atlas Lexicon lasted a good hour, during which I said my piece, restated my intentions to proceed with or without their blessing, weathered the arguments, the snide slurs (and the outright insults), and in the end was granted their 'permission' to save them from the Everlasting Dread Ash.

"I want Arlon and Caitlin back," I said. "They're good soldiers. Whatever you're paying them, it isn't enough."

"They serve at the pleasure of the Lexicon," Lord Tremaine snapped, a bitter fellow, early fifties, greying black hair, who had slung more than a little bit of mud at me during the meeting.

Chief Librarian Lady Waterwood, perhaps the only

one at the table who felt anything but hate for me—
and the organisation of cruel Knights Infernal I
represented, and the worst of them at that—hushed
him quiet and agreed to rouse my allies.

"What is your plan?" she asked.

I shook my head. "I don't know any of you, not
really, and the Everlasting can wear... well, any face
they want, so I'll keep that close to my chest for now.
But to get us started, I need maps—all the maps of
the Lexicon you can provide within a mile of the Vale
Crystalis."

"What are you looking for?" Lord Maerlyn asked.
"What do you hope to find?"

"Something buried a long, long time ago."

"You need to give us more than that," Tremaine
demanded.

"I don't need to give you a damn thing," I replied,
getting a little tired of the resistance. "You called me,
you need my help. Let's stop jerking each other off
and get to work."

So ended this mighty meeting of the great and
powerful.

~~*~*

I surveyed the maps surrounding the Atlas
Lexicon, matching records to my far from perfect
memory. What I was looking for was a needle in a
haystack... a haystack that had been buried ten
thousand years ago. So much had changed since then,
forests had disappeared and towers had sprung up,
though it had been just over a week for me—as
Dread Ash, my pixie-faced Fix, had been all too eager
to remind me when my plan faltered.

I'd get Tal back from her, as I had gotten Tal back from her brother, Lord Oblivion. Or die trying. Seems like everything I did was '*or die trying*'.

"What are you looking for?" Annie asked, lacing up her boots.

We'd been given chance to shower in preparation for what lay ahead. After the food, the rest, and the wash, I felt almost normal. Still a little drained from the power exertion, and the minor headache from the shield, but as close to normal as I could get. Hell, I felt like I had a hangover—without the awesome night of drinking that's meant to go along with that. It's a cruel, unfair universe, often ironic in its malice.

"Or is it another of those things you don't want to say aloud for now?" Annie finished with her boots and stood. She wandered over to the table and cast her pretty eye over the reams of parchment, the atlases, and modern print-outs of the region. With all power to the Lexicon down, this was the best we had.

"Partly," I said. "We're definitely being listened in on by someone—the room has basic surveillance enchantments, but I suspect its more benign than an attempt to move against us."

"So whoever's listening just heard you say you know they're listening?"

I nodded. "I suspect Lord Tremaine, but I'm sure he's got the best interests of the Atlas Lexicon at heart."

I felt the air in the room change and Annie shivered. "Feel that? The eavesdropping enchantment was just removed."

"Is that what that was? Felt like a tingle of electricity in the air."

I tapped the map in front of me, a section of the

city to the northwest, where a small forest climbed the foothills of the nearest mountain. A lot had changed in ten thousand years, but nothing so severe as a mountain. That took far more than ten lazy millenniums.

"Here," I said. "We need to head over to this part of the city."

Annie frowned and shook her head. "That's all the way across town… and then some. What? Two miles? Through streets infested with dead and worse?"

"I agree, it will be a challenge."

"You like a good challenge."

"That I do."

Annie giggled—a little nervously. "Have to say, I really don't want to go back out there."

"Stay here then. Eat soup. Wait for the world to end."

She punched me in my bicep. "You know I'm coming, but is there a smarter way we can do this? What about that book we used to get here—Road's Fire? Is there a portal?"

"No, not between two points so close together. Using portal magic like that would be like trying to squeeze into a pair of tight jeans four sizes too small. Lot of effort for nothing and something will tear or break."

"You've such a way with words."

"And the shield is messing with reality and the fabric of the world more than enough. The last thing we need is a few more holes in it. The canvas is burning around us. You can feel it, even hear it, if you listen." I cocked my head to the side and did just that. "If we don't stop this, Annie, and soon—within half a day—the shield will spread, the canvas will tear irreparably."

"What are you saying?"

"Oh, just the end of the world."

Annie cursed. "I don't think we've managed to spend more than a day together without things descending toward the end of the world."

I laughed and rolled up the map, folding the parchment in half and half again until the square fit in my back pocket. "You love it."

"I'm scared, Declan."

"Annie, me too."

~~*~*

The lords and ladies of the Atlas Lexicon—names I was already half-forgetting, as I met enough lords and ladies of various impossible cities before breakfast, it seemed, to start several tribute bands to the ponce and circumstance—outfitted us well from the armouries in the Vale Crystalis.

Arlon and Caitlin, looking a little rested, grim-faced but determined, had washed the grime away and were fully armed. The old grizzled soldier had strapped a rather modern looking assault rifle to his chest, something to counterbalance the light sabres he ignited from his hands, I supposed.

Along with the two Lexicon regulars who had stormed the city with me, Annie and I were joined by a fresh squad of bright-eyed and excited soldiers, bringing our total number of helpers to nine. A number of power, the number of the Everlasting. None of the new soldiers looked older than twenty, though perhaps that was more my problem than theirs.

Lady Waterwood met us on the balcony looking over the western tower blocks of the Lexicon, the city marching away into the west and climbing the foothills of the Swiss Alps—before stopping abruptly, a limb severed, by the ugly, malignant purple shield. I was in the process of clearing my shotgun and reloading when she pulled me aside for a quiet word.

"Is this sufficient?" she asked, a lot of the bravado and casualness from the meeting gone. We all wore masks—I struggled to wear one that surpassed indifference. Hard to care, sometimes, when the universe kept taking, rarely giving.

I nodded slowly, sighted the shotgun with my good eye. In the past, the enormous power I placed in the enchanted shells fractured the runes, the Will-work, in the silver gun. The barrel didn't look warped, but it had been hours since I last fired the gun and the metal was still warm to the touch. One way or another, I'd need to fall back on my Will and sword soon enough, and I was hoping to save that for the inevitable, earth-shattering battle against Dread Ash herself. I'd done a count of the enchanted shells I had left. Seven shots. Best I could hope for was seven shots, if the barrel lasted that long.

"It will have to be sufficient, Evelyn," I said. "Unless you strove to contact the Knights Infernal in Ascension City while we rested? No? I didn't think so."

Lady Waterwood scowled. "Many would rather see the Atlas Lexicon fall than ask your... organisation for aid."

"And yet here I am," I said, not unreasonably. "Your last best hope."

"You... are something else."

I feigned hurt. "A fella could take that the wrong way."

"Take it as you must, Hale."

"Are we going to be friends after this?"

"Once this incursion is resolved you are to be exiled from the Atlas Lexicon."

Exiled again. Great. My hurt was a little less feigned now, a little more angry. "No good deed goes unpunished, eh?"

The stillness in the air from the scarred sky, the groans of the dead echoing throughout the city, the ripples of purple lightning flashing in our eyes, turned the lady's grin into something devilish. For a moment, that instant between heartbeats, I was certain I was once again in the presence of the Everlasting. But then the clock ticked on, the petal in my heart remained unstirred, and I felt foolish.

Granted, I saw their machinations and spoke to the Everlasting more than any other Knight or poor son of a bitch across the Story Thread, but I'd quickly lose my mind if I started seeing them in every shadow.

"The Atlas Lexicon survives only so long as the Knights Infernal leave it alone," Lady Waterwood said. She thrust a sharp fingernail toward the sky. "This is Knightly business, is it not? Do your duty and be gone."

Lady Waterwood walked away, sparing a nod for the group of Lexicon soldiers, before disappearing back into the tower.

So ended the parade and fanfare to see us off to what would most likely be bloody death and unhappy endings.

"That looked unpleasant," Annie said, as I

returned to my group of allies. Eight pairs of eyes regarded me soberly. Far too soberly.

Still want that drink? whispered Emily's voice in the back of my mind. *You, me, a dimly lit cocktail lounge. Step back across the Void, leave all this behind, return to Atlantis. Oh the things we could talk about, Declan.*

"Lady Waterwood wishes us luck," I said to the group. "She fears for our safety, but knows we'll do what needs to be done to put an end to this mess."

One of the young soldiers—hell, it was the kid who had stopped us on the eastern skybridge—shuffled his feet and said, "Is it true we're facing one of the Everlasting?"

"Aye," Arlon grumbled. "Aye, lad, it is." Arlon clapped him on the shoulder. "Lucky for us, eh, that we've got the Story Thread's number one expert in dealing with those bastards in command."

I made a show of looking around the terrace for such an expert, and then pretended surprise when I realised it was me. That got a laugh from a few of the crew. Better to die laughing.

"What's the plan from here, Hale?" Caitlin asked.

I nodded. "Right, yes, the plan. We need to hit the north western foothills just beyond the city outskirts." I pointed over in that direction, most of the view obscured by the tall, silver towers of the Atlas Lexicon. "Annie's got a map and so do I, but we'll stick together for now. If I understand these skybridges right, we can move from here at the Vale Crystalis, through the currently occupied western accommodation blocks and beyond for about a quarter mile."

Arlon grunted. "Yeah, that's about right."

"We need to stay off street level as long as we

can," I said, stating the obvious. "There's just too many deadlings and creatures bleeding through the tear in reality. Our main objective is to pull this shield down—that will accomplish two things: One, it will cover the tear in scar tissue and stop any more enemies from coming through, and two, it will allow Lord Winter and the army he's commanding on the other side to sweep through the city and put an end to this mess." I saw a few glimmers of hope, of determination, on the youthful faces. "Any questions?"

"What do we do if the Everlasting attacks?" one of them asked.

"Stay out of her way. Leave that… to me. Anything else? No? Let's move out."

Our balcony led to a proper terrace sticking out from the side of the Vale Crystalis. I glanced up above, we were still a good ten floors below the summit of the tower, and I was bloody glad we didn't have to climb them. There'd be enough flights of stairs ahead. Knowing my luck, up as well as down. The squad moved across the crystal skybridge, bathed in that ugly purple light, connecting this level of the tower to the accommodation block on the other side.

"That was almost inspiring," Annie said, once the soldiers were out of earshot. "You're good at this, you know, when you want to be."

I laughed. "You mean I haven't impressed you so far with my grasp of command and leadership?"

Annie gave me one of her brilliant smiles. "You're too moody. Swings from high to low. Are you as confident as you sound?"

I thought about lying and then tilted my hand back and forth in the air. "So-so, I'd say. What lies ahead, well, I *can* get the shield down. I'm sure of that. If we recover what's to the northwest." I grew less certain. "After that, defeating Dread Ash, saving Tal again…"

"Not so certain?"

I shook my head. "Not so much that, as… Well, you've been around on one or two of these adventures, Annie. Seen more than most." *Lost more than most, though you don't know it yet.* "What I'm saying is, we never win without losing."

Annie considered that and then gave me a quick hug. "We'll manage," she said.

In my mind, Tal's words in the gardens of Atlantis played softly on repeat: *They won't be able to kill you. You survive, Declan. You always, always survive. Even when you die, you live. No, you won't die. But you'll change. I can see it. The war will take you and you'll become hard, harder than you've ever been. You'll sacrifice entire worlds for one inch of an advantage against the Everlasting. Don't tell me you won't, because I know you, and you have.*

I shouldered my shotgun, found half a smile, and together Annie and I quick marched to catch up with the squad of soldiers, now halfway across the impressive skybridge.

From the bridge, I surveyed the ever increasing number of fell creatures in the streets below. In my mind I pictured myself wielding the Roseblade from this crystal pedestal, far above the city, flooding the streets with cleansing fire. There was a time, many years ago and not so long ago in the grand scheme of things, where I could have done just that—and to hell with any living souls hiding down there, lost and scared. Acceptable losses.

Perhaps it was best I no longer had the Roseblade, that absurdly powerful weapon forged from celestial illusion.

The western accommodation tower was all hustle and bustle. The upper tiers, which we passed through to reach the next skybridge was teeming with teenagers, gangs of roaming youth and ne'er-do-wells, the students of the Lexicon. They seemed in good spirits, laughing and joking, but I noticed very few of them glanced upward, or out the windows. Pretending all was well was easy, but forgetting all was not well, a little harder. Each one of these kids had travelled to other worlds, at least once, and each one of them could feel the malice of the shield.

We endured our share of curious glances and took the stairs down a dozen floors to the next balcony and terrace, complete with defunct shuttle station, and the skybridge into the western quarter of the city.

"This would be easier if the shuttlecraft were operational," Arlon said.

"Yes and no," I replied. "All of us bunched up in one of those shuttles would make a fairly appealing target for anything, or any *god*, looking to take us off the playing field."

"Slow and steady then, sir?" one of the soldiers asked.

"Minimise the risk where we can, but don't forget we are on a clock here. This shield is pushing against the very fabric of True Earth, the reality that holds this planet together. If it's not unmade, the whole blue marble is going down the drain." I let that sink in—a bit of motivation for the crew. "The Void presses closer, ladies and gentlemen. Tell me you can't feel it? The ache in the air, in your bones, the *dread*."

And the hell of it was, they all could. The headaches, the oppressiveness, the sense that at any moment all of reality would just fracture. Like birds before an earthquake, we sensed the impending catastrophe at our base level of instinct. The same instinct that had served the human race for a million years, that screamed at us when there was a tiger in the trees, even when we couldn't see it—especially when we couldn't see it.

"Oh, is that what that is?" Annie said lightly. "Here I thought I was getting a touch of Void flu."

"Void flu." I managed a rough chuckle. We stepped out onto the second skybridge—which led to the roof of the smaller tower opposite. Beyond, our path through the maelstrom grew less certain. Northwest, sure, but the streets may become our only option. Which meant a fight, noise, more fighting, one or two or all of these green soldiers would die, no doubt heroically. Drudge work. A boring Sunday afternoon. "Void flu. That's like calling terminal cancer a touch of hay fever, Annie, but I like the humour in the face of utter annihilation. Good hustle."

A tremendous roar echoed across the length of the city, met by two, three, *four* accompanying roars. We came to a sudden stop halfway across the crystal skybridge, hearts leaping into throats, goose bumps rippling up and down my arms.

A gust of fetid, heavy air struck us all, making us stumble a few steps. From *within* the shield, directly over our heads, a good half a mile away, a bat-like creature fell through the sky, wingspan at least six-metres across, its face a ruin of bone and fire, elongated like a dragon's skull. It's body was mostly dead flesh fused to grey bones, rusted steel armour plates covering its heart.

"Oh. Oh, shit," I said. "If you're waiting for an order to fire, gang, *fire!*"

Four other bat-creatures circled the big bastard—Batsy—but they were smaller—wingspans at two, three metres at most. Much more reasonable.

Like an arrow loosed, Batsy shot straight towards us, and I had another one of my sneaking suspicions. This one told me Ash, bless her evil and ageless heart, had set a watch on all the skybridges in and out of the occupied towers. Clever, something I had hoped she would have overlooked, but so be it.

Game on.

"Heart or the brain?" Annie asked, standing tall and resplendent, her revolver aimed skyward.

She struck such a pose that one day I was certain I'd see her like this as a marble statue, perhaps here in the Atlas Lexicon itself, a memorial to the heroes who struck down the dark and terrible Everlasting. The Everlasting wearing the skin of the woman I loved and lost… so many times now. Diminishing return on investment, loving me.

"I've got Batsy—the big son of a bitch," I yelled. "Rest of you take down the pilot fish. Swat them like the vermin they are, ladies and gentlemen."

Arlon unclipped his assault rifle. "Right, you lot. Squad formation Delta-Delta. Caitlin, eastern flank. I'm on west. You two, protect the Arbiter and the Detective."

The six soldiers split into groups and spread out across the bridge. Two back toward the accommodation tower with Caitlin, two to stay with us, and two to the west with Arlon. Weapons were raised, safety switches were unsafetied, just as we were slammed with another gust of air carrying the stink of the fell creatures.

This is going to cost us, I thought. What I wouldn't have given for a handful of Knights Infernal just then. My old friends, my old allies, those of us that had swam through the ocean of blood that had been the Tome Wars and reached the other shore. Vrail, Tia—hell, even Marcus, who had betrayed me to the Renegade King eighteen months ago and gotten me killed. I still had to thank him for that. Everything that had followed had been by design, though hard to see that when I fell screaming and bleeding from the Vale Atlantia in the ruins of Atlantis, through a time rip, and into death.

Batsy and I only had eyes for each other. I ran to the edge of the crystal bridge, placed a foot up against the railing to balance the shotgun, nestled again in that bruised and abused nook below my right shoulder. "Come on…" I breathed.

The soldiers fired their weapons—sparks and tracer shots, enchanted rounds, ignited slivers of metal, lit up the ugly purple sky. The creatures surrounding Batsy peeled away, evasive manoeuvres, but the hail of bullets, the sheet of firepower, punctured wings and chipped bone. Roars turned to rage turned to pain.

Closer now, seconds away, I recognised Batsy as cousin to the beast Annie had taken down as we emerged from the forest to the south of the valley. That miscreation hadn't had enough rotten flesh left on its wings to fly. It's heart had also been exposed, unlike this beast, which had invested in some crude but effective armour plating over its bony chest.

Skeletal arms twice as long as I was tall reached for me, just beyond that snarl of a face, ending in massive hands tipped with sharp claws.

I gazed down the barrel of my shotgun, sighting the beast well. "Here, Batsy, Batsy, Batsy…" I whispered as the calm before the storm descended on me. The cold, calculating rage that had seen me survive battle after battle, war after war.

Berserker rage, some called it, but it was never loud, or angry. True rage was frozen, indifferent, without mercy.

After all the years, I could flip that rage switch like turning on a lamp.

A jet of orange flame burst from Batsy's maw, a wave of blistering heat set to sear me where I stood. The beast thought I'd move, dive to the side.

I grinned and moved my shotgun seven perfect inches to the left—and pulled the trigger.

Blue lightning burst from the barrel of the weapon, arcs of power leaping between four hundred or so nasty, bitey shot pellets. The blast tore a ragged hole the size of a soccer ball in Batsy's left wing, disrupting his aerodynamics entirely.

Batsy rolled in the air, the jet of flame veered away from me, striking and scorching the width of the crystal bridge on my right. With a tremendous *boom*, Batsy struck the bridge, knocking me back, almost knocking me from my feet, in a tangle of bone, steel, and flame.

"No, don't get up," I said, and realigned my shotgun. I fired again into the heap of monster.

The blast of the shotgun tore across the Lexicon, the fist of power—one of my last few enchanted shells—separated that left wing at the joint on the beast's decaying back. Batsy screamed, that all too familiar symphony of wrath and hurt.

I chambered again, the shotgun hot and heavy, smoke curling from the barrel and *along* the barrel.

Batsy turned his skull to face me, the red demon-light in his eyes flickering, narrowing.

As if I had all the time in the world, I fired again, wiping that smug look off his face, and sauntered over to the fallen creature. The torrent of light and fire from the shotgun ripped most of the beast's snout away—and took a good chunk of the crystal skybridge with it, punched a hole clean through to the quarter-mile drop below, where the streets still swarmed with deadlings.

"If you're the best Ash has," I said, hoping she could hear me, that she was watching, "this fight will be over before breakfast."

Knowing this would be my last shot, the shotgun vibrated in my hands, the business end of the barrel glowing white-hot, I shoved the barrel deep into Batsy's eye socket, getting an angle on his brain.

"Hey," I said. "Whatever your last thought is, I bet it's gonna blow your mind."

I pulled the trigger.

A rotten mix of bone and brain exited the back of Batsy's skull, along with the last torrent of redeeming blue lightning my shotgun would ever fire. The barrel bulged, broke. I turned away from the blinding light as Batsy, his form broken, ignited in that cleansing white fire, unable to hold its form together. *Good riddance.*

I held up my shotgun, the barrel had warped, twisted the steel and silver. The top foot or so had bloomed like in the cartoons, like a comical banana peel, or when Bugs Bunny blocked the end of Elmer Fudd's rifle with a carrot. I laughed and tossed the weapon aside. *Back to working with my hands.*

I turned to see how the others were faring, Annie mostly, and a stab of blinding pain pierced my right shoulder—I was yanked backwards, stabbed in the meat just below my shoulder, caught in the claws of one of the pilot fish.

Mini-Batsy roared in triumph, hurled me over the *edge* of the skybridge and out into open air. For the space of two long seconds I arced above the immense city without form or tether—or parachute. A second Mini-Batsy caught me properly, it's clawed feet closing around my chest, my legs, pinning me to its form. Leathery wings beat in heavy gusts, taking to the sky, flying me west and away from the skybridge and my allies.

I had time to glimpse Annie, her mouth fell open in an 'o' of shock, surprise, dismay, and see the other soldiers—Arlon and Caitlin—doing battle with the three remaining Mini-Batsy's, who were covering the retreat of the one that had me in its grip.

This was planned, I thought in a moment of rare clarity. *Planned to separate me from my friends.*

Well, fuck that.

CHAPTER TEN

They Come to Haunt Me

"I am the entertainer"

I had three real options, as best as I could see it, of dealing with my current predicament. And as predicaments went in my life, this one rated somewhere between a stubbed toe and a cut that needed stitches.

Only mildly bothersome in the long run, but in the shorter sprint hurt like a motherfucker.

The air howled past my ears as Mini-Batsy fled the skybridge, skirting west, diving between and around the silver towers of the Atlas Lexicon. The scent of decay, violent gusts of fetid air, whipped at my face. The world was a blur of silver and purple.

Option #1: I used my Will and burned the monster. Problem there was my arms were pinned to my sides by the beast's claws. We'd burn together, falling from the purple sky like a meteorite falling to earth, fiery contrail and all. Not ideal. Doomed to ruin. I didn't doubt I'd go down in flames one day, but there was still so much work left to do. Not yet.

Option #2: I broke the beast's grip, a wave of concussive force expanding outward from my palm—again, using my Will power. Problem there, of course, was that I'd only be free maybe twenty seconds before I slammed into the ground far below at terminal velocity. *If I could trick Mini-Batsy…* Wasted, pasted. Even if I survived the fall (I wouldn't), the beast would follow me and I'd be smack dab in the middle of a deadling army without my friends and their considerable firepower.

Option #3: I enjoyed the ride, let Mini-Batsy fly me where it had been instructed to fly me. Arguably the less risky option at the moment, but given that the odds Mini-Batsy was taking me anywhere decent—Paddy's on a Wednesday for the steak special and a pint of extra cold Guinness sprang to mind as pretty decent right now—that mid-level risk would head into the red rather swiftly.

Shit, I thought. *Boned by a bone-monster.*

I remember thinking I'd have given anything for a handful of Knights Infernal at my side on the bridge. Now I was glad they weren't here to see this embarrassment. I had one hell of a reputation out in the Story Thread, a thousand earned names and titles—hero, villain, genocidal librarian, the Shadowless Arbiter, saviour and destroyer… Declan Hale, the rightful king of Ascension City—cruel trophies, each one of them, but I had *earned* them. Bled and died for them. This predicament was best left out of the history books.

My shoulder hurt. The stab wound from the other Mini-Batsy's claws had punctured me deep, a good inch or more. Hot blood flowed sticky down my chest, staining my shirt crimson, and had completely ruined my favourite waistcoat. For that alone this beast would die.

We left the main towers of the Atlas Lexicon behind, swooping low toward the ground. I tried to free an arm, work it toward the sword I wore on my hip. If I could get that sword loose, my mockery of an Infernal blade, then the odds would change. Once we were close enough to the ground... or even a rooftop.

Mini-Batsy glared down at me, eyes red like the dying embers in a coal fire, as I wormed and wrestled in its grip. Shocking pain bellowed like a klaxon alarm from my pierced shoulder, but I was used to such nonsense. Pain was temporary, regret was forever. I forget who said that.

The city below gave way to more expansive parklands, of the sort we'd crossed to reach the Vale Crystalis in the heart of the Lexicon what felt like days, not hours, ago. A crimson rain of blood drops, my blood, watered the grass below. The towers were gone, more office blocks and buildings between the parks, and the ground sloped up to meet us as we entered the foothills of the mountains.

A small smattering of forest, sort of a palm with three fingers stretching out, creeping up the side of the mountains, swept beneath me. We were maybe ten metres above the tops of the trees. I had a terribly stupid thought. *I can survive ten metres...*

I'd worked my left hand to the hilt of the sword. I had no room to draw the blade or swing it, but then I didn't need to. My right hand I spun, palm outwards, placed flat against Mini-Batsy's crooked claws.

I summoned my Will, opened my mind to the currents of power, the ascending oils at the heart of the universe. Like a door swinging open, there was strength, power—*intent*. I snarled, gritting my teeth. This was going to hurt, possibly break bones, but so be it.

I summoned a blast of raw power, a concussive wave of strength, and the energy exploded from my hand—strong, but also tempered so as not to reduce my bones to jelly. A flash-bang lit up the sky, a crack like a whip, and Mini-Batsy's claw sprang open. The beast shrieked in surprise and pain.

So did I, as what felt like a hammer punched me in the side of my chest. I felt one or two ribs break, possibly just cracked, but I didn't hold out much hope for small mercies today.

Mini-Batsy let me go, let me fall.

But the beast recovered almost instantly.

I drew my sword as Mini-Batsy spun in the air, surprise turned to anger, and dove to recapture me. I'd been expecting that, grinning as it's skeletal arms extended to snatch me.

I let the snatch happen, let the beast pull me in close, and then *drove* my sword between its ribs, right through the flimsy armour that couldn't stand against an enchanted blade, and skewered the beast's rotten heart.

The light in Mini-Batsy's eyes blinked out, dead between heartbeats, and it's form erupted in that cool white fire anything with a pulse longed to see.

Snarling again, I spun the flaming corpse through the air, giving thanks to whatever god of fools and war criminals that watched over me that the fire was benign to the living. The white flame was a cool breeze, light and tingling, licking at my skin, almost refreshing.

We struck the treetops of the forest hard, but the disintegrating beast absorbed most of the impact. I bounced off its ruined husk—bruised, battered, bleeding—but alive. The tree canopy was nice and thick and my fall slowed almost instantly. Errant branches and twigs snapped under me before I came to a sudden stop, the air cast from my lungs, in a tangle of wood and leaves somewhere in the upper branches.

The world spun around my hand, a snowfall of white fire sparks danced around me, the last of Mini-Batsy. Everything was quiet, everything hurt. I took a careful breath, knotted as I was in the tree. My ribs protested the air, but that was the worst of it.

I turned my head, fearing a broken neck, a compound fracture, but everything worked as well as could be expected.

Through the branches, I could see the forest floor about five metres below. It was going to be one hell of a climb down, but I could make it.

First though, I took a minute to catch my breath.

I should have been dead ten times over.

The climb down out of the tree wasn't as agonising as expected—it was far worse. Annie always said I had a problem with my expectations. In this, at least, I was willing to concede the point.

What should have been the work of thirty seconds took me fifteen minutes, and by the time I fell into the bed of old crunchy leaves and dirt at the base of the tree near the remains of a long dead campfire, I was covered in a cold sweat, shivering with pain.

In need of a healer.

But given the purple sky, the utter hopelessness seeped into the air—the Void on its way, eager to devour my world—I was on my own.

Using my Will power to heal was more than possible. The only problem: I wasn't very good at that kind of subtle manipulation of energy. I was more of a blow-things-up Knight Infernal. If something needed destroying during the Tome Wars, King Morrow had sent me to destroy it. I'd earned such a reputation for destruction that he'd promoted me to lead the Cascade Fleet against the Renegades. The campaign of fire and death I had reigned down upon those armies was now legend and nightmare. Those memories hurt, but fondly.

"Sophie," I whispered. "Wish you were here, kid."

Sophie was the healer of the group, one of the few to stand by me during my exile. If I was a firework—big explosion that quickly burned away—she was an ever-burning flame. Her skill with the subtleties of Will manipulation was frightening.

Then I thought of Tal, Sophie's sister, and of Dread Ash corrupting Tal's body. Perhaps it was better Sophie wasn't here. I didn't think she could take another blow like that, not so soon after Tal was rescued from Lord Oblivion.

I sat and bled for a time.

Eventually, when I felt a little less faint, I hacked together a crude battlefield tourniquet for my shoulder, using some of the very same branches that had broken my fall and shreds of my waistcoat. Very rarely did my awesome waistcoats survive these adventures. My tailor back in Joondalup always smiled when I walked in, knowing he was about to make a week's worth of sales in a morning. Still, looking this good didn't come cheap—

I cried out as I tightened the tourniquet, disturbing my ribs, which after some inspection may have erred less toward broken, simply bruised and cracked. Small mercies, after all. I let the tourniquet sit until the blood oozing from the wound slowed to a trickle, began to clot. Only then did I attempt a few minor healing enchantments.

Nothing major, as I was likely to scramble my organs, but I pressed my hand against my shoulder and gently pulsed Will light against the wound, through the cloth. After about ten minutes of that, the wound looked a day old, instead of fresh. About the best I could do. The pain was substantially less, too. Enough that I could gain my feet, with the help of a convenient snapped branch serving as a walking cane.

My bones, my very soul, protested the movement, but there was still work to be done today. All too easy just to die under this tree. I worried on Annie and my allies. What was my next move?

The edge of the purple shield guided me through the forest, heading west, as planned. My progress was slow, but steady. I realised I'd lost my eye patch somewhere in the fall, and my ruined milky-white eye caught the occasional glimpse of light. Mildly disorientating, but I quickly adapted.

The forest was well trodden ground, plenty of dirt paths cut through the trees, and I headed inevitably upward, climbing the foothills, and emerged on a small rise overlooking the tops of the trees behind me—and within the shadow, if shadows without a sun had been possible, of the mighty towers of the Atlas Lexicon.

The mountain sloped above, the forest and the city rested below. I retrieved the map from my back pocket and got my bearings, using a small boulder as a natural table. It took me a minute, but I got there in the end.

Mini-Batsy had dragged me a good distance of the way I'd been planning to travel with Annie and the others. I was too far south, by about a mile and a half, but the area to the northwest, where I needed to be, was closer than ever. And, as I scanned the terrain ahead in that direction, looked clear—no deadlings, no tentacle monsters, or winged beasts. At least, none I could see.

"My luck's never this good…" I muttered.

And what about dear Annie? Emily whispered in the back of my mind.

Did I head back to the city? Make enough noise that they could find me? I didn't even know if they'd survived the attack on the bridge… But that wasn't true, was it? If Annie had fallen, if her injuries had overcome the petal in her heart—that little sliver of cruel immortality—I would have felt it. Hell, given the power in those petals, if one had been destroyed perhaps only a crater would have been left of the Atlas Lexicon.

Annie lived, and if I concentrated, I could even feel her, moving closer, heading west—she had her own map, and I'd shown her where we were heading.

I did something I probably shouldn't have then, not without explaining it to her first—that long overdue conversation. I used our connection, the twin petals, to send her a message. If I'd been asked *how* I did it, before I did it, I wouldn't have been able to say. Not really thinking about it, just expressing my intent—much like harnessing Will in its most fundamental capacity—I spoke to Annie through our shared immortality.

I'm alive. I'm heading on. Good luck, Detective.

The words left my heart and travelled to Annie's. I felt a moment of surprise from her, shared emotion, before the connection grew hazy, radio tuned to static, and I lost her. But it was enough. And, when all this was said and done, it would require some explaining. I worried I would lose a friend over that. But then, if I hadn't done it, Annie would be a year dead anyway.

It was most likely approaching the early hour before dawn outside of the shield, if my sense of time inside the purple prison was right. Time running out. I folded the map away and turned northwest—heading into the grassy green and rocky foothills below the mountains.

I'm coming Tal. Ten thousand years too late, I know. But better late than never.

THE THIRD RESOLVE

We're All of Us Bastards Now

"It is the wine that leads me on,
the wild wine
that sets the wisest man to sing
at the top of his lungs,
laugh like a fool – it drives the
man to dancing… it even
tempts him to blurt out stories
better never told."

~Homer (The Odyssey)

CHAPTER ELEVEN

The Cave of Blunders

"All these broken promises will end well for you, I'm sure"

When I'd been piecing together my dark and diabolical plan, I'd been worried that—after ten thousand years of lying in wait—the crux of the scheme, the key to the whole affair, would no longer be there. A lot can happen in ten thousand years, least of all to something as... delicate... as what I'd done in the past, in Atlantis, to cause this whole mess at the Atlas Lexicon in the first place.

And the nagging thought in the back of my mind, the one that never went away: whenever I'd tried to thwart the Everlasting, I'd lost more than I'd won. Every darn time.

But as I limped across those foothills, cursing every rise in the path, every boulder my bruised and battered legs had to climb over, leaning on my trusty walking branch and expecting it to snap every other step, I *felt* the plan—sensed, as only I could (and possibly Annie, if she knew the truth), what lay hidden ahead. The petal in my heart began to sing. I heard the gentle hum, as if the melody were blown in lightly on a breeze, an echo from a great distance. The voice was ethereal, angelic, light. The voice of a distant star.

Like that track in *The Return of the King*, where they crown Aragorn. Like that.

The song gave me strength, stood as a bulwark against the poisonous purple shield—the western edge of which sat less than a quarter mile away on my left, cutting clean through earth and rock as if it were butter, slicing a mountain in half.

From where I'd emerged from the forest and gained my bearings, it had taken me a cruel, agonising two hours to cover a mile in the foothills. If I'd been at my best, the same distance would have taken ten, fifteen minutes. Now I was close, I could feel it, to the cave. Seeds seeped in time, another legend if I pulled it off, were about to bear fruit.

And the path had remained unmolested. No deadlings, no monstrosities from the sky. I had the sense I was being watched, but that could have been good old healthy paranoia. If anything, I felt alone, isolated. My glimpses of the city, visible every time I crested another rise, and more so as the foothills started to give way to the mountain slope proper, showed monsters scuttling like ants through its streets, but other than that... nothing.

Not a bird in the sky.

OK, perhaps there was something to worry about. As painful as the trek had been, it was almost like someone—and we all know who, don't we—had laid out the red carpet and the welcome mat.

"Fix…" I sighed. "Ash."

In my current state, could I hope to stand against one of the Everlasting? Alone, broken, bleeding? Especially an Everlasting I had so effectively pissed off. I'd had worse odds, hadn't I? None that I could remember just then.

I'm walking to my death.

Well, not for the first time, perhaps not even the last. Time would tell.

A sheer cliff face rose on my left, and I limped behind a cascading waterfall of cool glacial water, which fell into a light blue pool—tainted by the shield—sixty feet or so below. Beyond that, I left the path behind and stumbled upward as best I could.

About ten minutes later, I recognised something I'd last seen ten thousand years ago.

On a sloping field of grass stood three obsidian stone pillars, bevelled toward one another, like the supports of a tent. Grim determination, what felt like excitement, rose in my chest. I was five minutes away, maybe more if the cave entrance had eroded or, well, caved in. Cross that hurdle when I stumbled into it.

The obsidian pillars were warm to the touch, as they had been ten thousand years ago. Under the right circumstances—the purple shield being very much the *wrong* circumstances—these pillars could act as a waypoint for Road's Fire, the network of portals that had brought Annie and me into the southern valley, what felt like weeks ago now. Had it only been the space of one night?

I shook my head, rubbed the pillar for luck, and soldiered on, feeling all too exposed on the hillside. I chanced a look back at the city and saw a great army of deadlings—several thousand strong—were on the march. A mass exodus from the city, a crawling flood of dead flesh and shambling bone. Three guesses which way they were heading. The answer rhymed with *forth-best*.

Cursing them all, dismissing the zombie army with a curt shrug and wave of my hand, I turned back to the bastard of a hillside and continued climbing. Minutes now, only minutes, but my legs, my shoulder, my ribs, every wound and bruise screamed at me to stop, just stop, lay down and die, you stubborn asshole.

Plenty of time to die later. Right now I wanted to see what ten thousand years had done to my carefully laid plans.

And that's a joke, isn't it? Nothing was carefully laid, Declan. Nothing. You were lucky, that's all. As you were nearly seven years ago, in the ruins of Atlantis, when you ended the Tome Wars. You were lucky—and Tal Levy wasn't. I didn't know which ghost was haunting my mind with those words, the voices all sounded the same, mixed into one. Perhaps I was talking to myself.

The song in my heart rose to a crescendo that was almost deafening, a shock of adrenaline flooded my system—most welcome—then faded away, as I rounded the hillside and reached the canyon between two towering peaks of ancient stone. Much had changed in the ten millenniums since I'd last been here. The canyon was wider, covered in green-yellow moss, and a small river trickled through the gulley, about three feet wide and only half a foot deep.

I kneeled on my haunches, using the branch for support, every joint in my knees protesting the movement, and scooped up some water. The climb had been hard, my throat burned. The water was the best salve I could hope for, alone on that mountain, and more than I deserved.

I felt better after a drink—though if the river had been flowing amber whisky I would have felt great—and hobbled further into the canyon, disappearing from the sight of the city. The rock overhead widened and narrowed, my progress slow, to the point of almost forming a ceiling pierced only by beams of rotten purple light through collapsed sections.

About two minutes later I reached a dead end, a face of rock no different from the other billion tonnes of rock all around me. I smiled sadly and limped *through* the rock face as if it wasn't there, because it wasn't. Emily Grace, may she rest in peace, had cast the illusion a long time ago. The fact that it had lasted across the length and breadth of time between here and Atlantis was a monument to her remarkable talent… and the reactor of power fuelling the deception.

Beyond the fake wall, I entered a natural cave and beheld perhaps the greatest wonder in the whole wide world.

"Ah…" I sighed softly, blinking against a landscape of stunning, ethereal white light, glowing in a grove of pure celestial illusion. The most potent, most volatile, most powerful alloy in existence.

Dread Ash sat waiting for me on one of the shards of celestial illusion jutting up through the earth. That shard alone, perhaps four feet wide and twice as high, was more alloy than had been discovered by the Knights Infernal since their inception centuries upon centuries ago. Ash swung her feet—Tal's feet—back and forth lazily, each time her heels struck the celestial alloy ripples of white light shivered through the gemstone.

"You should take up gardening more often," Ash said. "Look what you have made here."

I limped forward, further into the cave, away from the entrance, and beheld the cavern at large. From the entrance, the cave dropped away downward into the mountain, opening up into a space the size of a soccer field, curved like a wok, and on average about two storeys tall. Between the natural stone of the mountain, around streams of trickling, sparkling water, the source of the river I had drunk from, grew a field of celestial illusion—shards, crystals, gemstones of raw power, move valuable than anything in creation.

The sight stunned me—terrified me. Here was enough alloy to forge a million Roseblades. Enough celestial illusion to unmake the World Compass, to sever entire *universes* from the Story Thread. The potential in the cavern was limitless. Utterly limitless.

At the heart of the cavern, on a scorched dais of stone, hundreds of shattered pieces of alloy shone from the ruins of a central pillar of celestial illusion, what would have been the largest shard had it not erupted… from within.

"Were you… aware?" I asked Ash, not meeting her eyes.

"Every moment," she whispered, a quiver to her voice that couldn't be faked.

"I am sorry," I said. "Fix… Ash… I am sorry."

She hopped down from the shard and stepped over to me, tears brimming in her eyes above a large grin. I hated seeing Tal's face so corrupted by the ageless bitch, but it wasn't the first time. If she could bear it as long as she had, then I could bear it a little longer.

"I don't want your apology. You'd do it again, you know you would, and laugh while doing it. You know what I want."

"Ten thousand years," I whispered, shaking my head. "All that time, aware within that prison." How much strength would it have taken to escape from that enormous crystal at the heart of the cavern? Only possible once I returned from Atlantis... once the link was re-established. I'd bought the world ten thousand years without one of the Everlasting. On reflection, the price for that peace seemed far too steep.

"To the Everlasting, such a span of time is meaningless," Ash said, and I didn't believe her, not for a moment. "An hour, to me, to put it in a time frame you can grasp. Don't get sad on me, Declan. We've still so much left to do."

"I'm a little used up, Ash." I limped over to a low, flat boulder and took a heavy seat, leaning my walking branch against my leg and resting my head on it. I tried to make the effort look casual, my eyes focused on nothing, less she suspected...

"You know, the Orc-Mare would have brought you here," she said. "You didn't have to struggle."

Orc-Mare? Oh, Mini-Batsy. "If you didn't think I'd fight, then you don't know me at all."

"Tal knows you," she said idly, as if that wasn't a dagger to my heart. "And I have her memories. My,

207

the things Oblivion did to her. She never told you the half of it."

"I'll do for Oblivion one day," I said. "One day *soon.*"

"He's taken command of the Peace Arsenal." Ash reached down and picked up a sphere of celestial illusion. A tiny piece, light and wondersome, worth more than entire worlds. "Which you helped him unleash, I understand."

"It's usually my fault, yeah. I did it…" and here I laughed bitterly, "I did it to save Tal from being possessed by one of you nightmares. To free her from Oblivion."

Ash laughed, a clear sound that rang throughout the cavern. The light in the alloy responded, rippling and glowing. In its own way, celestial illusion was *alive.* "Even when you win, you lose."

"I was just thinking that on the walk over." Seeing as how the conversation hadn't yet descended into a fight, I pressed my luck. "What is the Peace Arsenal?"

Ash waved the question away. "Armies, interstellar battleships, war machines, ancient and powerful weapons. Everything the Everlasting would need to subdue resistance to our rule, and prepare for the battle beyond the Void."

"There's *nothing* beyond the Void. It's just… more Void."

She shrugged, not willing to argue, and I wondered.

The petal in my heart pulsed painfully and I rubbed at my chest, unable to suppress a wince. *Can the power run dry? What would happen to my heart if the petal ended?* I had one of my patented sneaking suspicions that the cause on my death certificate would read:

'Massive Coronary Failure', in polite words. 'Heart Fucking Exploded Somehow', in less polite words.

Eh, Future Declan's problem.

"Ah, yes," Ash said. She walked over and placed Tal's hand on my chest. Her fingers were cold, so cold, even through my bloodstained shirt. Everything in me shivered against that touch. The Everlasting weren't human, however close they could look, and I would do well to remember that. "This... annoyance. The 'why' of Declan Hale. My sister knew what she was doing, when she killed you."

"I may have given her the idea." I laughed harshly. "Time travel, chicken and egg bullshit."

"For this alone, your stolen grace, I should kill you."

I blinked and met her lovely green eyes. "Ashaya," I said, "if you were going to kill me, I would be long dead."

She pressed my chest harder, then scraped her fingernails across my skin, drawing blood. Ash turned away, licking my blood from her fingers.

"Know what I think," I said. "I think you're scared—all of you, your brothers and sisters. You don't know what will happen if you kill me. You don't know what I've got planned, what I may have set in motion, and what will happen if you snuff out the petal of the Infernal Clock in my heart. You're scared, for the first time in your lives, and that's got to sting."

"Shut up, Declan," Ash said tiredly.

"Why don't you ask Saturnia?"

Ash spun so quickly my eye couldn't follow it. She was facing one way, a blur happened, then the other. She moved in so close I could count the scattering of freckles on Tal's cheeks, our noses brushed, her breath warm against my mouth. "Where," she hissed, "did you learn that name?"

"Oh no," I said and grinned slowly, "something else a lowly human like myself is not supposed to know."

Ash slapped me. I fell back on the boulder, world spinning about my head, laughing and bleeding. Behind the boulder, I glimpsed the hilt of something last picked up ten thousand years ago.

"*How do I get out of here?*" she screamed. "*How do I escape the Atlas Lexicon?*"

"You don't!" I spat a mouthful of blood onto the stone and kept my face neutral, less she suspected I wasn't out of options just yet.

"Then my degradation around the city will grow, will consume, and tear True Earth apart!"

"Do what you gotta do, you spoilt brat."

She punched me in my dodgy eye, once, twice. I'd have quite the shiner in an hour.

Ash stormed away, hurled her sphere of celestial illusion across the cavern, where it bounced and chimed, bounced and chimed, sending cascading ripples through the priceless cache of alloy.

"You won't let this world die," she said, once an awkward moment had passed more awkwardly than most.

"Check my résumé, bitch, this world wouldn't be the first."

"This is different. True Earth is the heart of the Story Thread. If True Earth falls, the effect that would have... Eventually, *all* will be unmade, returned to the Void."

I nodded. "I'll be long dead, and won't care. Makes you wonder why no one else has come to stop you, though, doesn't it? Why it's just little old me standing against you, given how high the stakes are."

"It's only been two days since the shield fell around the city."

"Or perhaps those watching know I'm more than enough to stop you."

"You'll die here, Declan," Ash said, and her tone suggested she'd just come to a decision. "I'll tear your heart beating from your chest and cast it into the Void before the petal can wither. Any... fallout from the Infernal Clock will be consumed by the nothingness."

I nodded. "It's a plan, if you think you're quick enough. But I won't die easy, Ash."

A smile touched her face. "Remember our date in that tavern ten thousand years ago?"

"That wasn't a date."

She frowned. "Don't be cruel."

"Said the demon possessing the woman I love."

"You think yourself above affection for one of the Everlasting?"

I shrugged. "No, but your sister's hotter."

Ash's nostrils flared, eyes narrowed to pure murder. I sat up a little straighter, convinced that perhaps I'd just gone too far. I must be getting old, even wise, if I had the hindsight to realise that.

"There," she said. "Those words there. When I devour you, Hale, know that it was because of those words."

I stood and drew my sword, swaying a bit on the walking branch. My ribs burned pain and I nearly fell. My shoulder didn't want to support my sword arm for long. "I'm ready when you are."

The hate on her face lasted a few moments longer

before fading again. Her eyes, Tal's eyes, were drawn back to the cavern of celestial illusion. "Whoever controls this cavern," she said, "controls the future. Let me go, Declan. Please. And it's yours."

"It's mine anyway," I said. "I claim it on behalf of the Knights Infernal. Let all who would challenge my right stand against me. And you know what I want, Ash. What it'll cost you, to escape the Atlas Lexicon."

"Like you'll ever let me go," she sneered. "You are a liar—a liar from the moment I met you. How did you imprison me here? Escaping this cavern should have been the end of it. I still don't understand."

I shook my head. "It wasn't me."

"Gods damn you," she whispered, fighting back tears and failing. "I can escape in time. I'll fashion a blade from the celestial illusion and use it to sever the tether trapping me to this city."

I tried to keep the worry from my face. Her words struck dangerously close to the final play. "Well, you better remove the degradation shield then—sloppy work, by the way, Oblivion's was neater—because in a few hours it won't matter. We're all for the Void before brunch. You can sense that as well as me."

Ash bit her lip, slammed her fists against her legs, radiating frustration. "You're an awful creature," she said. "I can't believe I ever loved you."

I limped over to the edge of the cavern, around the nest of boulders I'd been sitting on, over shards of alloy, and leaned back against the wall of the cave entrance. *Soon now, soon...*

"You didn't love me, Ash. It was as much a game to you as it was to me. I'm just better at playing it."

On the ground, the tip of my left boot pointing in the right direction, just three feet away, the dull-silver hilt poked out of the smooth, wet stone under the boulder. The hilt differed from the one I held in my hand, though the ruby secured in the pommel was the same—a twin, both forged in Axis' starlight furnace a long time ago. My sword was mostly untarnished, whereas the guard on the hilt in the stone was old, at least ten thousand years old, and carved with intricate, enchanted runes designed to do one thing...

"Declan, please—"

I dove for the sword and grasped the ancient hilt. Expecting some resistance, I stumbled back a step when the blade slid from under the boulder as if the rock and glimmers of celestial illusion were nothing more than soft silk. Perhaps, to something as enchanted as this blade, they were.

Energy flowed down the twin swords I held, united again after an aeon, and flooded my system, masked my hurts and pains. I kicked the walking branch aside and stood tall.

Ash, no fool, took a careful step back. Her hands clapped together, arcs of wicked purple lightning dancing between her fingers.

"I *knew* you had something," she said. "I *knew* it!"

I advanced on the Everlasting, swords crossed in front of me, white light flaring up and down the silver-shined blades.

Ash thrust her arms forward and cast a rippling beam of sick purple flame at me. I swung the swords down through the air, caught the point of the flame, and hurled it back at her. Ash's eyes widened, she tried to dive out of the way, but the flame caught her in the face.

She screamed.

Oh, Tal...

When the smoke cleared, Ash was back on her feet—eyes seething with rage, teeth bared at me. Half her hair had been singed away, the side of her head a blistered-black mess.

"You…" Her lips trembled. "How could you?"

As I watched, the Everlasting's power healed the damage to Tal's head. I'd seen that before, in the Tomb of the Sleeping Goddess. Oblivion had attacked me and I'd blasted a hole through him—through Tal—with my shotgun. That had slowed him down a good half a minute while he knitted the damage back together.

"Surrender her to me, Ash!" I demanded. "End the degradation!"

I stepped across the cave entrance and Ash retreated. She snarled at me then turned on her heel to run.

Only she didn't. She *blurred*, as she had done earlier, and something that felt like a sledgehammer hit me in the chest. I was thrown backwards at the same time I felt my sword—the one I'd carried since this all started—wrenched from my grip.

I hit a shard of celestial illusion hard, the wind knocked out of me. Ash stood twenty feet away, holding up my sword, her stolen prize. "With this," she spat, "who needs you?"

Ash turned on her heel again and fled the cavern.

I screamed after her, raw and angry, forcing breath into my lungs and out again, the pain only dulled by the blade drawn from under the boulder.

CHAPTER TWELVE

The Older I am, the Wiser I'm Not

"My name is Declan, and I'm an alcoholic"

I stumbled from the cave of celestial illusion, giving chase to Ash, back along the canyon under the purple sky, which roiled and raged with arcs of lightning, thunder, destruction. A breath-taking cold gust spun throughout the dome, whistling with hurt and anger and pain. The shield *was* Dread Ash, and reflected her chaotic mind.

I emerged back on the sloped hill, pulling myself along in a limped sort of jog. The obsidian circle was struck by a thick fork of lightning and exploded, sharp spears of stone flying across the hillside.

Annie, Arlon, and Caitlin dove for cover on the other side of the pillars, the stone hurtling over their heads and cutting into the lines of shambling bone men and deadlings giving them chase.

Ash had my sword—and, worse, she knew it was capable of helping her escape. Pour enough power into that blade and it could sever the enchantment that had kept her imprisoned here at the Lexicon for the last ten millennia. The celestial illusion had been her maximum-security cell within the prison, but with the sword she could cut right through the perimeter fence.

Ah, hell. Never a dull moment, no, no, no.

"Annie!" I shouted. "Which way did she go?"

The wind stole my words, but Annie looked up sharply. She grinned to see me alive and I felt a similar fierce smile on my own face.

I limp-jogged down the hillside and helped her to her feet, as Arlon and Caitlin struggled to theirs. They were all battered, bruised, bleeding. Annie's leather jacket was torn down the front. A field bandage had been wrapped around her scalp. Blood seeped from the wound underneath.

The army of deadlings had been hurled back by the explosion, but more were stumbling over the corpses of the fallen—a lot more, thousands more. We had a minute, maybe two, before they were upon us.

"Where the hell have you been?" I asked, pulling her to me.

Annie laughed and kissed me quickly on the lips. "Doing all the hard work, it looks like."

"Did you see Ash?" I asked.

Annie thrust her finger at the slopes above. "She came out of that canyon, gave us a scowl, and headed up the mountain. She had a sword. Your sword. I thought for a moment you were gone."

"We need that sword back," I said. "It's the only

chance we've got to put an end to all this mess."

"Arbiter!" Arlon said. "Can you slow the rabble?"

He waved at the ascending army. The wind rolled down the mountain at our backs, thankfully carrying most of the stink and decay away from us—back toward the city.

"Can we expect reinforcements?" I asked.

Caitlin shook her head. "We lost the squad getting here. It was hard fought."

"Just the original band then," I muttered, and glanced down at the blade in my hand, seeped in ten thousand years of softly soaring celestial illusion.

The blade glinted untouched by the purple light poisoning everything else. Indeed, a small pale-blue shield seemed to repel the dark radiance.

"What is that?" Annie asked, following my gaze.

One of those god-awful ideas occurred to me. A sordid plan to defeat the deadlings, pursue Ash, and cut her off from anything but a final confrontation. *So be it...*

"Right, we need to head back up the hill, quick as we can." I pointed to the ridge above the canyon that led to the cavern of celestial illusion. "We need to get up there. Looks like if we circle round from the left the climb won't be too bad."

"Then what?" Arlon asked.

I shrugged, honestly racked my mind for another option, but came up blank. I think my sigh could have been heard across entire worlds. "Then I'm going to set this mountain on fire. Quickly now."

So it was a race.

Ash in the lead, somewhere up above. I'd be able to track her down, so long as she had the sword. I had time there, time to stop her, but not much.

Myself and my allies in the middle, used and abused, at the final reserves of our strength, even bolstered as I was by stolen energy. And bringing up the rear, thousands upon thousands of deadlings, befouled corpses set to dark work. They'd never stop coming, never tire. We would run until we collapsed and then we'd be devoured.

"I'm almost out!" Annie shouted, turning and firing, the barrel of her revolver shooting flame and smoke. Each shot found a mark, though, on those deadlings too close for comfort.

"Save what you've got left," I said, panting. "Quickly now, quickly."

From the mouth of the canyon we crested the hillside, moving up to the left. The going was slow, steep, and we had to crawl, leap, scuttle up the side, but two minutes later and we stood atop of the canyon's edge, gazing down at the frightful army, and beheld a commanding view of the Atlas Lexicon beyond.

"Whatever you're going to do," Caitlin said, picking off deadlings climbing in our wake with single shots from her rifle, "you've got a minute, maybe less."

Working mostly on instinct, on *intent*, I held my sword up high, the silver-steel glinting against the tortured sky, against the cries of the damned. Beneath me, a hundred feet below my boots, sat the immense cavern of celestial illusion, all that strength and power, all that... immensity. I didn't have the words to describe the potential. I never would.

With a cry, I thrust my sword down through the air and punctured the stone at my feet. The blade crackled with power as it bit through the rock. I fell to one knee, focusing my Will, my intent, and sent a bolt of energy from the hilt of the sword and down through the side of the mountain—into the wealth of stored power and energy in the cavern of celestial illusion.

A terrifying heartbeat passed, then another. The first rotten hands crested the hillside, the vanguard of the thousands more to come.

I've miscalculated, I thought. *It wasn't—*

The ground began to shake.

A torrent of liquid hot flame exploded along the length of the canyon, a dozen feet high, twice as thick, like the world's most devastating beam of energy.

We were thrown from out feet, back against the ground, and I scrambled away with Annie, holding her close, my sword still thrust into the rock, which now rattled in earthquake.

"*Back!*" I roared. "*Move back!*"

Arlon and Caitlin didn't need telling, shuffling back on their hands and knees away from the canyon, further up the mountain.

The torrent of white-hot flame shooting along the canyon became a flood, a cascading waterfall of silver energy, an avalanche of power, which swept along the hillside and devastated the deadling army. The canyon served as a barrel, directing the colossal amount of energy I'd unleashed like a burst fire hydrant.

In a way, I'd managed to get one more shell off from my shotgun, after all. I'd turned the mountain into a shotgun, my sword the trigger.

Liquid energy, a flow of celestial magma, ate the hillside, fell downward, glassing the landscape. The deadling army broke, scattered, as thousands of them were simply ignited.

A wave of tremendous heat blasted up out of the cavern, the world's biggest steam vent.

Minutes later, only minutes, the ground stopped shaking, the torrent of flame receded, but the damage was done.

Deep below, in the once priceless cavern, the field of celestial illusion burned and consumed, a fire that would last... well, long after I was dead and forgotten.

The cavern would burn for aeons.

I smiled grimly and gained my feet. Annie and the others gave me one of those looks that could only be read as somewhere between terror and awe, disbelief and careful respect.

I collected my sword, smoke rising from the blade in idle wisps, and gazed up the mountain. White fire burst in gouts from the natural chimneys in the rock, chimneys which would lead back down to the cavern beneath us. Ash was up there somewhere, no doubt seething, planning to remove my head from my shoulders.

This fight wasn't over. Not yet.

"Come on," I said. "Annie, you and I have a story to finish on the way."

REMINISCENCE THE FOURTH

(Eight days before Declan sets fire to the mountain, in his measure of time. Half a day before he travels back to his proper time. Six days before Dread Ash's degradation strangles the Atlas Lexicon. One week before Declan and Annie share Jasmine tea)

The End Game,
A Most Subtle Cruelty

After nearly one year in Atlantis, plotting and planning, Tal slapped me, hard, dislodging my eye patch and sending me reeling. The pain rang in my ears.

"You... *bastard*," she hissed, eyes angry and hurt. "After everything, you spring this on me now? I thought..." Her face crumpled. "I thought you were changing. I thought sobering up had given you a new perspective. But all this time, this last year, you've been planning this."

I held up the two swords I'd crafted in the forges of the Vale Celestia, Scarred Axis' forges, pure starlight and power. The Everlasting wasn't here at the moment, not quite yet, the forges swirling away on their own, which was for the best, as when I did find Axis the conversation was going to be short, sweet, and to the *point*.

Tal swatted away a tear and pushed me in the shoulder, but with no real strength. I put the twin swords down, the runes on one complete, still some work to do on the other, and took her hand between mine.

"Is this where you tell me the less I knew the better?" she asked, not quite meeting my eyes. Sad. Sad was worse than anger. "Trying to protect me, spare me the pain?" She hitched a breath. "Years too late for that, Declan."

"No," I said softly. Overhead the interstellar clouds drifted slowly, a million points of light swirled between emerald greens, sapphire blues, ruby reds... A real gem of a sky, that one. "Protect you, always, but never with falsehood. I didn't tell you, Tal, because you didn't want a part of this—you made that clear a year ago, in the gardens, where I drank my last drink."

She touched a finger to the silver-shined blades resting on the forge edge. A wave of cool energy cast us half in pale light, half in dark. "How many of them are here?" she asked. "Is... he here?"

"I haven't run into Oblivion, as best as I can tell." I frowned. "But most of them are here, Tal. Astoria, Axis, Ash—the A-Team, heh. Scion... perhaps." I picked up the sword with the complete runes, flipped it, and handed it hilt-first to Tal. "This is for you, if you want it."

"Why on earth would I want *that*?"

A flare of something that wasn't sympathy, or even empathy, but something crueller—the part of me that could burn worlds—but an emotion mostly condescending and arrogant shivered through me.

"You want to stay here in Atlantis, don't you?" I said, and Tal flinched at my tone. "You want the city to survive, to escape its fate a while longer yet. Then pick up the sword, Tal, and fight. The Everlasting are here for one reason, and one reason only, to ensure Atlantis falls. The city—the Vale towers we've claimed as our own—are a monument to humanity's potential. As a species, we're getting too uppity. The Everlasting are here to course-correct that, to cast us into a dark age."

"We know they manage it," she whispered. "We've stood in the ruins."

"Yes, but not today. Not for a hundred years or more, if I have my way." I picked up the other sword, the ring of steel on stone more than familiar. "I've a dark and terrible plan, Tal. It involves you, and Emily—Fair Astoria, herself—and Switzerland, and celestial illusion."

Tal blinked. "Switzerland?"

I concentrated on the petal in my heart, caught a glimpse of Annie ten thousand years from now, sitting at her desk in Joondalup Police Station, scrawling on some paperwork. If I wanted to, I could cut a path through the Void right now across that length and breadth of time, of impossible space, and appear next to her at her desk. Getting home was the easy part.

"The Vale Crystalis, where the Atlas Lexicon will one day stand. I'm baiting the trap."

Tal considered that, then sighed. "You'll never tell me the whole truth, will you?"

Tal took the rune sword from my hand, stepped away, and practiced a few of the old moves they'd taught us at the Infernal Academy, over ten years ago now. *Late twenties snuck up fast*, I thought. *You'll be thirty soon, old man.* A small part of me was convinced I'd never hit that mile marker, not with my life of excess. *Ah well, I've done enough living for ten men.* Ten miserable men.

"What's the plan then?" Tal asked.

I grinned a not-so-pleasant grin. "He'll be here soon."

"Who?"

"The Forge Master, a man calling himself Alexas, and when he gets here…" I clenched my fist around the sword. "I'm going to take something from him."

"What?"

"His sight."

Tal shivered and took a step away from me, turning her shoulder my way. "We should probably find some cover until then."

I agreed. We moved away from the four swirling forges of starlight, away from the central chimney of billowing frost and cold steam, and crouched down behind a materials cache of steel and what looked like mythril, a blue-silver alloy good for weapons and armour. Tal looked like she wanted to speak, no doubt tell me what a bastard I was, but then I already knew that.

Though the sky here was an eternal, bright night, I kept a good account of the time in my head. Shortly after midnight, the Forge Master strolled into the space between his starlight forges. Alexas—Yet-to-be-Scarred Axis of the Everlasting—six and a half feet tall, silver-grey hair tied back in a short ponytail, skin alabaster pale, wearing loose-fitting breeches and a leather jerkin, exposing his heavily muscled arms.

The bear in the bear trap.

I looked to Tal, who nodded. The light in her eyes had changed from sad, weary, to a look I knew well from the Tome Wars—the look of a killer, a soldier, a Knight. Red work to be done, that look said. They'd almost made us eager for such work, back in the academy days.

Axis placed a hand on his central forge and frowned. He knew someone, someone handsome and wearing an eye patch, had been at work with his tools. A sneer crossed his face, a glimpse of the true creature within, then faded back to something near-human. In the dim light, his skin grew even paler—I could see veins, arteries, pumping purple ichor through his body. *His mask's slipping*, I thought, as something that felt like a wave of ice washed over me and Tal. *He knows you're here*, I thought, a split second before Axis spoke.

"I know you're here," he said, his voice echoing across the vast open forge, rattling the tools on the workbenches, sending a shot of pure fear coursing through my body. "Show yourself."

Tal closed her eyes and whispered a short prayer.

"Me first," I whispered and picked up both of my freshly forged swords. "Step in if it looks like I'm struggling."

Tal cursed and I stepped out into the forge, skirting the edge of one of the starlight pools. Axis spun to face me, his face hard and then softening slightly when he saw me sauntering toward him, closing the space between us. I held my swords low, at the ready, but not hostile.

"Arbiter Hale," Axis said, and if I hadn't known the truth I could have mistaken the jovial hostility in his tone for curiosity. "What brings you out this evening?"

"I've been using your forges," I said, and lifted my swords. "You like them?"

Axis scanned my work with a masterful eye, noting the runes on one, the incomplete work on the other. He crossed his massive arms and shrugged. "Adequate work," he said. "Fit to purpose… but whatever purpose would that be?"

Knight's bite repels the blight, I thought, the snatch of old rhyme that revealed one of the few weaknesses of the Everlasting. An Infernal blade, forged with pieces of star-silver, star-iron, and enchanted with the right runes could wound an elder god. I couldn't kill Axis with these blades, but then I knew he didn't die here anyway. I could make him wish for death.

"Thought I'd give one of the Everlasting a haircut."

Axis's face changed in a heartbeat and he charged me, lightning-faced, getting inside my guard, hands extended to crush my throat.

I was quick—just quick enough—to sidestep the attack and bring the rune blade down across his heavy arm. The blade sung as it carved a neat slice across Axis's bicep.

Knight's bite.

He stumbled, looked stunned at the line of rosy red blood on his arm, and then his face shuddered with rage. I'd taken a smart handful of steps away, putting about ten feet between us. He turned to face me and clenched his fists together.

"How do you know of me?" he asked, his voice dropping all pretence of friendliness—of humanity.

"We've met in the future," I said. "I knew you the moment I saw you in this forge."

Axis thrust his arms forward and a colossal wave of air slammed into me, tore one of the blades from my hand, and I rolled ragdoll across the forge. I grasped the edge of the furnace, thankful it was cool, to stop from falling into one of the starlight pools.

Axis moved in to finish me, as easy as that, when he was struck in the back by a glowing green sphere of energy. He stumbled, his leather jerkin sizzling, and spun.

Tal sighed. "Looked like you were struggling, Declan."

Axis the Bear, the yet-to-be-Scarred, strode across his forge, the flames from Tal's attack eating at his vest and back. The burning flesh didn't seem to bother him.

"You as well, girl?" he spat. "Your bones will make a poor morsel for my dogs."

I stood, held my remaining sword above my head, the other lying out of reach, and enchanted my throwing arm with strength, accuracy, a dash of fucking hope.

I hurled the sword across the forge, about twenty feet, and it struck Axis behind his thigh, a glancing blow that cut a neat slice in his muscle. He roared and fell to one knee, the sword clattering away.

"Enough!" he shouted. "You both die. *Now*."

He gathered dark energy in his palms, fuelled from tendrils of starlight from the pools of his forge, which rose to meet him, a dozen tentacles of power. I felt the strength in his attack, the purgative fire. We were about to be obliterated, Tal and I both, after barely any fight. This had been a dumb idea, really.

A column of white fire struck Axis in the chest and severed his connection to the starlight pools. The

Everlasting staggered, eyes bulged, pain etched across his face.

Emily Grace stepped out from around the other side of the furnace, the beam of white light flowing down her arm, from her palm, striking the Forge Master.

Axis's face fell. "Sister, what are you doing?"

Emily smiled sadly. "Safeguarding the Story Thread, brother. Safeguarding the future."

"You throw your lot in with this *human*? What is he? A gnat, a mosquito soon swatted. His lifespan is the smallest sliver of a second compared to yours."

Emily looked at me, then back to Axis. She clenched a fist and sent another stream of power at the fallen god. Axis slammed back into the stone of his forge, cracked the paving beneath him. Blood dribbled from his nostrils.

With some clever gestures, twisted finger movements, Emily tied a knot in her power, securing Axis to the ground. "I think," she said softly, a look of utter sorrow on her face, "that I do not want to be here for this. Declan, I shall meet you at the shuttle."

Emily swept away from the forge, not a mark on her flawless white gown. The stars shone in her spill of auburn hair. I thought on all the history we shared, all the history we *would* share, before she died in my arms on Voraskel, our new-born son hidden in the nearby glade so his uncle, Lord Oblivion, wouldn't devour him. Oblivion slaughtering Astoria, Emily, made a whole lot more sense to me now.

I approached Axis and knelt on my haunches, blade resting just on my knee. Axis glared pure hate at me, an anger so deep and unfathomable it was hard to meet his gaze. But meet it I did. I'd been glared at that way before, after all.

"When I'm loosed from these bonds," he said, "your head will sit smoking on a spear forged from your bones."

"Do you know where you'll spend the next ten thousand years?" I asked quietly. I felt Tal appear at my side, glimpsed the tips of her boots on the edge of my vision. Her hand fell lightly on my shoulder. "Do you know what they call you in the future?"

Axis smirked. "I gave your paltry race access to the light that fuels the universe," he said. "I forged the great gears that turn the very essence of creation into magic. And I will take it from you, if I choose. You think I fear your future?"

I sighed with a shrug. "You said that the first time we spoke, as I measure time. Ten thousand years from now, bound to the same stone you're bound to now, in a prison hidden in the storm clouds of Jupiter. You don't get loose, Axis. Not for an age."

His smirk became more of a sneer, more of a frown.

"I need the seed of celestial illusion," I said, and patted the pockets of his leather apron. "Wouldn't have that on you, would you?"

"Declan Hale, you will burn—"

I drove the tip of my sword into Axis's left eye. The wide, blue orb popped like a grape, spilling white-grey jelly down his cheek. He screamed, of course, and I worried at the part of me that enjoyed hearing him wail.

Tal's hand left my shoulder and she turned away.

"The seed?" I asked, whispered, withdrawing the sword. The blade shone, eager for more.

"*Never! Never, never, never, nev—!*"

So I blinded the Everlasting Scarred Axis, cutting scarecrow eyes into his face, scars I would see as ragged scabs in his temple prison within the storm clouds of Jupiter, so very far away from now. What followed after that, five minutes of blade graft, drawing intricate patterns in his skin, peeling flesh away, was some of the grisliest work I'd ever done.

At the end of it, and the elder god had lasted far longer than anyone I'd… interrogated, he revealed to me the location of the celestial illusion orb.

The central crucible housed several secret compartments, hidden functions, a network of vents, pipes, and chimneys for creating wonders—the forge was a piece of master craftsmanship. If nothing else, Axis had been a skilled engineer. Shame I'd taken a few of his fingers. He was of the Everlasting though. Given enough time, I'm sure he'd heal enough to get back to work. Not that he'd have such time, trapped away at the far reaches of the solar system.

"One down," I said to Tal, cradling the sphere of celestial illusion in my blood-soaked hands as we left the forge behind.

Tal eyed the precious alloy with a look of hunger in her eyes. She knew its value, its potential, perhaps even better than I did myself. Tal had always been the dreamer, back when we loved each other honestly.

"What next?" she asked.

"Gardening," I muttered.

Behind us, Axis screamed my name into the night—"*HAALLEEE!*"—screamed pain and anger and regret.

"What about him?"

I shrugged.

I didn't know the specifics, didn't really care—I

imagined Emily may have a part to play—but Axis, Scarred Axis now, would be taken from here and imprisoned for a very long time. He would be loosed one day, the shadowless part of me, my Void-twin, responsible for that, and no doubt would have thought of some creative punishments for my defiance in ten thousand years. So be it. At a certain point, when your enemies numbered so many, fear of the future lost all meaning.

"Future Declan's problem," I said. "Come on, we've got at least one more god to put down tonight."

"Declan, you let your work get in the way of your happiness. You do it on purpose, I think. You keep busy. Busy is numb." Tal shrugged, as we jogged across the grounds of the Vale Celestia and back toward Atlantis. "You've been lying so long you've made the unhappiness true. Never mind. Seven years between us, many of those spent dead or dying, and you've made loving me an obligation."

"My work? You understand, more than any, what would happen if I gave the bastards an inch, Tal." I scoffed. "You speak to me as if I were a banker, or a plumber, or if I worked a nine-to-five in some office on True Earth. As if my work didn't carry the fate of the Story Thread."

Tal sighed. "That's just it. You put the weight of this conflict on your shoulders. You, and no one else. What would happen if you dropped dead of a heart attack tomorrow? Or an aneurysm? If you were hit by a bus? Something tragic, yes, but normal? The Story

Thread would go on without you. It existed for aeons before you were born." She cupped my cheek. My rough, stubbly cheek. "Sometimes you force the conflict, the confrontation with gods or demons or evil men, and people get hurt. Those closest to you, more often than not. Me, most of all."

"The Story Thread is as much a nightmare as it is a dream," I said. "Hellish wastelands of time forgotten and horror to come. Creatures born for the sole purpose of conquering True Earth. They must be fought. That is our duty as Knights Infernal."

She smiled in the sad way that meant goodbye. "I love you so much, Declan Hale."

"Then stand with me."

We stepped through the portal doorway, the inter-dimensional connection between this world and the heart of Atlantis on True Earth. We went from eternal night to the first taste of dawn, spilling across the Lost City in shades of orange. From our vantage point, high up above the rest of Atlantis, a slow fog wound through the streets.

This early, few were out and about, which was all to the good. I looked like I'd been in a fight. Having been here just under a year, ingrained into the society, learning a bit of the language, I was more or less trusted—but I didn't doubt we were still under some sort of observation. Our warnings of the dire future alone would be enough to ensure that.

Never mind that I'm fairly certain the lords of this city are Everlasting. At least one of them, for certain. That High Lord wouldn't like that I'd just gutted his brother, the blood still wet on my hands. I had ten thousand years of time but not a moment to spare.

We made it out of the Vale Atlantia unmolested. I

kept one hand on the hilt of my sword, sheathed now, and the other on the golf ball of celestial illusion warm and certain in my pocket. If I lost that, the game was over… the Everlasting would win. All would fall to ruin. Tal carried her sword, twin of my own, wrapped in a fold of tanned leather. Despite her objections, her admonishments, she was still at my side.

As if reading my thoughts, she said, "I'm with you because anything that puts a burr in their plans is the right move. I just wish it didn't have to be you, Declan."

"Who else?" I asked. The roads were quiet, a few vehicles, hovercraft, early morning cafes and restaurants opening for the day—scant few folk on the streets—we moved as quickly, as silently, as we dared through the fog. "Honestly, Tal, who else is there?"

"I don't remember you being this arrogant when we were young."

"That's not an answer. You used to love my arrogance."

"I mistook it for confidence."

That stung, but then I had roped her into a torture-murder plot against at least two gods, all with about five minutes' notice, so I let the excuses, the ugly truth, die on my tongue.

The city's eastern shuttle station was busier than the CBD had been, but not by much. Neat rows of sleek, silver shuttlecraft stood in bays, some on idle, cold blue fusion engines alight. The sweet scent of ozone clung to the air, as the sun rose to blast away more of the low hanging cloud.

Hustle and bustle, I thought. *Enough to get lost in.*

Engineers, pilots, shouted instructions at one another. People lined up, reminiscent of every airport in history, waiting to board their flights.

We were travellin' in a bit more style. Emily had secured us the Atlantean equivalent of a private jet.

It took a moment to find her, standing in the doorway to the craft like a pale, beautiful marble statue—save for that auburn hair, burnished by the sun. She raised a hand to get our attention and we hurried over.

"Come along now, Declan Hale," she said, pointedly staring at the blood on my hands, my shirt. "You retrieved the sphere?"

"I did."

"May I see it?"

I considered, then nodded. As if it were nothing more than a golf ball, I tossed Emily the orb of celestial illusion from the bottom of the steps below the shuttle craft. Her eyes widened slightly, but she plucked it from the air with grace.

Emily stared at the gemstone, the precious alloy, for a long ten seconds, during which time I carefully climbed the first few steps of the shuttle, Tal just behind me. When she showed no sign of letting it go, I climbed the last two steps between us and placed a careful hand on her shoulder.

Emily startled, blinked beautiful eyes at me, and then found a sheepish smile. It looked funny on her face, out of place. I realised that was because it made her seem young—younger. She gained a lot more… Emily-*ness*… over the next ten millenniums. My hand left a red smear on the white cloth covering her shoulder.

She sighed and carefully handed me back the seed.

"We don't have much time. Ashaya already hunts you. Word of what you did to Axis has spread quickly between my siblings."

Tal gasped. "Ashaya? We're going up against Dread Ash?"

"We're not being hunted," I said harshly. "Not even close. All aboard."

The interior of the craft was small, enough room for about six comfortably, but elegant. The seats were white leather, the walls adorned with screens, interfaces. A small kitchen fully stocked with drink and food. There was even a tiny bathroom toward the rear of the craft.

Emily approached the control console and began pushing buttons. I'd been trained as a pilot on all manner of ship and craft in the Knight Infernal arsenal, and recognised some of the controls here, but only some. *Navigational console… primary thrust… what the hell is that?* Emily placed a hand either side of a large, glowing-white sphere about the size of basketball. Once the door hissed closed behind us and sealed seamlessly against the wall, Emily pushed on the sphere and we rose into the sky.

There we hovered about twenty feet off the ground, as Emily communicated with ground control to allow us passage into the sky proper. Airports, always the same. She even had to log a flight plan, which was part of the main plan. Anyone, god or human, man or woman, would be able to follow…

After a tense ten minutes, during which I expected something to go wrong, our shuttle to be grounded, the Atlantis army to attack, or the Everlasting—those not flayed and blind—to descend from the sky in chariots of vengeful bone, we were given clearance to ascend.

Emily ascended.

And kept on ascending. The shuttle was fast, the engines barely making a hum, and the inertial dampeners making the ride no bumpier than travelling down the highway on a motorcycle. We punched through the stratosphere, the upper atmosphere, and beheld a commanding view of the glittering blue marble several hundred miles below.

Emily flew us into orbit above the Earth and I got a good look at the continents for the first time. Atlantis, for all that mattered once it was swept away in the Voidflood, was built on a landmass roughly the size of Japan. The Lost City was situated in the middle of the Pacific Ocean, around chains of islands that would, in my time, be known as Fiji and French Polynesia. About halfway between Australia and North America, give or take a thumb's width at this height.

As it stood now, the land was whole and hearty. In the future, all that remained were scatterings, patches, of the continent. The Void would eat Atlantis, flood the surrounding land, and leave only pieces—like an acid thrown against skin, or the tide washing away a sandcastle. The ocean would rush in to hide the scar tissue left behind and all that would survive across the years would be myth and less than myth.

Atlantis was doomed.

The greatest city the world had ever known would be swept from the face of the planet and wash up in ruin further down the Story Thread. A needle in a stack of needles, until some dumb kid named Declan Hale, searching for fortune and glory, came along and uncovered a path to the city.

Almost like I was meant to find it.

"Does it look familiar to you?" Emily asked.

Tal's hand had found its way in to my own. That was nice, and unexpected. We shared a significant look and I nodded. Over to the west, I could see the coastline of Western Australia and the spot of land that would, in about nine thousand and eight hundred years, become Perth. My little bookshop was a long way away. And Paddy's, oh Paddy's.

"Holy hell," I said with a terrified start. "The Guinness factory. I just realised there's no Guinness factory."

Tal squeezed my shoulder. "You're an idiot."

"Shall we be about our business?" Fair Astoria of the Everlasting asked, her gaze ancient, unsettling, all too familiar.

Emily steered us north, chasing the curve of True Earth, a flight plan on the console blinking for the Vale tower hidden in what would one day become Switzerland.

Either way, hell or high water, death or dismay, I was committed to seeing this through.

As was Tal.

~~*~*

The flight across the face of the world took less than fifteen minutes, as the planet spun lazily beneath us, as ancient and as indifferent as any of the Everlasting I'd had the misfortune to meet. Save Emily, of course, but that was a whole other kettle of wasps.

Our shuttle descended back through the atmosphere, over the ocean at first, before heading inland. The lush, green fields below soon began to rise, became tremendous mountain peaks, chains of snow-capped highlands surrounding hundreds of untouched, pristine valleys coated in forest, rushing with rivers and blue ice flow.

"Why did the Vale build a tower here?" Tal asked, mostly herself, but Emily had an answer.

"The towers are… antennas, I suppose you could say. Forces for keeping power in balance, in check. Gates against the Void. They're built on human worlds, on Vale worlds, across creation, as sentinels, guardians. If you were to dig a hole from the base of the tower here, straight down, you'd find another tower on the other side of the planet."

"I was told there are three towers on this world," I said. "Only one survives in the future."

Emily frowned, worried. "Three towers, yes. One just ahead, one in the sea on the other side of the world. And the Vale Atlantia, in Atlantis—that tower is the keystone, the anchor. The three towers together form a net of protection around True Earth." She paused. "If what you say is true, Declan, and only the Vale Crystalis survives in your time, then the world is in great danger."

I shrugged. "That's nothing really new."

We flew low between the peaks, above thousands of acres of wild forest. No sign of human habitation, no sign of anything. The shuttle rose with the foothills, crested a rise and a craggy peak of grey, snowless stone, and our objective came into sight. Emily flew us in from the south, heading north up the valley to where a monumental silver tower, at least a mile high, rested in the arms of the surrounding mountains.

The Vale Crystalis, what would one day be the heart of the Atlas Lexicon—a city dedicated to saving the poor souls flung across the Story Thread, the children who stumbled back to this world having caught a glimpse of the infinite. The kind of glimpse that could fuck you up irreparably, if you weren't careful with the fallout.

I intended some dark work for this place. *This school*, whispered my conscience, which I'd long since thought reduced to rubble. *What if some little bastard nine thousand years from now stumbles across your little plan?*

Well, it was a worry. A risk I'd have to take. That said, if what I had planned here *worked*, then I would have heard long since about the details being discovered in the future.

Maybe that meant it wouldn't work, but I had to try.

Emily looked at me as we hovered just above the summit of the Vale Crystalis, an empty tower, an antenna, keeping the Void at bay. "Well, hero, what now?" she asked.

"Scan the area," I said. "Can we do that? Sure we can. I want a cave in one of those mountains, the more hidden the better, and the bigger the better—a cavern."

"What's the play, Declan?" Tal asked, as Emily turned back to the control column and began shuffling glowing crystal buttons about. The screens on the wall showed topographical maps of the area, and started to zoom in on certain mountains, scanning the enormous piles of rock and snow.

I tapped the celestial illusion in my pocket. "Spot of gardening. Is she following, Emily?"

Emily said nothing, concentrating on the console.

"Astoria?" I said, an edge to my voice.

"Yes," she snapped. "You'll have your chance to hurt my sister soon enough."

It's my party, I thought, *I can cry if I want to.* I left Emily be and took a seat next to Tal while she worked, offering her my hand.

Tal didn't take it. She hauled her legs up and rested her chin on her knees. "I've got a bad feeling about all this."

I thought of about a dozen things to say, from reassurance to worry, and chose to say nothing, which was a touch of that wisdom again, that sharp spear of sanity. Emily worked away up at the control column. I didn't want to just sit around, so I got up and went to the bathroom at the rear of the shuttle. It took a good few minutes, but I scrubbed the dried blood from my hands and forearms, from under my fingernails, rubbing the skin raw. Looking in the mirror, I caught splotches on my face, dried flecks—some of it my own, from the fight—and cleaned that away, too.

"I think I've found what you need," Emily said. The shuttle glided away from the Vale Crystalis and toward the north west, over hill and dale.

Emily landed us on a sloping hillside, just above the foothills, of a mountain overlooking the valley and the towering silver spire built by the Vale, those enigmatic blue aliens. Exiting the shuttle, millions of stars overhead and a fat moon lit up the hillside, and revealed three crudely curved obsidian stone pillars. The pillars didn't seem natural—perhaps something Vale-related—and were warm to the touch. I sensed the potential within, the foundation of possible enchantment. *Portal stones,* I thought. *Grown portal stones.*

"Which way?" I asked Emily. My words echoed on the air, down the mountainside. Birds and animals that hadn't ever heard a human voice startled in the night.

Emily, standing just in the doorway of our transport craft, pushed an interior button and a half dozen beams of light emanated from the roof of the shuttle, lighting up the hillside and a good chunk of the forest below. High beams. Neat.

"Up there, Declan," she said, directing a single beam toward our destination. "See that canyon cut between the two rising thrusts of stone? If we follow that, scale a few boulders, you should find what you came to find."

"Very well."

The walk was pleasant, if a little eerie. It still blew my mind that this was True Earth, ten thousand years or so before I'd be born. Time travel was a dangerous thing. One I could get used to—and that was a scary thought. I was a man held together by regret, after all, and little else. If I had the opportunity to undo some of those mistakes... I shook my head. No, it didn't work like that. I couldn't pretend to know the rules, but there was no changing the past—or, in this case, the future. What happened will happen, because of what we did now, not *despite* it. I created my own problems, and so would have to create my own solutions.

Which made time travel, now that I thought on it, not so dangerous—merely part of the narrative. Still, still... I wondered. If I pushed hard enough, could I snap the thread, retie it toward some brighter, less bloody future? Dangerous thoughts, after all.

The canyon was narrow, and as Emily predicted

we had to haul ourselves up and over a few low-lying boulders, gripping the mossy-wet walls for purchase. Tal cast a few spheres of light to hover above our heads and illuminate the way. We twisted and curved, Emily ever so graceful, until we reached the entrance to a vast cave system.

I cast one of my nets of detection, half-expecting a cave troll or something equally absurd to hamper our way, but the net came back negative. We entered the cave, Tal thrusting her arms forward, casting another half dozen spheres of light, floating orbs of warmth and white radiance. The light illuminated the entrance to the cave, a small plateau a few feet above a massive cavern which stretched back, and back... beyond the edge of the light.

"Yeah," I said. "Yeah, this will do nicely."

Emily tilted her head, listening to something only she could hear. "Ashaya draws near, Declan. We have minutes, at best." She met my eyes and I saw something merry dancing in hers. "Are you ready?"

I hefted my sword onto my shoulder, like it was the barrel of a shotgun, and retrieved the orb of celestial illusion from my pocket. "Guess we'll find out. Where do you think, Tal? I think that small pedestal near the centre of the cavern will do nicely."

I hopped down into the cavern, my two companions—one a stunning beautifully goddess, the other an Everlasting—watching my back.

Water drip, drip, dripped overhead, forming small cool pools on the stone. I stepped carefully but quickly across the cavern and reached a naturally smooth jut of rock, a tiny dais, about ten feet across by the same wide. Stalagmites, tapering columns of calcium deposits, rose in a mini range of mountains around the dais.

I stepped onto the stone and knelt at its centre, brushing the cold surface, feeling its pulse. I summoned a globule of hot fire, liquid energy, then took a step back as it heated up, first red-hot then white-hot, and turned the stone to slag, to molten rock.

"This better work like I think it does, Axis, you blind bastard," I muttered. Once the smoke had cleared, I held up the orb of celestial illusion and then—*plunk*—dropped the priceless gemstone into the fast-cooling melted stone.

Something, some foreign urge, came over me, and I whispered a small prayer, though even through my surprise the words felt strong, powerful. In a language I didn't know, had never heard before, would never hear again. I stepped back—stumbled—off the dais, almost falling over a small stalagmite, as the entire platform shone with ethereal light.

Seconds ticked by like the slow turning of the earth itself.

From the centre of the dais, a perfect stem of glowing crystal breached the cooling stone and stretched up toward the roof of the cavern, like the first tiny shoot of a plant breaching the soil. I relaxed. I didn't know what to expect, what a good sign looked like in this caper, but that had to be one.

"OK," I called across the cavern, "I'd say that—"

A wave of rippling, greasy purple smoke surged into the cavern, a torrent of dark energy speckled with black oil. A beautiful young woman rode within that wave of power, bright-eyed and pixie-faced.

Dread Ash of the Everlasting. Fix, that was.

She howled through the cavern, shook the

foundations of the mountain, and when her eyes fell on me they narrowed. "*You!*" Her feet barely touched the ground as she ran at me, a storm of menace clouding her movements. "*You blinded my brother!*"

I braced for the attack, for the impact, shielding my face with my arms, but it never came.

Tal stood in front of me, holding Ash in a binding of power I'd never seen—something unique, clever. She held one hand up against the Everlasting, smooth light flowing from her palm and into the shackles, and in her other hand Tal held one of my swords, the blade covered in runes.

I had a sneaking suspicion—no, a terrible certainty gripped me—and I knew what was about to happen mere moments before it did.

"I learnt this trick from Oblivion, bitch," Tal snarled, and the light in her palm changed, darkened. She wrenched a mass of purple shadow from Fix's body, from the form the Everlasting had chosen, and with a wild sweep of the blade forged in Atlantis *severed* the purple entity from the whole.

"Tal, Tal, no…" I said. I tried to move but the force of power rolling off Tal as Ash struggled, as her power buckled, couldn't be surmounted.

"This one's my job, Declan," Tal whispered, and stepped back over the stalagmites and onto the pedestal that held the blossom of celestial illusion. "You think you're the only one who hates them?"

She grinned at me as Fix's body—Ash's vessel—disintegrated.

I laughed—it was, perhaps, the saddest sound I'd ever made.

Tal stepped back *onto* the growing stem of celestial illusion and tossed the rune blade aside. It whistled over my head and I ducked to avoid its infinitely sharp edge. She looked at me once, for what would be the last time in a very long time, and then released Ash from the impossibly complex net of Will that had snared an elder god.

Robbed of her form, Ash did exactly as Tal had expected her to do—she possessed her. The purple shadow roiled into Tal, just as the celestial illusion under her foot seized her ankle.

"No…" I whispered, already knowing it was too late.

Dread Ash and the celestial illusion claimed Tal at the same moment—the silver-clear alloy rising up her legs, sealing her in an immense crystal of divine light. Ash had enough time to assume control of Tal, to understand what had happened, and spin her new, stolen eyes to find me before the crystal solidified and trapped them both in the eternal prison.

That hadn't been the plan.

Not by a long shot.

I had hoped to ensnare Ash, yes, but not at the cost of Tal.

"You stupid…" I began and trailed away, not knowing whether I was talking to myself or Tal or to the gods that weren't listening.

I stepped closer and placed a hand against the cooling crystal of celestial illusion. Already other tendrils, stems and blossoms, were creeping across the cavern. I couldn't stay here, not without being consumed and imprisoned alongside Tal. Perhaps that would be for the best…

I leaned down and collected the rune blade.

Emily Grace, Ash's sister, stood in the entrance to the cavern. She hadn't lifted a finger to stop what had just happened, not moved an inch as the purple flood of malice her sister had rode in on had taken away the love of my life.

I probably should have felt angry at that, but I didn't. Already a plan was forming in my head, a way to undo this mess. It would take… well, it would take thousands of years to pull off. And would mean releasing Dread Ash, which wasn't ideal. Good. Luckily I had thousands of years and specialised in less than ideal.

"I'm sorry for your loss, Declan," Emily said. "Truly."

I scanned the entrance to the cavern, spied a boulder with a small groove in the base back against the eastern wall. I shoved the rune blade under that boulder, leaving just the hilt sticking out. That would do—no one would come here, I'd make sure of it— and even if they did, they wouldn't be looking for a sword.

"I haven't lost anything," I said.

Emily read my thoughts. "You cannot release her, Declan. You would need to wait until the celestial illusion is done growing. To tamper with it now… would be catastrophic." She glanced at my hidden sword. "What are you planning?"

"Feels right to leave it here," I said. "Perhaps the blade will gain a boost from the celestial illusion, the beginnings of another Roseblade to replace the one I destroyed." My chin trembled and I gritted my teeth together. "Perhaps, if Tal awakes, she'll need something to protect herself."

"Tal is lost, Declan," Emily said. "Ashaya will devour her mind, torment her for as long as they're entwined."

"She's survived that before."

"What will you do now?"

"Head on home, I suppose," I said. "Back across the Void, to the future, to my time, and undo this travesty. I will *save* her, Astoria. I swear it."

Emily said nothing, though her eyes said enough. After a long moment, "I admire your tenacity," she said. "Hope in the face of hopelessness. A final resolve."

THE FINAL RESOLVE

What Have We Not Fucked Up Yet?

"How often have I lain beneath rain on a strange
roof, thinking of home."

~William Faulkner

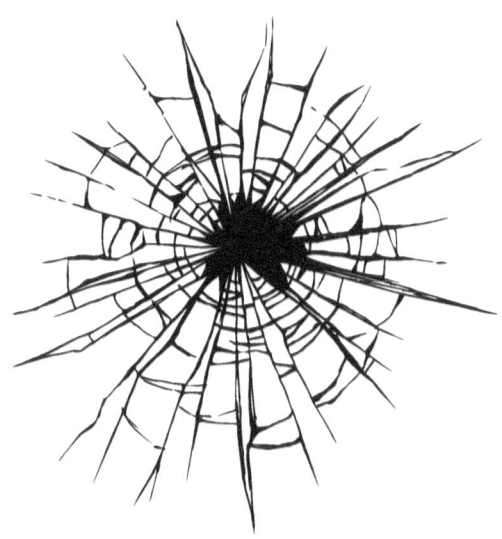

CHAPTER THIRTEEN

Upon the Lilac Precipice

"And the world did applaud our folly"

Half a mile of burning mountain behind us, half a mile of burning mountain ahead, rising to a snowy peak already being licked by curls of smoke, steam, and fire from the scorched cavern within the mountainside. Small tremors, little aftershocks, of the ignited celestial illusion shook the ground, sent boulders tumbling around us, snapped trees from the hills, and made our going slow.

I'm coming for you, Tal.

"And that brings us to now," I said, mostly to Annie, though Caitlin and Arlon were listening on in, of course. Should they survive what lay ahead—and I would do my best to see it so—they would relay the truth of my sordid plan to the Atlas Lexicon. I was responsible for everything that had happened here over the last two days. "You see the choice I have to make, Annie, what it's all been for."

"You may have to kill Tal," she said. "If Ash won't let her go, you'll have to imprison them both again."

I climbed over a shaking boulder, scrambled up a small rock fall. Only the energy from the sword sustained me now. My aches and pains, pierced shoulder and broken ribs, were distant but getting closer, returning—on the express train to pain. Before long, I'd collapse. This had to end before then.

"I never meant for this to happen. I just… wanted to stop the Everlasting. It's all I've ever wanted."

"Tal made her choice," Annie said. "She chose to stand with you. I'm making the same choice."

To that, I had nothing to say. She was right, but that didn't make living with the cost any easier. If anything, I should have been better, cleverer. "It was a multifaceted plan," I said. "All clever and conceited. Tal was never meant to suffer, not again. I'd have died first, but like she said… I don't die. I go on."

"You drew Dread Ash in," Annie said. "So you could defeat her, like you did Axis, and if nothing else you'd have a cavern of priceless celestial illusion to come back to." She sighed, half-breathless as we climbed the mountain, taking twisted paths to follow Ash's trail.

"It was a trap with benefits, yeah," I said. "Should have known better."

"And Ash is stuck here? Tied to the Lexicon?"

I shrugged. "Didn't actually plan for that, I think it must be something to do with the grove of celestial illusion, being imprisoned in it for so long. So long as the grove exists she can't stray too far. Or maybe its

Tal, still fighting for me."

"You don't sound sure of that, and not to forget you just set that grove on fire."

The mountain groaned, strained its burning joints, as if to drive the point home. I nodded. "The tether will snap—she will be freed, before too long. We have to wrench Ashaya's essence from Tal before that happens."

"And make her pull down the shield before it eats the world," Annie said.

"Yes, thank you. The two go hand in hand. If we defeat Ash, wound her enough, the Everlasting may be beyond actual death unless they give up their grace, as Emily did, but she won't have the focus, the strength, to maintain the shield."

Arlon grunted. He looked at me with something approaching disdain. "All or nothing then, is it? And all we must do is destroy an elder god. You make it sound so simple, Arbiter."

I shrugged and grinned. "Standard Tuesday afternoon most weeks for me, Arlon. Chin up, they'll write stories and sing songs about us after this."

He looked troubled at the prospect. "You, perhaps, Hale. The rest of us are just along for the ride."

Caitlin, breathing heavy and hard, rubbed the blood from her eyes. Her forehead had split open again. "This is all your fault," she said.

"Caitlin," Arlon warned. "Not now."

"You're right," I said. "I put the Lexicon in this position. I'm responsible for every death since that shield fell, every lost Lexicon soldier and student. Tell me, though, how would you defeat my enemies?" I felt that old familiar arrogance, the hot, jealous poison inside of me that Tal, sweet Tal, had once mistaken for confidence. "None of you would stand a chance. This world would be for the Void long ago, if I hadn't acted."

"OK," Annie said, stretching the word out into a low whistle. "Let's not argue. We're all still friends here."

"Allies," Arlon said. "We're allies."

The mountainside rose ever higher, the Atlas Lexicon far below us now—save for the Vale Crystalis, we hadn't quite summited past the height of that tower yet—but was quickly becoming less of a scramble and more of an actual climb. If we had to go much higher, if Ash had fled beyond us, we were doomed. The world would crumple and die.

But she wouldn't have fled much farther, not while she still needed me, needed the sword. Sheer spite and rage would ensure we had our last battle—I wanted to see what she had to say about burning the grove of celestial illusion, perhaps the greatest treasure in all creation. Entire worlds and universes prayed to that alloy, saw it as divine. Which made what I'd done an act of incomparable blasphemy. When word spread, as word always did, I'd have more than a few new bounties on my head.

And what do we say to that? Well, heck, sure sounds like Future Declan's problem.

I clung to the hilt of the rune sword, created only last week and ten thousand years ago in the starlit forges of the Vale Celestia, willing it to keep me going. The pain was returning now, my legs and arms trembled from the exertion. Soon, very soon, I'd pass out. And there was still a god to fight. Climbing this mountain felt rather biblical, though, so if nothing else at least our thematic narrative was in order.

All that was left was sacrifice, selflessness, someone nailed to a cross… This time, if such a ransom was required, it would be me paying the bill. No more friends, or allies, to suffer for my arrogance. My clever little plans spanning worlds, space, and time.

That thought gave me strength as we summited a small, sheer cliff face and reached a plateau—a wide space covered in black rock and rivulets of fast-melting snow. Steam rose in quick curls from the narrow gullets breaching back to the cavern below.

Dread Ash of the Everlasting stood on the edge of the plateau, on a precipice of sharp stone, a knob of rock overlooking the entire landscape within the purple shield—and a drop of about a thousand feet to the glassed hillside of deadlings and monsters below.

Her back was to us, but I had no doubt she knew we were there. A light breeze swept her golden-brown hair around her head, as red lightning tore across the canopy of the shield. Dread Ash looked like what she was—an ageless god, surveying the world as if it were just being forged from the fire. Only this wasn't the beginning of something, this was the end.

With Annie at my side, Arlon and Caitlin at my back, I strode across the plateau and held my rune sword before me. My voice, a tone of raw command, echoed across the space—punctuated and somehow enforced by the lightning strikes and the shaking mountain.

"Ashaya D'levaney, Seventh Born of the Everlasting, you will surrender to me. You will unmake the degradation surrounding the Atlas Lexicon, and you will release your prisoner, Tal Levy of the Knights Infernal. *Do this now or be destroyed.*"

Dread Ash, pixie-faced Fix, sweet Tal—names upon names, disguises within disguises—

took a delicate step forward until her toes brushed the very edge of the thousand-foot drop. She spun, elegance and grace, and smiled at me below cheeks tear-stained and flushed. Her eyes, Tal's lovely eyes, were as black as midnight on a night with no moon.

With a cry that shook the heavens, she thrust the stolen sword down between her feet, into the stone, burying the blade halfway along its length. "Give me your sword, Declan. You made the blades as twins. I require both to escape this hateful place."

"No," I said. "That doesn't work for me."

"Then I'll tear it from you."

"Bitch, come at me."

She laughed and that was all manner of unnerving. We had jumped back and forth between advantage and disadvantage so much over this long night and dark morning that I didn't know where we stood— probably best to assume I was arguing from the low ground. Safe to assume I was screwed. "You are the most infuriating, the most unpredictable, man I have ever known." She blinked her coal-black eyes. "I'm going to miss you, I think."

I straightened my posture, stood tall, and cut my blade down through the air. "Talking's done," I said.

Dread Ash inclined her head and clapped her hands together, fusing purple fire with dark light, and shot five spiralling arcs of energy across the plateau. I swung my sword again, focused my Will tied to the petal in my heart—acting on a foreign prayer—and a wave of force repelled the sickly beams of fire, shooting them skyward, where they were lost against the purple sky.

Arlon and Caitlin opened fire but Dread Ash moved fast, faster than fast, a blur on the wind, zig-zagging across the plateau. My allies were thrown aside, back against the cliff face, save Annie, who drew a level bead on the demigod in human form and placed a hot inch of spinning lead in her lung.

Dread Ash blinked in surprise, in pain, and fell to her knees before me, blood blossoming on her chest, spilling down her blouse. She looked furious as Annie calmly pulled back the hammer on her revolver again.

"That…" Ash laughed, coughed up a mouthful of heart's blood. "That shot was impressive." She looked at Annie, tilted her head, and grinned twin rows of bloody teeth. "Ah, I see, you are like him."

Annie held the barrel of her gun between Ash's eyes. She paused. "What?"

"It's not important," I said.

Ash laughed. "She doesn't know, Declan?"

"Know what?" Annie said, though something flickered in her eyes, something scared, something *knowing*. An oh so sneaky, sneaking suspicion. "Talk, bitch."

Ash's skin began to knit itself back together, healing, I levelled the blade against her neck, ready and willing to take Tal's head from her shoulders. Better that than another minute slave to the Everlasting. I tried to tell myself it was what she would want, that it wasn't murder, but such blurred distinctions were so much bullshit. Loving me had cost Tal everything, more than once, and here I was to put her out of her misery.

Still, I hesitated.

And Dread Ash told Annie Brie the truth.

"A petal of the Infernal Clock rests in your heart, child," Ash said around her wicked grin. "You died and were brought back to life, an immortal half-life. Your doing, Declan? Were you lonely?"

Annie's grip on her revolver slackened, hardened again. She glared at me. "That true?"

I nodded slowly. "On Diablo Beach. Scion killed you. You were dead for maybe ten minutes. Emily had seen it, or perhaps I told her in the past, and she had slipped a petal of the Infernal Clock into your jacket. I used it to heal you. To bring you back."

Annie considered all of that, a range of emotions warring across her face. "Oh. OK, thanks." She looked back to Ash. "What do we do with her?"

I blinked—and thought that, perhaps, if we survived the next few hours, Annie and I were not done with this conversation—but matters at hand demanded our attention.

"Please, Ash, don't make me do this. Let her go."

The blade twitched in my hand, drawing a thin line of blood against the Everlasting's neck. Pearl droplets trickled into her collar, staining the soft cotton crimson.

"Even when you win, you lose," she said, and wasn't that my curse, my obscene truth. "Are you going to *peel* me as you did Axis, Declan? Drive me mad as you did my brother? He rages about you— across time and space, echoing through the great machinations and gears at the heart of the universe, I can hear him. He's coming for you."

"I'll do for all you Everlasting before too long," I said. "I'm giving you a chance to save yourself, Ash."

"Don't you want me dead, sweet thing?" she said, tossing my own words back at me, pulled no doubt from Tal's mind.

Across the plateau, Caitlin cradled Arlon in her lap, pressing a bandage to a hell of a scalp wound on the side of his head. She looked at me, eyes wild, unfocused, lost, as the shield howled overhead. We had minutes, perhaps less—I honestly didn't know—before the canvas around the Atlas Lexicon tore and the Void spilled across True Earth and simply unmade the world.

A decision was about to be cast, one way or the other. An end to a plan set in motion ten thousand years ago on this blasted mountain.

Ash closed her eyes, whispered a harsh word in an alien, guttural tongue—dark speech, if ever I heard it—and a crimson bolt of lightning flashed down from the shield and struck the hilt of my sword, the one embedded on the precipice in the stone. A shockwave of energy burst outwards, riding a blinding flash of light, and we were all tossed across the plateau, scattered in the explosion.

I held on to my rune sword, the beginnings of something that, if all would be well, could one day be a weapon to rival the Roseblade, but it was a near thing. I landed hard on my back, sharp rock digging into my spine. My shoulder wound bled fresh across my chest. I wheezed against broken ribs. The pain receded again as I clutched the hilt of the sword, borrowing the blade's celestial energy.

Then Dread Ash was upon me—she leapt through the air like a lion, and came down atop of me, pinning my sides between her legs, holding my shoulders against the rock with her knees. She dug her thumb into my pierced shoulder and I screamed. My hand holding the sword jerked and tossed the blade aside.

At once, I was flooded with fatigue, pain so blinding I nearly passed out, but Ash held me, brought me back.

"No, no," she said. "You don't get to slip away. The tether weakens, Declan. I thought you a fool to burn the grove of celestial illusion, but no, you've freed me. I can escape. In time, Axis will create another seed, and millennia from now we shall have a new grove. What's a few thousand more years after so long? Nothing to me, and you will be ages dead… buried and forgotten."

She laughed and closed her hand around my throat. Her legs pressed against my cracked ribs, drawing the breath from my lungs. I gasped and Dread Ash squeezed, cutting off my air.

I stared up into those black eyes, that bloody grin, as the world grew white and hazy at the edges, in defiance of the purple sky, the ash on the wind, the strikes of vicious lightning and the scent of burnt copper, the tang of the Void, all around us. The last of my defiance. I felt the cavern burning beneath us, a slow vibration that would last forever.

"You lose, Declan," Ash whispered.

My lungs screamed for air, my heart pounded against my chest, fast and desperate.

My heart…

Ah, shit, a terribly awful plan occurred to me, as consciousness faded.

Annie, I thought. *Annie… do this for me.*

I sent my terrible plan from my heart to hers, along the celestial petals that joined us together beyond life and death. I couldn't speak, couldn't even whisper, but the thought may as well have been shouted from the mountaintops for Annie. I knew she heard me. I knew it.

As my sight dwindled, the world reduced to a narrow corridor, where all I could see was Dread Ash's snarling face, Tal's corrupted expression, and beyond that the awful purple sky, I readied myself to die—and to stay dead this time. I didn't feel anger, or hate, or anything except relief. If this was the end, so be it. I'd earned a death like this a thousand times over, some would argue it was too quick.

Someone blocked the purple sky over Ash's shoulder—someone wearing a killer leather jacket, with jade-green eyes and sharp black hair. Detective Annie Brie, blood-spattered and bruised, tears in her eyes, raised my rune blade over her head behind Dread Ash.

Her chin trembled, she sniffed, and whispered, "I hear you, Declan."

Annie drove the infinitely sharp point of the blade through Dread Ash's back, right through her heart, and out the front of her chest.

Ash's eyes widened—in fury, in pain—and her grip on my throat slackened. I felt that for half a second before Annie completed my terrible thought and *kept driving the blade downward* and into my chest.

There was no pain, nothing, as the tip pierced my heart and struck hard against what was hidden. A chime, church bells on high, echoed across the plateau, up the mountain, and down into the Atlas Lexicon. For just a moment, the lightning in the shield recoiled as if stung, shying away from that pure sound.

Finish it, I thought.

With a cry, Annie wrenched the blade up and back out of me. The sword left my chest—coated not in my blood, but in glowing, ghostly, silver-blue divine light. The petal of the Infernal Clock, my stolen immortality, left my chest, and I felt a great sadness, an infinite regret, at its passing. As if I'd lost something I'd never know again, a glimpse of the true turning of the world. I was robbed of its protection.

Annie wrenched the sword upwards and dragged the tip back through Ash's chest. The petal passed into her heart—Tal's heart—and when the blade exited her back it was clean, bloodless, and *without* the petal.

Ash's hands fell from my throat and I sucked in a gasp of air like a man nearly drowned. My lungs strained, shot and abused, but the air was good, redeeming. I blinked and the world came back into focus, as Dread Ash fell from me, fell next to me against the hard ground.

Her eyes flickered from pure black, to swirls of white, to Tal's eyes. She convulsed on the rock as if in seizure, and her chest—her heart—blazed with celestial light.

Ash turned to look at me, quivering, crying. Afraid. Her hand found mine and she squeezed it hard enough to snap my fingers. I embraced that pain, I'd earned it. The look on her face was terrible to behold, sad and miserable.

"I'm scared," she whispered. "Oh, Declan, I'm scared."

Though it cost me, I reached over with my free hand and gently cupped her cheek. Dread Ash leaned into my palm, her tears mixed with my blood, and I pulled her close.

For the second time in my life, I held one of the Everlasting as she died.

CHAPTER FOURTEEN

Like Rain on a Sunny Day

"One day, when this is all over, I'm going to Disneyland"

Annie knelt next to me as I felt Ash's grip slacken and watched the life leave her eyes. I held that lifeless gaze a long moment as cold fingers fell still. Annie ripped my shirt open and ran her hands over my chest, over my heart.

"There's no wound," she said, and placed her warm hand flat against my chest. "Declan, I stabbed you in the heart, and there's no wound."

"The petal healed me on its way out." *Or whatever.* A dozen aches and pains, broken bones and stab wounds remained, but not my heart. "Parting gift, for all the trouble it cost me."

Annie took a deep breath and exhaled. "Is she… gone?"

"You just killed one of the Everlasting, Annie," I

said, not quite willing to let go of Tal's hand just yet. "As far as I know, you're the only person in the history of creation ever to do such a thing. That's going to bite us later, I'm sure."

The purple sky screamed, rippling with lightning. I'd hoped Ash dying—and there were four sad words—would have severed that monstrosity of a shield, but no, it was beyond that now—self-sustaining, and work still to be done. I needed to get up and get on with that work, mill the last of the day's grist, but I was tired, beaten, at what could only be described as an utter loss. If the world was about to end in Voidflame, then so be it. I'd been robbed of death again.

You survive, Declan. You always survive. Oh, how right you'd been, dear.

A howling wind swept across the plateau, rife with ash and the swirling dust from the glassed deadling army below.

Tal Levy opened her eyes.

"Hey there, sweet thing," she whispered, her voice a rasp almost stolen by the maelstrom. "You do like to keep a girl waiting."

~~*~*

Annie and Tal helped me over to the edge of the cliff face, over the knob of jutting rock where Ash had driven my sword into the stone, twin and brother to the proto-Roseblade, the rune blade that was already going to be infamous for slaying an Everlasting. And, perhaps, for stealing the scant-understood immortality of the infamous Declan Hale.

There was one hell of a headline for the *Ascension*

City Times tomorrow morning: *EVERLASTING KILLED BY IMMORTALITY.* This and other bitter ironies in the news at eleven.

Tal and Annie carried me between them, as gently as they could.

Arlon and Caitlin stood back, ready to help if any of us fell, but knowing this one was out of their depth, above their pay grade. Hell, we'd all been out of our depth most of the night, just doing the best we could with the tatters of that oh-so-clever plan devised one should-have-been-drunken night in a quiet tavern of the Vale Celestia, ten millenniums ago in time's true measure.

"Are you sure you're up to this?" Annie asked.

"Nope."

A haunted look lurked in the back of Tal's eyes, and I imagined it would be there for some time. But she was strong, stronger than I could ever hope to be. "There's no one else, Detective Brie," she said. "Declan started this, and Declan *will* finish it. No love of mine will stumble at the finish line."

And if there was little mercy in her voice, a resentment in the word 'love', was that any one's fault but my own?

I gripped the hilt of the rune blade and felt a trickle of its power. Enough to stand on my feet.

The shield raged overhead, great forks of lightning scoured the landscape, smashed into the towers of the Atlas Lexicon and sent marble, glass, and steel raining to the ground—we were in the eye of the storm, the Void so close now that great patches of darkness were bleeding across the sky. Holes in the very canvas of our reality—thin enough that anything, simply anything, could break through. I glimpsed a monumental, lidless eye in one of the dark patches, some abomination beyond reckoning, staring into our world.

That wouldn't do.

At the last of my strength, I held the rune blade up over my head and brought it crashing down into the rock next to its twin. The blades sung a swift harmony as I fell and I gripped both hilts in my hands, down on one knee, proposing quite the engagement to the purple sky. I poured Will into the swords, focused my intent, and bolstered by the sheer amount of energy burning within the heart of the mountain, I cast that intent *against* the shield surrounding the Atlas Lexicon.

That's all any real Will casting was, at the end of the day—intent, focus, energy.

I threw my Will against that of the Everlasting Dread Ash—a contest under normal circumstances I could never win, a puppy trying to fight a bear, but Ash was dead. Nine were now eight—seven, without Emily Grace. The shield roiled against my power, bucked like some wild thing caught in a snare.

The degradation around the Atlas Lexicon wailed. Nothing ever died easy in my line of work.

And then it split.

Right across the top of the dome the purple shield *split*, and a great scar of blue sky, honest golden sunlight, poured into the Atlas Lexicon, flooded the landscape, lit up the city and made the silver towers shine magnificently.

The stitch broken, the thread severed, the ugly shield exploded outwards on all sides, dissipating into nothingness stolen on the air. Ragged, oily chunks of the shield fell like burnt cloth over miles of valley, a blizzard of tainted lilac snow, burning to nothing before it struck the ground. In the space of three seconds the purple sky faded and was replaced with bright sunshine, a cloudless blue sky.

A pressure I'd almost grown used to, the terrible weight of the Void, disappeared with the shield. The terrible patches of impending doom and Lovecraftian horrors winking at me from beyond the stars fused, scarred over. There'd be weak spots, places that would need to be monitored for years to come, as what I'd done was nothing more than a field medic's attempt at triage, but I thought it would hold. For what felt like the first time in days, I took a breath of clear, fresh air, rolling down off the pristine peaks of the Swiss Alps, and beheld the entire valley of the Atlas Lexicon—emerald forests, glacial blue rivers, mountains capped with pure white snow.

I managed a rough chuckle, blood ran from my nose, the whole world spun about my head. I stumbled back from the twin swords as the blades folded and then melted from the surge of heat and power I had channelled through them, rivulets of molten steel pooling on the precipice, the last stolen starlight of Atlantis. The best laid plans, and all that nonsense. No new Roseblade for me.

I don't remember falling, I don't remember Annie and Tal catching me in their arms, or being wrapped in the warm, blissful embrace of some well-earned unconsciousness.

Which was a flowery way of saying I fainted just after saving the whole worthless world.

It had been a long night.

~~*~*

Warm healing light, the sun at noon on a spring day, flooded my body and I sat up with a start, reaching for the sword on my hip, the shotgun at my side, and finding neither.

"Welcome back to the land of the living," Lady Evelyn Waterwood said, her hands still glowing with the power she'd used to rouse me from troubled dreams.

I'd dreamt of a field of sunflowers, a familiar face sitting amongst the blooms, my lost Valentine. Clare had smiled, in a sad sort of way that seemed par for the course around me, and told me the worst was yet to come.

I recalled a similar dream, during my first few weeks in Atlantis, recalled pulling one of those sunflowers *from* the dream.

"Where are Tal and Annie?" I asked, and speaking hurt my throat. Lady Waterwood handed me a glass of water and I sipped at it carefully. My head was pounding.

"Your friends are well. Resting."

I swung my legs off the cot and found spongy grass beneath my feet. I was alone with Lady Waterwood inside a three-walled white canvas tent. Through the open wall, I glimpsed rolling green fields, the edge of a forest, and in the distance the silver towers of the Atlas Lexicon. I was in the mobile command centre where Annie and I had been brought after arriving in the valley.

Someone had changed me out of my bloodstained jeans and shirt, removed the rags of my waistcoat, and healed the worst of my wounds. I was dressed in a simple pair of board shorts to hide my shame, shirtless and barefoot. I felt all kinds of out of sorts.

The worst of my wounds, the pierced shoulder, looked about three weeks healed. I prodded at the lump of red scar tissue gently, felt a faint twinge but nothing severe, and examined the rest of my body. A wicked swath of purple bruises covered my chest and along my side. Over my heart were four new scars, lines drawn like claw marks—Dread Ash's fingernails. She'd left her mark on me, for sure.

"I don't think I've ever seen a man with so many scars," Lady Waterwood said. She stood above me in some fancy blue ceremonial robe, a small flap cap on her head. Her hair was pulled back in a tight bun, highlighting her severe face, her sharp nose and sparklingly clever eyes. "You cannot be happy, living the life you do."

On a small table next to the cot I spied a pile of clean clothing—shirts, socks, a pair of thin boat shoes. I shrugged into a white T-shirt and slipped on the shoes. The movement cost me in aches and pains. I wished for a patch to cover my dead eye and the hideous network of scar tissue around it, but we don't always get what we want.

"I spoke with Sergeant Grenn before healing you. Arlon, that is," she said at my frown, "and he informed me of everything that happened after you left the Vale Crystalis. How you defeated the Everlasting and destroyed the majority of the deadling army."

Had I done all of that? I supposed I had, but it hadn't been done alone, and a lot of good soldiers had died. But then that's what soldiers did. So the rest of the worlds could sleep easy in their beds. Someone had to bleed. If I'd learnt nothing else in my life, I'd learnt that—someone had to bleed.

"Honestly," Lady Waterwood said, "I took a moment to decide whether to heal you or to slit your throat."

"You will recall," I said, taking another sip of water. I wasn't quite ready to stand yet. "You will recall that I was invited here, and my assistance was formerly requested by all available lords and ladies of the Atlas Lexicon. More than once, even."

Lady Waterwood scowled. "If we'd known you were here to clean up a mess you were *responsible* for, Arbiter—"

"You would have done nothing differently," I snapped. "Let's skip to the punchline, my lady. You sat out most of the Tome Wars, and that's good, and the work the Lexicon does in saving children from the Story Thread is admirable, but you are Willful, you *are* travellers of the Story Thread." Now I stood. "What on this or any world makes you think you're exempt from being called to fight when the Knights Infernal *demand* it?"

She took a step back, not in fear, but to work herself up into quite a storm. Lord Towré Winter strode into the tent wearing a similar blue robe of importance, handsome if grave, leaning on his tall black-glass staff.

"Our accords with your people, Arbiter," Lady Waterwood spat, "recognise the Atlas Lexicon as an independent city-state. You violated those accords by tethering one of the godforsaken Everlasting to a school for children! You declared war on us!"

"No," I said.

"No?"

"When were the accords signed?" I asked softly.

"Ah," Lord Winter said. He chuckled without

mirth. "I see I've come at the right time to defuse this particular time bomb."

"Lord Winter," Lady Waterwood said. "We should arrest this man. He should be tried under our laws. His people won't protect him—he broke the accords."

Lord Winter stared at me and I saw that I didn't have a friend there, no, not at all. But I also saw that he got it. That I hadn't broken a single law, not one letter of the accords.

"Our treaties with the Knights were signed over four hundred years ago, during the last conflict we had with them," Lord Winter said.

"Exactly," Lady Waterwood said. "And the travesty Hale brought down on us two days ago is in direct violation…" She trailed away, I saw the light of understanding dawn in her eyes, then fade to sullenness. "You *monster*," she whispered. "You knew there would be children here, but still you did it."

"No accords were broken," Lord Winter said tightly. "As when Arbiter Hale imprisoned the Everlasting Dread Ash here at the Atlas Lexicon, there was no Atlas Lexicon. No accords."

Almost like I planned it…

"As I said, Lady Waterwood, Lord Winter." I crossed my arms over my chest. "You don't get to choose when to fight and when not to—the Everlasting threaten the entire Story Thread, and this world most of all. I am their sworn enemy, and I will use *any* means to ensure they do not get a foothold on True Earth."

"Tell that to the people who died for your strategy here," Lady Waterwood said, as if sucking on something sour. "The soldiers we lost, the teachers and students."

"War is coming for all of us," I said. "And you will be called into service. But look on the bright side. Now instead of eight vicious and malignant elder gods darkening the universe, there are only seven. Today was a win, and could have come at a far greater cost."

"The cost *was* too great!"

I was ready to leave, but I wanted to make sure they understood, that they got it. "I would have let the entire Atlas Lexicon fall into the Void if it meant one of the Everlasting fell with it," I said. "I would have burned you all, every last man, woman, and child, to gain an inch of ground against Dread Ash. Count your blessings the city still stands at all."

I left them gaping and strolled out into the sunlight on that cool autumn afternoon. How long I had been unconscious, I didn't know, but I felt it was still the same day. The sun was like a kiss against my skin, the breeze and fresh air even more pleasant.

Unarmed—well, without a physical weapon—I strolled across the lush green fields in search of my friends.

CHAPTER FIFTEEN

You Can't Go Home Again

"For everything a price to pay, for everything in its time"

Sensing I'd worn out my welcome at the Atlas Lexicon, and not wanting to push these good people any further (or risk the soldiers turning on me), we left the picturesque mountain valley not one hour after I'd awoken in the field tent. Annie and Tal at my side, we headed back into the forest and the portal that would take us down to Western Australia.

As we strolled through the pleasant forest glades, dashes of sunlight falling through the green canopy, carpets of wildflowers either side, they told me about all that had happened during my unconscious hours.

After destroying the shield and heroically passing out, the four of them had carried me a little ways down the mountain, but found the path beyond the canyon, the hillside where I'd glassed the deadling army, impassable. The celestial illusion still burned hot, scorchingly so, and would for a very long time to come. The potential energy and power in that cavern would outlast the sun.

Thankfully, Arlon had made a call—all the electronics and devices had started working again once the shield fell—and a shuttle craft had collected us from the mountainside. The city, still rife with scatterings of deadlings and a few other ugly creatures, was deemed an active battle zone, so we had been brought to the command centre just outside of Spire-Brunnen.

Lord Winter had been waiting for the shield to fall, and had led his soldiers and mercenaries into the city almost the moment the purple bastard disappeared. He swept the streets clear of the dead.

The fighters among those that had been trapped in the city emerged, too, led by the lords and ladies. It was a short, swift, decisive battle over in a matter of hours. Mostly because I'd burned ninety-five percent of the army on the mountain. *You're welcome,* I thought, but didn't say.

Annie, Tal, and I walked through the forest in various states of slow injury. Scrapes and bruises, mostly, after all the healing, but a seeping fatigue had stolen over me and I wanted nothing more than to get home, back to my bookshop, and put this matter to bed. I had a feeling there was still work to be done, though. I hoped I was wrong about that.

I collected the black duffel bag I'd stashed near the Road's Fire portal when we'd arrived, full of weaponry and shells for a shotgun I'd have to remake, and opened the portal back to Rottnest Island just as the sun began to slip behind the tallest peaks to the west.

The little quokka who had bounded through ahead of us at the start of this sordid adventure was waiting nearby, and once again the furry marsupial took lead and hopped back through the portal, back to his natural habitat on that tiny spit of island just off the coast of Western Australia.

It was a warm night on Rottnest, we'd jumped forward about six or seven time zones, making it close to midnight. Stars blazed overhead, reflected in still portrait against the salt lakes.

After all that happened, it felt good to be away from the Atlas Lexicon. No doubt there would be ramifications for all I'd done, all I'd *wrought*, and the Knights Infernal would want to talk. But, as discussed, none of the accords or treaties had been broken. I was a bastard, but an honest bastard.

"Can't believe we've been gone less than a day," Annie said, as we headed through the main settlement on the island and toward the ferry jetty. "Declan," she asked, "did we do good?"

I glanced at Tal, who had said little, who stared not at the world around her but I feared at the world behind, at the long ago.

"The Everlasting are…" I sighed. "They are more human than they care to admit. They love and hate, just like the rest of us. I would have let Ash go, I truly would have, if she had released Tal and dropped the shield. I had hoped to imprison her forever in that cavern, that was the plan, back in Atlantis, but it wasn't meant to be. Not once she took Tal."

"I didn't ask you to save me," Tal said, but with no heart to the argument. Done was done.

"You never need to ask."

She looked at me sideways, her angular face in profile against the night sky as we walked along the coastal path to the ferry terminal. Gentle waves from the Indian Ocean crashed against the sandy shores. Tal looked away.

"Killing her was the only option," Annie said, as if trying to convince herself. After all, it had been Annie's blade work that had ended the Everlasting.

"I know they can die," I said. "Because I watched Emily die. But killing Ash was never part of the terribly awful plan. We got lucky, really lucky. It won't happen again."

"Am I in danger, Declan?" Annie asked.

"More than you've ever been. I'll try to deflect as much of it my way as I can, but you removed one of the *Everlasting* from the board." I took a deep breath and exhaled slowly. The bruises on my chest twitched, a dull ache. "There will be trouble for that. You will be noticed. I'm sorry, Annie."

She brushed some imaginary dust from the arms of her torn leather jacket and fell into thought, the frown creasing her brow both pretty and worried.

"How do you feel being back among the mortal?" Tal asked, a hand over her heart where my tiny sliver of immortality now resided. The lights of the main jetty loomed ahead, about two minutes' walk away. No ferries were parked up alongside the jetty, which was irksome.

I dwelled on Tal's question. I'd been dwelling on little else, actually, since awaking in the field tent.

"With the petal gone, I'm vulnerable," I said, thinking of the Everlasting, of their ability to *possess.* Without the petal, I was just as exposed as any other poor soul in creation. The damage the Everlasting could do, our powers combined, was unfathomable.

And also Future Declan's problem.

If there was a silver lining to that dark cloud, it was that the petal now resided in Tal's heart, and so long as it was there she could never be slave to the Everlasting again. If there was any soul so deserving of such protection, it was Tal.

"I guess we'll just have to see what's next," I said.

We were informed by the sleepy caretaker at the Visitor's Centre next to the main jetty that there were no ferries to the mainland until the morning. He offered us accommodation in a chalet on the island for the night at a discounted rate, so long as we were on the first ferry, but none of us were in a mood to spend the night on Rottnest.

The caretaker called up an after-hours number and arranged a private boat to take us back to Perth within the hour. It cost an arm and a leg, both limbs placed neatly on Annie's credit card after much grumbling, but soon we were zipping across the dark ocean on a speedy little six-metre boat captained by a short, heavily tattooed man with an impressive wiry grey beard, which whipped over his shoulder as we headed into the wind. Ocean spray and salt stung my face and arms, but it was a good sting, a sensation of being alive after such matters had been so uncertain.

We didn't speak on the voyage over. Speaking was done for now as there was too much to say.

~~*~*

After a call made during the boat crossing, Ethan Reilly, my wayward apprentice, met us in the carpark of Hillarys Boat Harbour on Sorrento Quay. He sported a head of bed hair, his eyes heavy with sleep.

That fatigue was washed away in an instant when he laid eyes on Tal—Sophie's sister. Sophie and Ethan had been arguing a lot since we disappeared, cast back in time to fabled Atlantis. I could see a thousand and one question bristling on his lips, but I gave him a look that suggested such enquiries were better left to the morning.

We piled into Ethan's beaten up old '87 Astra, the floor of the car covered in pizza receipts from his part-time job, a long-since dispersed pine tree air freshener swinging from the rear-view mirror.

"No trouble while you were gone, boss," he said, turning the engine over and looking relieved when the old car started. "I spent last night and all of today at the shop. Had the glazier round to fix the window. You owe me two-fifty."

I blinked, only just remembering that an hour or two before the whole business of the Atlas Lexicon had kicked off, someone had thrown an enchanted Molotov cocktail through the window of my little bookshop. "That's worrisome," I said, but my heart wasn't in it.

I was done in, knackered, and wanted nothing more than to sleep for a week. I thought, I hoped, Tal might spend the night with me at the shop. I could use a cuddle. And a drink.

I could really, really use a drink.

But, and this was a pleasant realisation, I thought I probably wouldn't have one.

True what they say, you gotta hit rock bottom before you can quit your demons. Drowning them in blood or whisky doesn't work. Those bastards can swim.

The drive along the coast up to Joondalup and Riverwood Plaza, the small nestle of shops and restaurants, was only five minutes, but I began to doze in those minutes and they ticked by as if in dream. I awoke as the battered old Astra pulled into the street parking on the side road across from my shop, cold and feeling a touch adrift, out of sorts.

"Cup of tea before bed?" I asked the car and got a few nods and mutters.

We stepped out into the warm night, lit only by two streetlamps, casting shadows all across Riverwood Plaza—all save mine, me without my shadow.

We reached the marble fountain, spouts of water trickling softly in the clear waters, our boot heels clicking on the cobblestones, and here Annie hesitated. She wrapped her arms around herself and gazed at my bookshop just across the way. I could read the look on her face well.

"I should probably head home," she said. "Via the station, of course. Need to explain where I was today."

"Surely not the truth," I said.

She smiled sadly. "Not if I want a job in an hour, no."

Tal and Ethan hung back in the space between the fountain and the bookshop, giving Annie and I a chance to chat. There was far too much to be said.

"Annie," I began, "we should talk."

She nodded, black hair spilling over her shoulders, eyes not quite hostile but... guarded. She tapped her chest, her heart. "You should have told me about this a long time ago."

"How would you begin such a conversation? I..."

I shook my head. "I had hoped you would never need to know, that you would be free of my world."

Annie sighed. "I've only known you a year and a bit," she said, "but even I can see you're kidding yourself."

"Yeah," I said. "Sorry."

"We're not OK, Declan," Annie said, then she stepped forward and gave me a quick hug. "But our hearts are in the right place."

She kissed me on the cheek.

And my bookshop exploded.

A great torrent of emerald-green flame burst outwards from the store, wrenching the front face of the building away entirely. A deadly rain of splintered wood and glass blasted outwards.

I fell on my instincts and threw my arm up to conjure a shield—but Tal, sweet Tal, had always been faster. She and Ethan stood closer to the explosion, but Tal still managed to get a half-arc of invisible energy, a force field of Will, in between herself and the explosion. The shield arced back over her head, over to Annie and me.

A storm of green flame and debris shot past us, tore into the fountain, and scattered across Riverwood Plaza. The dark restaurants across the plaza took the brunt of the fragments and wreckage, shattering windows and annihilating support pillars. For the space of about ten seconds, the whole plaza blazed and burned, tumbled and fell—the quiet of the early hours pierced beyond repair.

The green flames receded back to the heart of the explosion, my poor old shop, as Tal and Ethan stumbled over to us. A thin sheen of sweat coated Tal's face—the quick shield had cost her, but saved our lives.

All around us, hundreds of books fell fiery from the sky amidst thousands upon thousands of torn pages. A blizzard of ruined, flame-scorched stories. We stood at the heart of that blizzard, in disbelief and, for me, raw fury.

A figure stumbled from the burning façade of my bookshop, wrapped in a smouldering grey cloak, smoke and flame licking its edges. The figure staggered from the fire, hooded, small, clearly in pain, scrambling over piles of burnt books, through the thick scent of acrid scorched paper and the dispersion of all the carefully laid wards. Protections I had placed around my shop to prevent *this* from happening.

The figure saw us, standing just thirty feet away around the rim of the fountain, and threw the hood back from her face.

Tylia Vale, the beautiful, blue-skinned girl, one of the last of her alien race, my student in the Vale Celestia of Atlantis, stood before the devastating wall of green flames that had been my refuge, my home for the last seven years.

She swayed, her eyes found mine, and she managed a small, pained smile. "Declan," she rasped, "I found you."

Tylia fell forward onto her knees, scraping her palms on the ground, crying out as she pressed her arm against a burning book, and then fell back.

I dashed across the plaza and caught her before her head could smack the cobblestones. Her eyes, glazed and confused, sought me out between the heat of the flame and the spiralling clouds of smoke.

"Declan," I heard Tal say, as if from a great distance. "That's n—"

Tylia's soft blue hand came up to brush my cheek and in that moment her eyes changed—the whites flooded with blood, crimson-red, and the pupils disappeared entirely.

I gasped as she grinned, a terrible grin, and her hand snaked behind my head and pulled my lips down to hers.

A cold, dead tongue, what I imagined kissing a corpse would feel like, wormed into my mouth. A blistering cold swept my body, I froze, unable to break the embrace, and heard terrible laughter echoing in my head as something, some malevolent force I knew all too well, passed from Tylia's mouth and into mine.

A spear of ice thrust itself into the back of my throat and I broke away from Tylia with a cry for the ages, one that pierced the night in a vicious wail they would have heard back in Switzerland.

A presence entered my mind, *overwhelmed* my mind, and I was sent raving into the back of my own consciousness. It felt, in a very real sense, that I was dragged screaming away from the controls of an immense, powerful battleship by a force of irresistible hate and power.

"Boss," Ethan said, first to reach me as I lay curled on the ground, on books and pages alight with flame. "Boss, you OK? You need to get up. Come on."

Ethan picked me up under my arms, hauled me to my feet. I watched his face come into focus, saw the concern in his eyes.

And then I grasped his shoulder with one hand and used my other arm to close around his neck, so his head sat in the crook of my elbow. His eyes widened, I laughed—an awful, hollow sound—and tore his head from his neck in one vicious, all-powerful tug.

'*No!*' I screamed, though no words escaped my mouth. It was no longer my mouth.

A gout of blood fountained up from the ragged stump of Ethan's neck as his body fell away, still twitching. I held up his head against the night, against the flickering green flames, his eyes blinking their last, and laughed again—at Annie, at Tal, who stared at me from the marble fountain in disbelief and fear.

Between us, Tylia Vale stirred on the cobblestones. Her eyes flew open, her normal eyes, and she scrambled back away from me, the monster shrouded in green flame, covered in the blood of his friends, holding up a severed head for the whole world to see.

With my free hand, I conjured a spear of dark metal from the air—something far beyond my abilities—and thrust the bitter point into the cobblestones, shattering rock, creating a pike upon which to mount my awful trophy.

I placed Ethan's head upon the tip of the spear and laughed again, feeding the flames.

Tal moved first. She fell to the ground and grasped the nearest burning book—*run*, I thought, *you have to run*. She didn't need telling. Tal was a Knight Infernal, trained alongside the best of us. To me, she had always been the best of us.

"*Annie!*" Tal shouted. "*Hold on to me!*"

Annie didn't disobey the command. She stared at me terrified, one hand resting uselessly on the handle of her revolver. She didn't understand, not yet.

With the burning book in one hand, her free hand grasping Tylia's burnt arm, and Annie holding her shoulder, Tal Levy used the book to open a 'way across the Story Thread, to the world contained within the book—one of the first tricks they taught a knight at the Infernal Academy. Like so much ash on the wind, my friends disappeared, faded from reality, travelling god knew how far across the Story Thread.

Tal knew what I knew—anywhere was better than Riverwood Plaza in that moment.

I laughed again, laughter escaped my throat, but I didn't make the sound.

Sauntering, at ease with nowhere to be, I walked over to the space my friends had occupied just moments ago, sniffing the air, kicking aside burning books. Here I paused a moment before leaning forward and considering the reflective water of the fountains. Lit by the emerald green flames from behind, I could see my face well in the water. Very well.

My eyes were twin orbs of deepest, darkest heart's blood. Pure crimson and malice. They stared back at me alien and hostile—and in triumph.

"Hello, Declan," Lord Oblivion of the Everlasting said, and I watched my mouth work and form the words, heard my own voice ring back at me. "What's new with you?"

'What do you want?' I asked, raging, screaming, against the cage in my mind. The Everlasting had possessed me, as I had feared. *Possessed me!* I couldn't budge, not an inch. I was locked in bands harder than star iron. I felt Oblivion's amusement and my struggle and redoubled my efforts. *'RELEASE ME!'*

"Dominion, territory, control," Oblivion said and ran his/my hand back through his/my hair. "A little blackberry farm in the country where I can grow old in peace. Oh, really, Declan, is that what you thought would happen? That you deserved anything close to such harmony?"

'Get out of my thoughts!'

Lord Oblivion grinned, my teeth bloodstained and awful, stretched from ear to ear in the waters of the fountain. "What do I want, you ask? First and foremost, I am here to extend you an invitation."

'To what?' I snarled, doing the mental equivalent of hurling my shoulder into the locked door.

"My sisters' funeral," Lord Oblivion whispered.

That stopped my struggling for a moment.

'You killed Astoria,' I said.

"And you Ashaya with the blight in your heart."

'Can't help but feel I won't be welcome at such a memorial.'

Lord Oblivion laughed, harsh and bitter. "You have no say in the matter. We will attend, Declan Hale, an event that hasn't occurred since before time was new. You're my plus-one. I fear we will cause quite the sensation."

I felt the heat of a million burning books scorch my back, a cleansing fire for my oft corrupted soul. *'And then?'*

"I will use you as my vessel to destroy the Knights Infernal and claim the Story Thread for my own."

With a tremendous roar heard by none, I hurled myself against the shackles in my mind, hard enough to shock and jar limbs I no longer had, a body I couldn't see nor feel. I was a ghost, adrift in an Everlasting prison. I reached for my Will and found nothing. I grasped, scrambled for the edges of the bonds that held me, clawed at locks I couldn't see or touch.

The Everlasting laughed and turned from the fountain. My vision swayed, I was merely along for the ride, as Lord Oblivion stepped sideways into the Void and cast us together, master and puppet, across the ragged edge of the Story Thread.

We were off to start a war.

~~*~*

The End of
Book Four

Declan Hale will return in:

ELDER SHADOW

The Reminiscent Exile #5

Coming November, 2017

Follow Joe at www.joeducie.com